A TEMPTING LOVE NOVEL
SWEETEST SIN
USA TODAY BESTSELLING AUTHOR
NIKKI ASH

She illuminates my dark world.

SWEETEST SIN PLAYLIST

Sure thing-Miguel

Rock Bottom-Hailee Steinfeld

Stay-Rihanna

Complicated-Avril Lavigne

Consequences-Camila Cabello

If I can't have you-Shawn Mendes

In the Name of Love-Martin Garrix & Bebe Rexha

Hate Me-Ellie Goulding & Juice WRLD

Takeaway-The Chainsmokers & Illenium

Sabotage-Bebe Rexha

Listen to the *Sweetest Sin* playlist on Nikki's website

To the women who love a green-flag man but are
craving something a bit darker.

AUTHOR'S NOTE: *Like real life, the characters are far from perfect, make morally gray decisions, and deal with subjects that may be sensitive for some readers. If you are looking for a safe romance, this series is not for you. Content warnings, which contain spoilers, can be found on my website.*

PASSPORT
HGK815
25 DEC 18
15:45
JFK
JOHN
from New
to London
gate 35

ONE

Dominick

"WHAT DID HE DO NOW?" I ASK OVER THE SPEAKERPHONE as I wipe the blood splatter off my hands, checking to make sure I didn't get any on my suit while I wait for my younger brother to tell me what our father did this time.

There are only two reasons Matteo sends a 911 text when I don't answer his call—he's in trouble, or our dad fucked something up. And since Matteo can handle himself better than anyone I know, it's usually the latter.

"He took a meeting with Rothschild behind our backs."

That gets my attention. Joseph Rothschild and our father haven't been anything more than business associates in many years, and everyone knows if it's business-related, I'm the person they should contact. It's been that way for the past year, since our father was diagnosed with Alzheimer's—information only our immediate family is aware of—and he had no choice but to go into an early retirement, despite refusing to officially hand the title over to me until I either meet his absurd requirements or he dies. I'm banking on his death.

So, the fact that they're meeting only means one thing …

The body on the floor groans, reminding me that I'm in the middle of something.

"Hey, Matteo, let me call you right back."

He hangs up, and I pull my gun out of its holster, aiming it at the man who betrayed me … betrayed my family. His face is mangled, to the point that I can't tell if he's looking at me. But it doesn't matter because, in a moment, he won't be looking at anyone.

I glance at the gentlemen standing around the room—some with terrified expressions, others neutral.

"Take this as a warning," I tell them. "When you steal from my family's casino, you're stealing from me, and there's only one way it will end." The bullet goes straight into the thief's chest, and I look at the other employees. "Any questions?"

They all shake their heads.

"Good. Now, get back to work."

They scurry back to wherever they belong, and I glance at Franco, who runs our underground casino. It's invite-only, and only the most wealthy and influential are considered.

"You did good," I tell him, reaching out to shake his hand. "Expect a bonus for your loyalty."

When he contacted me to let me know he believed someone in the accounting department was stealing from the casino, I told him to handle it. It took a couple of weeks, but he figured out who it was and called me with proof.

Unfortunately, shit like this happens all too often.

And then Matteo or I have to step in.

People get greedy and try to get away with skimming off the top. They think because we have our hands in so many pots, we're not watching. But you don't get to where we are by being stupid.

"Thank you, sir." Franco nods and then scurries out while I text my cleanup crew to let them know where they need to pick up the trash.

Once that's handled, I head back to my office in downtown North Harbor Point, calling my brother back once I'm situated.

"Sorry about that," I say when he answers. "Issue at the casino, but I handled it. Now, where were we?"

"Andrey meeting with Joseph."

Ah, yes. I lean back in my seat. Our father took a meeting with Joseph Rothschild behind our backs.

"Let me guess. Joseph was asking when our sister would be ready for marriage."

"Worse," Matteo says, his tone laced with venom. "Anthony doesn't want to wait. He wants to marry her now."

"How do you know that?"

"I ran into him at Pasquale's," Matteo growls through the phone. "He was bragging about how it won't be long until we're family. That Dad agreed Brielle would marry him this spring. Not fucking summer, Dominick. Spring! I think they know Dad's health is declining, and they want it to happen before he dies."

I clench my fist around my phone, trying to tamp down my anger. "I'll talk to Joseph when I get back. He agreed to wait. I don't give a shit what deal our father made with his friends thirty-five fucking years ago. It's not supposed to happen until after she has graduated, and she still has five months to go."

Hopefully, by then, Dad will be dead, and I can renegotiate so our little sister isn't forced to marry that dumbass Anthony. He wouldn't know the first thing about keeping my sister safe, and the last thing I want is our family name tied to him.

"All right," Matteo concedes. "But don't prolong it. That asshole sounded like it was a sure thing."

Of course Anthony did. Because he's been counting down the days until he can claim our sister as his own. The Rothschilds are practically champing at the bit to secure ties to the Antonov name. He would've tried to make it happen sooner, but with the twelve-year age difference between them, Dad told him he had to wait until Brielle turned eighteen.

Then, thankfully, I convinced Joseph to make his son delay the wedding. It took some negotiating and sacrifices on our end, but he agreed.

"He can say whatever he wants," I tell him. "But she's not signing a marriage license until after she walks across the stage."

If everything goes according to plan, our father will be dead, and I can tell Joseph and his son to go fuck themselves. Dad's deteriorating quickly on his own, but Matteo and I have already discussed ending him if we need to.

"Speaking of which," Matteo says, the humor in his voice telling me exactly where this conversation is going.

"Don't go there," I warn, but my brother never fucking listens. I might be feared by damn near everyone who knows our family, but there's one person they fear more—Matteo Antonov.

"Lorenzo went to visit Daniella at boarding school," he taunts.

"I said, don't go there."

I don't want to know anything about the seventeen-year-old I've been arranged to marry. I'm not a good guy by any means. My family deals in drugs and weapons and has as many, if not more, illegal businesses as we do legal. I sold my soul a long time ago. But even I have my limits, and pedophilia is a hard one.

Not too long ago, our men found out a few guys in South Harbor Point were selling underage sex tapes on the dark web from their basement. We wiped them from the face of the earth and made an example out of them. Nobody fucks with underage women in this city. So, just the thought of marrying Daniella Russo, who's fourteen years younger than me, makes my stomach churn.

It was supposed to happen when she turned eighteen, but when my father and I renegotiated the terms for Brielle, Giuseppe— Daniella's father—insisted his daughter be allowed to go to college as well, thanks to me putting that bug in his ear. While I did it for Brielle, a small part of me made the deal in hope of avoiding having to spend my life with a woman I have no desire to be with.

"You can live in denial all you want," Matteo says, "but in four years—"

"Anything can happen."

Don't get me wrong. She might be pretty—hell, she might even be beautiful, but I wouldn't know since I haven't seen her in years since her parents sent her off to boarding school when she was younger—but regardless of her age, I'll always see Daniella Russo as the little girl with pigtails and braces, running around the back-yard at our parents' annual Fourth of July party.

Not that our fathers give a shit about that. Andrey Antonov, Giuseppe Russo, and Joseph Rothschild only care about three things: money, power, and control.

Even when they were younger, when most guys their age were fucking around, they were building their empires and strategizing how to make them stronger. And I gotta give it to them—they succeeded in owning damn near the entire city we live in, as well as the surrounding area and the port that controls most of the import and export to major countries, like the Dominican Republic, Peru, and Colombia.

"Anything can happen," Matteo agrees, "but you know they're hell-bent on seeing their plan through."

Their plan …

My thoughts go back to when I was a teenager and learned of my father's ludicrous scheme.

"One day, this empire will rest on your shoulders, son," Dad said in a tone that conveyed his seriousness. "And when that day comes, you're going to have to do things to ensure our power and control remain."

"Like what?" I asked curiously.

I was no stranger to the shady shit my father had done over the years. While some dads tried to keep their children's innocence for as long as possible, Andrey Antonov believed in tough love. He might be rich and powerful now, but it hadn't always been that way, and he thought that if he took it easy on us, he'd make us soft.

I had been five the first time I watched him slice a man's neck for betraying him.

At ten, I'd witnessed him murder a city official because he was going to come between him and a development my dad was passionate about.

At twelve, I'd killed for the first time—a motel owner who had been lying to Dad about what he was up to. He'd paid Dad for protection, and in doing so, Dad got a cut of the women he prostituted. But he hadn't been honest about how much he was bringing in, and Dad had said an example needed to be made out of him.

And when I'd been thirteen, he'd forced me to go with him to a sex club, where he got footage to blackmail a politician. While there, he insisted I lose my virginity so I would become a man—his words, not mine.

Up until that day, I'd thought my father loved my mother—despite how shitty he treated her—but when I saw him go into a room with a woman who wasn't her, making her scream so loud that I could hear it through the walls, I'd realized my father wasn't capable of loving anyone or anything that didn't help push his agenda.

"For one," Dad said, snapping me from my thoughts, "you know Daniella Russo?"

"Lorenzo's baby sister?" I asked in confusion, unsure of what she had to do with anything.

Dad always said this was a man's world and girls like my mom and sister, Brielle, belonged at home. I wasn't sure if I agreed since my mom was one of the smartest women I knew—even if she preferred to act stupid around my dad—but I wouldn't ever argue with him, not if I wanted my heart to continue beating.

"Yes," Dad said with a grin that sent chills up my spine. "Once she's of age, you're going to marry her."

"What the fuck? Why?"

"Watch your fucking tone with me, boy," Dad warned. "Before you were born, an agreement was made between Giuseppe, Joseph, and me," he explained. "You will marry Daniella, and your sister will marry Anthony."

"But you don't even like Joseph," I accused.

I might've only been sixteen, but everyone knew about Joseph knocking up his now wife, Maria, when Giuseppe had been in love with her. Apparently, it was a drunken mistake, but Joseph wasn't about to abort his own flesh and blood. So, they got married, and she had his baby.

Giuseppe and Joseph had refused to let it ruin their business partnership, but when Dad and Giuseppe were alone, they talked shit about how much they couldn't stand Joseph and that he was untrustworthy.

"That's neither here nor there," Dad said, his cold gray eyes locking with mine. "We agreed that our families would come together for the sake of power, and I am nothing if not a man of my word."

"But she's only a baby," I pointed out.

"She won't always be young," Dad deadpanned. "And once she's old enough, you will marry her and produce an heir, forever linking our families."

"No way!" I argued. "I'm not doing that, and you can't fucking make me!"

I knew the grave error I'd made the second my dad stood and grabbed me by my throat, shoving me against the wall.

"Yes, you will, Dominick," he said, his voice menacing yet unbothered. "You will marry Daniella, just like your sister will marry Anthony. And you want to know why?"

He didn't wait for me to answer.

"You both will do as you're told because if you don't, then you're no good to me, and what do I do to people I have no use for?"

When I didn't answer him quick enough, he tightened his hold on my throat, cutting off the air supply to my lungs.

"What do I do?" he demanded.

"You kill them," I choked out.

After Dad was done threatening me, he calmly explained that he, Giuseppe, and Joseph were a force to be reckoned with, but united, they would become the three most powerful families in Harbor Point—the city we live in,—and one day, if they continued down that path, they would be the most powerful families in South Florida, maybe even the East Coast.

They didn't know how it would play out when they made the deal, but once the girls were born, they decided Brielle would marry Anthony since Giuseppe and Joseph didn't get along, and because I was the oldest, that left me with Daniella.

I would respect him if it wasn't for the fact that he wasn't even loyal to his own family. He cheats on Mom and is willing to sell his own flesh and blood for power, and I wouldn't put it past him to kill us all for going against him. He takes being a psychopath to another level.

Hell, once, when Matteo was younger, he said he wanted to be a marine biologist after learning about the ocean in school, and our father tortured him for a week, saying that if he wasn't part of the family business, he might as well be dead. After that, Matteo never again mentioned wanting to do anything other than work for our father.

"I need to get going," I tell Matteo, pocketing my wallet and keys. "Since Lorenzo is using the plane, I have to fly commercial. So, if you need to get ahold of me, text me. I don't even know if those planes allow for phone calls."

Like the dick he is, Matteo laughs, knowing I hate flying anything but private.

With how insane my life is, I crave consistency and order. And commercial flights are anything but. Add to that how dirty they are—with the thousands of people sitting in the seats, kids with their snot and germs—and I avoid them at all cost.

I'd cancel this meeting just so I wouldn't have to fly commercial if it wasn't so important.

But it is.

A real estate developer I'm looking to do business with on the west coast of Florida requested a meeting, and since time was of the essence, I agreed to fly out to meet him. There are very few people I would jump through hoops for, but Jaimie Sanchez is a genius when it comes to expanding his territory.

Dad's goal has always been to own the city he grew up in, but I have bigger plans than slinging drugs and dealing weapons, owning a few hotels and underground casinos. And now that I'm running shit—and half the time, my father can't remember to wipe his ass—I can make decisions as I see fit without him questioning me.

After hanging up with Matteo, I call Fernando, my driver, to take me to the airport. Traffic is a bitch, but I get a bunch of work done on the way.

We're about five minutes out when my phone rings. I consider declining my sister's call, knowing what she wants to talk about and not wanting to listen to her freak out, but she won't stop until I answer.

"Brielle, how—"

"Tell me it's not true!" she shrieks, forcing me to turn my volume down. "Tell me you're not going to force me to marry that slimy piece of shit!"

"Brielle." I sigh.

"Don't *Brielle* me!" she screams through the phone. "You said you would get me out of this, Dominick. You promised!"

"Enough!" I bark. "I said I would try, and I'm working on it. Shit like this takes time."

Despite me now being in charge of Antonov Enterprises, our father still legally owns the company and refuses to relinquish his rights until the deals are finalized—Brielle marrying Anthony and me marrying Daniella.

And even if I did have full rein of the company, because my father's ties with Giuseppe and Joseph are so thick, it's going to take a helluva lot to cut them.

Thankfully, Giuseppe will be stepping down soon from Russo Property Group, handing the reins over to his son, Lorenzo—who is also Matteo's best friend—but he's as fucking stubborn as our father, and he won't do it until the marriages are finalized.

On the other hand, Joseph has no plans to hand Rothschild International over to Anthony anytime soon—not that I blame him since his son is a few bricks shy of a load. But that means I'm going to have to deal with him for the foreseeable future, and since he's as hell-bent on this arrangement as Giuseppe and my dad, it won't be easy to convince him that we could be just as strong without intertwining our families and blood.

My dad, Giuseppe, and Joseph are old school—my parents were part of an arranged marriage that was beneficial to both sides in terms of money and power, Giuseppe only married his wife, Tanya, because she came from an influential family, and Joseph married Maria, despite not being in love with her, because she was pregnant with Anthony.

"Dominick," my sister pleads, "I can't marry him. I'm in lo—"

She cuts herself off, but I can piece together the rest of what she didn't say. My sister is in love. She met someone, probably in college.

"Brielle," I warn, my patience running thin, "when Dad agreed to let you go away to school—"

"I know," she snaps. "I know, Dominick. I'm allowed to get my degree as long as I understand that I'm never allowed to actually use it because I'll be too busy pushing out Anthony's babies."

Dad wouldn't let her leave the state, but he compromised and let her go to a university that required her to live closer to the school, which meant she could move out of the house, provided that she come home on Sunday nights for family dinner—surprisingly, he did that for our mother, who had said she was afraid Brielle would leave and never come home—and that she understood once she graduated, she would be required to move back home and marry Anthony.

"It's just so unfair," she cries, and despite how hard this life has made me, my heart softens for her the way it always does.

I'm eight years older than Brielle, but because our father is incapable of love and our mother spends most of her time trying to avoid our father's abuse, Matteo and I have had a hand in raising and protecting her.

Since the day I found out my baby sister would have to marry Anthony, Matteo and I have been planning how to prevent it from happening, but the men we're dealing with didn't get to where they are by being rash, and their contracts are ironclad. If I go about this the wrong way, we can potentially lose everything, and I've worked too damn hard and long, putting up with my father's shit, for that to happen.

"I'm going to figure it out," I tell her as Fernando pulls up to my terminal. "Just focus on school. Nothing is happening right now."

"Okay," she sighs. "Where are you?"

"I'm heading to Coral Bay for a meeting. I'll see you on Sunday for dinner."

We hang up, and with only my briefcase in hand since this is a day trip, I head into the airport, wondering if Matteo and I could get away with killing three of the most powerful men in Harbor Point.

Check-in is quick and painless, as is security. I spend the short time I have before the flight working in the airline's designated lounge until business class is called.

Between dealing with my family, checking the books for discrepancies now that it's been brought to my attention, and preparing for the business meeting I'm about to have in a few hours—and add to that, the screaming toddler, whose mom is trying and failing to soothe her child before we've even had a seat on the plane—my head is all over the place.

So, when I step onto the plane, I'm not paying attention when a woman appears out of nowhere. With both of us on a mission to get to where we're going, our bodies collide. She shrieks, her hands flailing about as she attempts to right herself in the small space, and I reach out, trying to save her from falling.

But in doing so, instead of keeping her upright, I hit the plush cushion—thanks to the airline sparing no expense on the business-class accommodations—and she lands directly on my lap.

Before I can help her up, she scrambles off me. Her mortified eyes meet mine—emerald, like the gem, shiny and bright and filled with enchantment—and I'm instantly mesmerized by her green orbs.

Her skin looks like porcelain, similar to the dolls Brielle used to collect when she was little. She swore they were real, but Matteo used to tell her that nobody's skin was that flawless. But this woman's is, and it makes me want to reach out and touch her to find out if it's as smooth as it looks.

Her hair, which is up in a tight ponytail, is fiery red and matches the color of her plump lips, which are shiny, like she recently applied lip gloss. Her makeup is done to perfection. Her cheeks are flushed, and her lashes are thick.

There's a fine line between a woman who uses makeup to highlight her beauty and one who's trying to create it. I have no doubt this woman is naturally gorgeous, and the makeup only enhances that.

My eyes trail down her face to her slim neck and then to her rounded breasts, which are accentuated by her formfitting button-down blouse. I continue my descent to her long, shapely legs and stop at her black heels, which I imagine her still wearing as I fuck her against the wall in the private restroom on the plane.

"I'm so sorry," she says, quickly ending my fantasy and reminding me where I am—on a commercial flight.

I glance up, and her cheeks have turned a beautiful peach shade, the same color as the flowers my mom keeps all over the house.

Peaches and cream, she calls them—the bouquets filled with white and peach roses.

In our world, it's easy to get sucked into the dark, so Mom fills the house with flowers, swearing they help keep the light in.

"Are you okay, Mr. …"

"Dominick." I chuckle. "And I think I should be asking you that."

She might be five foot eight, give or take an inch or two, but she's got nothing on my six-foot-three self, especially since I have a good fifty pounds of muscle on her.

"I'm okay," she breathes, stepping into the aisle. "I'm just so sorry." She laughs, and the melodic sound—as enchanting as her eyes—goes straight to my cock.

"It's all good," I tell her, glancing up at the row designation and realizing we fell into my assigned seat. "I needed to sit anyway. And if one of the perks of flying commercial is having a beautiful woman fall into my lap, I might need to stop flying private."

She snorts out a laugh and rolls her eyes. "I haven't heard that pickup line before," she says, narrowing her gaze at me. "So, I'll give it an eight for originality and the fact that you came up with it so quickly."

She moves to the side so the other passengers can get down the aisle and flips through the papers in her hand. "Dominick Antonov?" she asks, her tone all business.

When I raise a questioning brow, she says, "You said this is your seat, and since I have the seating chart for those in business class …"

It's then I realize that the woman didn't appear out of nowhere. She was coming out of the galley … because she's a flight attendant.

"That's me," I say, waiting for her to recognize my name and react.

The second a woman learns who I am, she either retreats in fear or dollar signs appear in her eyes, like a slot machine at a casino, hoping that with one pull, she'll hit the jackpot.

But the recognition from this woman doesn't come. Not the fear or the attraction. If she does know who I am, she's doing a damn good job of hiding it.

"I'm Peyton," she says with a smile that causes twin dimples in her cheeks to pop out, adding to her beauty. "I'm your flight attendant today. So, if you need anything, please let me know."

Normally, I would assume those words held an insinuation somewhere in there, but this woman has transformed from embarrassed to professional in the blink of an eye.

"Can I get you something to drink? A glass of champagne or …"

"An old-fashioned, please," I tell her. "Kingston Limited Black Label."

"Unfortunately, we don't carry Kingston on this flight," she says, "but I can make it with Maker's Mark."

I'm about to argue that Kingston is definitely kept in stock—I make sure of it—when I remember once again that I'm not on our private plane.

"That would be great. Thanks."

She nods and turns, and I can't help but lean to the side so I can watch as she walks away, her luscious ass swaying in her tight skirt as she goes.

Peyton returns a few minutes later, places a napkin on my armrest, and then sets my drink down.

"For the record," she says, her voice low and her green eyes filled with mirth, "I prefer Kingston as well. It goes down smooth."

Well, fuck me sideways, maybe there is hope for me fucking her against the wall in the restroom on this flight.

PASSPORT
HGKB15
29 DEC 18
15:45
JFK
JOHN
New
Lond
gate
35

TWO

Peyton

TODAY HAS BEEN A DAY FROM HELL.

It started with my now ex–best friend from college, Sara, messaging me to let me know that I should get tested. She'd found out that Brent, my ex-boyfriend—who cheated on me with Sara while I took some time off from college to move back home to take care of my sick mom—had given her chlamydia. Because she apparently cares so much about me, she wanted to make sure I knew in case he had given it to me as well.

I had already been tested after I found out he'd cheated, and thankfully, everything came back clean. But after her call, I scheduled a doctor's appointment because I wouldn't stop thinking about it until I knew for sure that the asshole hadn't given me one last parting gift before I dumped his ass and then blocked him.

After receiving that wonderful message, I arrived at work, only to be accosted by Dale the Douche. He's one of the pilots on my route who has decided that I'm his new conquest.

Gag.

At first, when Dale had asked me out—swearing he only wanted to get to know me on a friendly basis since we'd be working together—I'd agreed, thinking it would be nice to make a friend, until I learned he was married with three kids and did this shit to all the new hires, hoping to get laid.

What is it about me that attracts all the assholes? I swear it's genetic.

My mom fell for a cocky professional boxer's charms, let him in her pants and into her heart, and he promised her the world. For a short time, she thought they were forever, until a few years after they had me—when she found out he'd been cheating on her. From there, things went downhill.

Instead of keeping the violence in the ring, he started to take his temper out on my mom, and she knew she needed to leave him. It took her a few years to get out of the abusive situation, but she did.

I read somewhere that kids who come from abusive homes are more likely to continue the cycle, and while I want to be, like, *fuck that*, the fact that I keep meeting cheating assholes feels like I'm dodging bullets left and right. If the cycle is trying to continue, it can eat shit because it's not getting me.

But I digress …

Where was I?

Ex-boyfriend and ex–best friend with chlamydia …

Cheating pilot douche …

Oh yeah, my day from hell.

The pilot is pissed because I won't sleep with him, and now, he's determined to make my life miserable. Like, he thinks if he harasses me enough, I'll get so fed up that I'll give in and spread my legs. That's not happening.

On top of all that, my mom's doctor has requested our presence in her office to go over her test results. And everyone knows that the only time a doctor forces you to come in is when they have bad news.

Despite all this going on, I was trying to focus on getting the flight ready—because I need this job—but my head was all over the place, and I wasn't watching where I was going when I ran smack into a passenger. A ridiculously handsome—with his chiseled jaw, gray eyes, perfect amount of scruff—business-class passenger.

It shouldn't surprise me. I'm the least coordinated person you'll ever meet. Honestly, if it wasn't for a friend of mine pushing me to get a job as a flight attendant, I never would've considered this as a career. Planes sway and dip, and my hand-eye coordination is not good. The number of times I've tripped and stumbled while the plane was in motion is embarrassing.

Too bad I couldn't use that as an excuse when I ran into the good-looking man since the plane hadn't even left the runway yet.

Thankfully, he was nice about it—because the last thing I need is to be reported. With Dale on my case, it wouldn't take much for HR to fire me. And I need the money from this job to support my mom since she can't work, and her disability isn't anywhere near enough to cover our expenses.

Once I was no longer perched on his lap, I introduced myself and offered to get him a drink. He ordered an old-fashioned—a drink I haven't heard of in years—and I was immediately brought back to my childhood, sitting on the floor, playing with my toys, while my dad demanded my mom make him an old-fashioned.

I loved him so much, and I'd be lying if I said I wasn't a daddy's girl, but he didn't know how to keep his temper limited to the ring and his dick in his pants when he left the house. And when he drank, it only got worse.

He never hurt me, but I witnessed him hurt my mom on several occasions, and when she threatened to out him to the media—having enough evidence to prove that he was abusive—he agreed to let us go if she walked away without a dime. He thought she would choose the money over our safety and stay, but my mom was stronger than that. With my hand in hers, she walked away and never looked back.

"Unfortunately, we don't carry Kingston on this flight," I choke out, pushing the memories of the past aside, "but I can make it with Maker's Mark."

Mr. Antonov agrees, and I head to the galley to make the drink. Aside from him ordering an old-fashioned, I noticed that he preferred Kingston Limited liquor. I'm not a huge drinker, but I know a lot about liquor, thanks to years of working as a bartender, and that's an expensive one.

"For the record," I tell him when I set his drink down, without thinking about what I'm saying, "I prefer Kingston as well. It goes down smooth."

The moment the words are out of my mouth, I immediately regret them. I never flirt, especially on a flight. The fantasies men have about fucking flight attendants to earn their Mile High badge is a real thing, and I never want to lead anyone on.

But there's something about the gray-eyed man that has me not thinking clearly. Maybe it's because it's been months since I've gotten laid or it's the stress from my mother's doctor requesting that we meet with her, but when he looks at me with a gleam in his eye, I almost consider telling him to meet me in the restroom.

But I don't because anybody who's been on a commercial flight knows the restrooms are small and gross, and between my five-foot-seven self and him being well over six feet, we would never fit, let alone successfully get off.

So, instead, I smile and walk away, feeling his gaze on my ass as I sway my hips a little more than usual. Tonight, when I'm home, I'll use him as a visual when I get myself off. At least with my vibrator, I won't risk getting a goddamn STD.

PASSPORT
HGK815
JFK
25 DEC 18
15:45
New
Lond
35
JOH
AI

THREE

Dominick

THERE WILL BE NO FUCKING ANYONE IN THE RESTROOM OF the plane. For one, the restroom is so small that it should be illegal. And two, aside from Peyton making sure I'm comfortable throughout the flight, she hasn't indicated that she's interested in me.

The pilot announces that we'll be arriving in Coral Bay shortly, and the flight attendants come around to collect everyone's trash. I've considered asking Peyton for her number several times, but I've refrained because she doesn't seem like a one-night-stand type of woman, and with my unknown future, that's all I could give her.

When the passengers begin to deplane, our eyes meet, and Peyton smiles warmly at me. But then one of the pilots steps out of the cockpit, and her smile drops. The guy says something to her, and she shakes her head, her features morphing from warm to annoyed. I can't make out what is being said, but it's clear from here that she's uncomfortable. She walks away, thanking everyone for flying with their airline, and the entire time, the asshole stares at her like he wants to devour her.

Normally, I'd mind my own business, but this woman has me intrigued, so instead of getting off the plane and heading to my meeting, I hang back as everyone else gets off.

Once the rows have emptied, I take my briefcase and make my way toward the front. Only, instead of heading through the loading bridge, I wait for Peyton since there is only one exit she can go through.

Sure enough, a few minutes later, Peyton rounds the corner with the asshole on her tail. When she spots me, her eyes widen in shock.

"Is everything okay?" she asks, her tone professional even if she appears to be uncomfortable.

"Peyton, is this guy giving you a hard time?" the guy asks, making me chuckle at the irony.

"I feel like I should be asking her that question about you," I say, eyeing him as he glares my way.

"Excuse me?" He reaches up and places his hand on Peyton's shoulder, and his wedding ring catches my eye.

"Come," I say to Peyton, ignoring him. "I believe you owe me a drink, one that goes down a bit smoother."

I smirk, and she flushes that beautiful shade of peach.

"She's on the clock," the asshole says.

"Shouldn't you be focused less on your flight attendant and more on your wife?" I ask him.

The guy's face reddens as he takes a step back.

"Now, if you don't mind, Peyton and I have plans."

He looks at her, hoping she'll deny it, but when she doesn't, he huffs and storms away.

"Ugh, thank you," Peyton says, her shoulders sagging in relief. "Dale is such a douche. He's the first officer, and he thinks he's God's gift to women. He's married with three kids, and he tries to sleep with every attendant like he's single."

"No problem," I tell her. "Have you considered reporting him?"

"So many attendants have, but the airline is short-staffed." She rolls her eyes. "So, of course, they do nothing about it because it would mean firing a pilot that they need." She shrugs. "Anyway, I appreciate you saving me. We're off the clock until our trip back to Harbor Point later, so he was trying to convince me to go back to his place in Coral Bay." She visibly shivers. "I'd rather dry up from lack of use and risk getting attacked by spiders from the cobwebs that have developed down there than consider letting that man inside me."

The second she realizes what she just said, her face flushes in embarrassment. She looks like a fish out of water, with her wide eyes and mouth agape, as she tries to backtrack, but when she can't come up with anything, she shakes her head and laughs.

"Okay, now that you know I've gone so long without sex that I've dried up and I have cobwebs, I'm just going to go." She points to the airport exit, and I chuckle at how adorable this woman is when she's flustered.

"You said you're on the flight back to Harbor Point?" I ask, walking with her down the gangway.

"Yeah." She smiles and nods, then stops when we get to the gate. "Maybe I'll see you on another flight."

With a playful wink, she takes off, rolling her small bag behind her, while I stand in my spot, watching her walk away. For the first time, I want to get to know a woman beyond how deep her gag reflex goes.

But then my phone goes off, reminding me of my meeting, and I shake the thoughts away because I don't have time to get to know a woman, especially not one who isn't a part of my world.

"I look forward to doing business with you," Jaimie Sanchez says, shaking my hand.

The meeting went better than planned, and if all goes well, in a few weeks, several investors and I will be signing a contract to partner on one of the biggest real estate projects Coral Bay has ever seen. With over fifty acres of land that we own between the two of us and three other investors, the project will include two office buildings, a shopping mall, five residential buildings with high-end condominiums, as well as dozens of restaurants and a hotel. And the best part is that this project has nothing to do with my father. It's the first business deal I'll make without him.

"I'll see you soon," I tell him before getting into the town car.

When I arrive at the airport, I have time to spare before my flight, so I head straight to the lounge to get some work done. But before I enter, the sound of a woman in distress hits my ears, and I find myself walking toward where the commotion is coming from.

I'm usually one to keep to myself, but I have a sister I'm protective of and a mom who's been abused by my father for years—while I had to sit by and watch or risk being killed—so women tend to be a soft spot for me.

The door reads *PRIVATE*, but I ignore it as I swing it open and come face-to-face with the pilot from earlier, towering over Peyton. Her eyes are filled with a mixture of anger and fear as she stands helplessly against a wall while Dale corners her, his fingers wrapped around her throat.

"I suggest you remove your hand from around her neck," I warn, getting his attention.

"Fuck you!" he barks. "This is between me and the tease."

"See, that's where you're wrong." I stalk over to him and get in his face. "The moment you put your hands on a woman without permission, you made it my business."

I shove him, grabbing ahold of his lapel, and it forces him to let go of Peyton. "Now, explain to me," I say, pushing him against the wall, "why Peyton is a tease."

"Because I took her out on a date and the bitch didn't even let me feel her up," he chokes out.

He clearly has no self-preservation because the more he keeps talking, the more he pisses me off, and the deeper he digs his grave.

"I didn't know you were married!" she hisses. "I had just started, and you asked me out, making it seem like you were trying to welcome me to your crew. I didn't know you meant for it to be romantic."

"You know, Dale," I tell him, slamming him harder against the wall and wrapping my hand around his throat so he can feel what he did to Peyton, "it's men like you who give guys a bad name. Now, I'm only going to tell you this once. You're not to be anywhere near Peyton after today, and if I find out you are, I'm going to make sure you never fly a plane again."

Dale scoffs. "You can't do that."

I chuckle. "I can." I squeeze his throat harder, and he starts to panic as the air from his lungs is cut off. "And I will," I promise.

I lean in so only he can hear. "Do you have any idea who I am? My name is Dominick Antonov."

His eyes widen in fear, and I smirk, happy that he knows who I am.

"That's right," I whisper. "And whatever you've heard about me and my family, I can assure you, the truth is worse."

I wait until I know he's about to pass out from the lack of oxygen, and then I release his throat.

"Consider this your only warning." I step back and grin. "I'm glad we had this chat."

Then, I turn around and walk toward Peyton. "C'mon, Peaches. Let's grab something to eat before the flight. You have a little bit of time, right?"

"Uh, yeah." She nods, allowing me to thread my fingers through hers and guide her out of the room.

When we get a good distance away from that asshole, Peyton looks at me and says, "Did you call me Peaches?"

I stop in my tracks, shocked by her question. "What?"

"You called me Peaches."

I turn to face her and stare at her for a few seconds. I just threatened a man, and the only thing she clung to was the nickname I'd mistakenly called her.

The term of endearment had just slipped out—but it didn't

surprise me because I'd been thinking about her nonstop since we'd collided on the plane.

I could lie to her, come up with some ridiculous excuse, but I've never been one to run from the truth. "When you blush, your cheeks turn a beautiful shade of peach, reminding me of my mom's favorite flowers," I say, gliding my knuckles down her cheek. "A glimpse of light in an otherwise dark world."

Her brows furrow in confusion because she doesn't know who I am or the world I'm a part of, and I like that. I like her innocence, and I'll be damned if anyone ruins it—including that piece-of-shit pilot.

"Nobody's ever given me a nickname before," she murmurs, her cheeks deepening in color.

"I can assure you, it's a compliment," I tell her, taking a small step toward her.

This close, I can smell her sweet floral scent, only adding to her allure.

"Are you hungry?" I ask to change the subject.

"I could eat," she admits. "I know a good restaurant not too far from our gate," she says, looking up at me through her lashes. "And I'm almost positive they carry Kingston." She smiles softly. "My treat," she adds with a shrug. "I owe you for coming to my rescue back there."

"You don't owe me shit," I tell her, palming her cheek. "And what kind of man would I be if I didn't buy our meal?"

"One that's not sexist," she volleys.

"It's not about being sexist. I was raised by a man who treats women like inanimate objects. That'll never be me, but I'm also not going to let a beautiful woman pay for her meal when I'm capable of doing so."

She nods in understanding.

"And, Peaches …" I lock eyes with her. "I meant what I said. If that asshole comes anywhere near you, I'll make sure he's never able to fly again."

"Mmm, this place seriously makes the best burgers," Peyton moans after swallowing the last of her food and wiping her mouth. "How's yours?"

I had already eaten during my business meeting, so I wasn't hungry. I wasn't about to tell her that though, so I ordered the same thing as her and then regretted it when I saw how massive the burger was.

"It's good, and so is the drink." I hold up the old-fashioned, made with Kingston Limited's Black Label. "Are you from around here?" I ask conversationally.

The entire meal, we've talked about her job and how she fell into it after she dropped out of college, just before her senior year, to move back home to take care of her mom, who had fallen sick, but she's yet to give me anything more.

"I am," she says vaguely, leaving it at that.

I've noticed that while she talks about herself, she keeps the details to a minimum. I'm not sure if it's because I'm a stranger or what, but it's almost like she doesn't want me to know anything significant about her.

"What about you? Are you from Harbor Point or Coral Bay?"

"Harbor Point. I flew to Coral Bay for a business meeting."

She takes another bite of her burger, and I laugh at the moan she makes.

"Are burgers your favorite food?" I ask, wanting to know more about her.

"One of them. But I love anything breakfast-related the most." Her eyes light up. "When I was growing up, after my parents divorced, Mom would do breakfast for dinner sometimes. It was a cheap way to feed us when money was tight. She felt bad, but I loved it. Pancakes, sausage, bacon, biscuits and gravy, and toast with jam.

It became my go-to meal." She shrugs. "When I have a family of my own, I'm serving breakfast for dinner, even if we're not broke."

I chuckle, trying to imagine eating breakfast for dinner. When I was growing up, we had a housekeeper who cooked for us—and still does—and I'm pretty sure she'd have smacked me upside the head if I'd requested breakfast for dinner.

Her phone starts to beep, and she glances down at it, turning it off.

"Time for work," she says with a smile.

She reaches into her bag and pulls out a couple of bills, but I'm already shaking my head.

"You're really not going to let me at least pay for my own meal?" she asks.

"No." I chuckle and then lean in so our faces are close. "Since I'm paying, I can call this our first date, and it'll be harder for you to argue when I ask you for your number to arrange a second date."

It takes her a second to wrap her head around my words, but once she does, she throws her head back with a laugh. "That was good," she says. "But it's not happening."

"Me paying?" I ask, even though I already know what she meant.

"You getting my number or taking me out on a date," she clarifies. "Why not?"

I can think of a dozen reasons why I shouldn't pursue this woman, starting with the fact that until I sort out this arranged-marriage bullshit, I'm technically promised to another woman. Yet I still want Peyton to say yes.

"We don't live near each other, so it would never work."

I open my mouth to argue, but before I can come up with a rebuttal, she adds, "And if you tell me it doesn't matter, it does. I know we both feel it. The chemistry sizzling between us. Add in the fact that I haven't had sex in months, and it would be easy for me to get caught up in the moment. But I tried the long-distance thing with my ex, who swore he loved me, only for him to cheat on me with my best friend. Three years wasted." She sighs. "You're handsome, and from what I can tell, you're sweet and chivalrous, but I have my mom to take care of, and I'm just not in a place to start something that will ultimately lead to heartbreak."

I want to argue with her, but everything she's saying is spot-on. I can't give her what she needs, and it would be selfish of me to say otherwise.

So, instead, I pull a hundred out of my money clip, drop it onto the table, and then stand. "It was great to meet you, Peyton, and I enjoyed getting to know you."

She nods in understanding and stands as well. "It was great to meet you, Dominick. Thank you again for what you did with Dale. I really appreciate it."

When we reach the gate, Peyton disappears behind the door, and soon after, business class is called to board. The entire trip, she's professional. She smiles and says all the right things when getting me a couple of drinks. But I can see a hint of sadness hidden behind her expression and I can't help but wonder if maybe she was hoping that instead of agreeing with her, I would fight for her.

And I wish I were in a position to do so.

PASSPORT

FOUR

Dominick

"Is Brielle coming?" I ask when I walk into the kitchen on Sunday afternoon, fresh out of the shower after my workout session in our private gym.

I'd rather spend my afternoon doing anything but hanging out with my father, but Sunday dinners make Mom happy—and she deserves whatever happiness she can find, being married to the Devil himself. And it also means seeing my sister, who rarely comes home from college unless she's forced to do so.

Mom and Brielle always cook a delicious meal and dessert. We have drinks and talk over dinner, and even though I can't stand being in the same room as my father, I get a bit of satisfaction from watching his health rapidly decline.

Only Brielle hasn't shown up for the past three Sundays, and I'm starting to worry. After she missed the first dinner, feigning illness, I offered to visit her, but she insisted I stay away, claiming to be contagious.

The following Sunday, she used the excuse that she was behind on her studies due to being sick and couldn't make the drive home.

Last Sunday, she didn't even bother with a decent excuse. When she didn't show up, I called, and she said she forgot but promised she would see me this Sunday. Something sounded off in her tone, but she hung up before I could question her. I know she's having a hard time with the thought of having to marry Anthony, but she knows that Matteo and I are working on it.

"She's not coming," Mom chokes out.

When she turns around, I notice the tears in her eyes.

"What's wrong?" I ask, walking over to her to make sure she's not hurt.

The only time I've seen her cry is when Dad's hurt her, and it's clear from her splotchy face and puffy eyes that she's been crying for some time.

"Your sister and father had a falling-out. She turned off her phone, which led him to believe she was going to run away, so he had his men go to her apartment to bring her home."

"Do they have her?" Matteo asks, walking in and joining the conversation.

As much as we'd prefer to have our own places, in order to keep Mom safe from our asshole father, we still live at home, knowing he won't touch her while we're here now that we're capable of knocking him on his ass if he lays a finger on her.

"No," she whispers. "I don't know the details since your father doesn't feel the need to keep me informed, but I heard him yelling about her not being at her apartment, and then he took off to go after her himself. I'm worried," she says, her gaze flitting from Matteo to me. "I've never seen him this mad before. And he knows about her boyfriend."

"What the hell do you mean, her boyfriend?" Matteo yells, then turns to me. "Did you know about this?" he accuses.

"I had my suspicions, but she never confirmed," I say sharply. "And I didn't think she'd be dumb enough to flaunt it in public, where our father could find out."

"Can you locate her?" Mom asks Matteo, who's already typing away on his phone.

"Fuck, her location is off." He glances up at me. "We can't let Dad get to her. You know he'll stop at nothing to see his fucking plan through."

"We'll find her first," I tell him. "Mom, let us know if you hear anything."

"I will," she says, wrapping her arms around me. "Please find her first," she pleads, hugging Matteo next. "If your father does, I don't know what the outcome will be. He was so mad. When Anthony told him that he saw her with another man, your dad lost it. His violent tendencies have been getting worse, and I'm scared he might hurt her."

Fucking Anthony.

This is worse than I thought. Brielle being seen with another man is the equivalent of Dad going back on his word, which is viewed as the highest disrespect in our world.

If he finds her first, he's not only going to drag her back here and lock her up until it's time for her to marry Anthony, but he'll also find a way to punish her. And with his health at an all-time low, who knows what state of mind he'll be in or how badly he'll hurt her?

"Don't think the worst," Matteo says, reading my thoughts. "We'll find her. I've already spread the word on the streets that if anyone sees her, they're to grab her quietly and bring her to us. And, Mom"—he looks at her, his features filled with remorse and anger—"once we get her back, we're going to take care of Andrey once and for all. Enough with this bullshit."

"Any news?" I ask Matteo when he walks into my office.

"No. None of her friends or my contacts have seen or heard from her."

It's been a little over a week since Brielle went missing. We've pulled our resources in search of her, but we haven't had any luck in locating her. Thankfully, our father hasn't had any either, so at this point, it's a race to see who will find her first. Matteo and I hope she'll reach out to one of us so we can help her before our father gets ahold of her.

"We'll find her," he says, dropping into the visitor seat on the other side of my desk.

"I know. I just hate the thought of her being out there alone."

"It's a shitty situation," he says. "But our sister is tough."

"What if she's …" I begin, unable to finish my thought because imagining a world without Brielle in it makes me sick to my stomach.

"She's okay," Matteo says, his tone brooking no argument.

We're both silent for several minutes—the only sound in the room is from him typing away on his phone and me finishing an email I need to send out—until Matteo speaks again, moving on to another subject.

"So, you're leaving for Coral Bay … and flying commercial again?"

"What?" I glance up from my computer, trying to stall and think of an excuse my observant brother will buy.

"Your assistant emailed your agenda and copied me since she had to move a meeting we had to another day. It said you're flying commercial, which is strange since I know for a fact that our plane is available. Care to share why?"

"Saving gas," I mutter, going back to typing up my email and hoping he'll drop it.

As much as I don't want to leave Harbor Point until our sister is found, I also have a business to run, which means flying to Coral Bay to finalize the contracts for the real estate development deal with Jaimie.

Only, instead of having my assistant, Janet, secure the private plane, I told her I would handle it—and then found myself booking a flight with the same company Peyton worked for, telling myself that I was only doing it to make sure that cheating fucking pilot had heeded my warning.

It's been a month since I met Peyton, and I'd be lying if I said I haven't thought about her damn near every day. I wanted to find a way to reach out and make sure that fucker was no longer working directly with her, but I told myself it was for the best that I kept my distance.

But now that I need to go to Coral Bay … two birds, one stone, and all that shit.

"So, now, you're all about the environment?" Matteo barks out a laugh. "Stop with the bullshit and try again."

He leans back, crossing his arms over his chest, and I sigh, knowing he's not going to stop until I throw him a bone.

Our dad thinks Matteo is dumb because he struggled in school. He constantly got in trouble for not paying attention and for failing assignments, and when he got older, he barely showed up until he eventually dropped out. Once, a teacher tried to tell our parents that she thought Matteo had some kind of learning disability, and Dad beat the hell out of him for "being stupid and lazy."

But he never took the time to see Matteo's strengths. Instead, our father wrote him off and threw him onto the streets, thinking he wasn't capable of anything more than slinging drugs and enforcing our protection payments.

While Dad was grooming me to take over the company, Matteo was running the streets and creating a name for himself, making deals that fattened his pockets and establishing connections with men who wouldn't give Dad the time of day.

He has natural gut instincts and street smarts. He's intuitive, and he picks up on people's nuances that most wouldn't notice. You give him a problem, and he'll solve it—you just might not like how it's solved.

While I make sure our mom and sister are cared for, he protects them. Because that's what Matteo does. He protects. On the outside, it looks like he's a ruthless bastard, and while that's true when it comes to business, when it comes to our family, Matteo cares enough that he'll stop at nothing to ensure our mom, Brielle, and me are safe—which is why I know that Brielle missing is eating away at him and he's using my situation to distract himself.

Matteo's not only my brother and best friend, but he's my business partner in everything that doesn't involve our father. And the day I get complete control of the company, I'll make our business partnership official in every aspect.

"If you must know, I finally met someone who could hold my interest for longer than thirty seconds," I admit, shutting my laptop and giving Matteo my attention.

"And she'd rather fly commercial than private?" He chuckles. "Damn, bro. I need to find someone like that. The woman I took out a few weeks ago wanted dinner before she let me take her back to her place to fuck her." He shakes his head, actually looking put out over the fact that a woman wanted to be treated like a lady.

"And she bitched when I took her to Pasquale's," he adds, referring to his favorite hole-in-the-wall Italian restaurant in South Harbor Point. "Insisted we leave and I take her to the country club instead. She wouldn't know what a good meal looked like if it smacked her in the head."

"Did you take her to the country club?" I ask, curiosity getting the better of me.

Our entire family belongs to North Harbor Point Country Club. It's where all the wealthy who's who of Harbor Point socialize, including many politicians and public officials. Usually, I'm the one who frequents the club since I manage the business side of things while Matteo handles the underground shit.

"Of course I did." He grins wolfishly. "Then, I fucked her in their fancy-ass restroom after dinner."

"You're such a dog. At this rate, you're going to run out of women in Harbor Point soon."

Matteo just shrugs. "Maybe I'll go to wherever you went to meet this woman. Which was where exactly?" He tilts his head, curious.

"She was the flight attendant on my flight to Coral Bay."

"Ah, did you become a member of the Mile High Club?"

"I'm not a pubescent boy," I drawl.

Matteo cracks up. "Okay, Mr. Grown-Up. So, where did you *maturely* fuck her?"

"I didn't. It wasn't like that. Besides, have you seen the restrooms on a commercial flight?" I cringe, remembering how small it was. "It could barely fit me, let alone a woman too."

Matteo laughs. "Challenge accepted."

"You know, every woman you treat like shit is someone's daughter or sister," I point out.

"Who's treating anyone like shit?" he scoffs. "The women who come to me know exactly what they're getting—a good fucking that ends with multiple orgasms. If they wanted a gentleman, they'd go to you instead. Speaking of which … this mystery flight attendant— what are you doing with her? Because unless something's changed—"

"I'm not marrying her," I snap, referring to Daniella Russo. "But, to answer your question, nothing is going on with the flight attendant. The pilot—who is married, I might add—was harassing her, so I helped her out. Threatened his livelihood if he went anywhere near her again. I just figured since I need to go back to Coral Bay, I might as well make sure he's staying the hell away from her."

"Do you need any help?" Matteo asks, sitting up straight.

My brother might be a playboy who fucks around, but he would never stand for a woman being harmed in any way.

"Nah," I tell him. "Guy would be crazy not to heed my warning. I'll fly to Coral Bay, make sure she's not being hassled, and my good deed for the year will be done."

The motherfucker did not heed my warning.

How do I know that? Because I'm currently standing in the airport, watching him harass Peyton—like his life wasn't threatened— right in front of everyone.

While he speaks to her, his brow furrowed in annoyance, she attempts to ignore him as she goes about doing her job.

"Let me guess," Matteo says when he answers the phone on the first ring, "you need my help."

"His name is Dale Stuart, resides in Coral Bay, Florida, and I want to make sure he can never fly a plane again."

"Dominick," Peyton says in surprise when she arrives at my seat. She glances back nervously—no doubt to see if Dale is in the vicinity—and then plasters a smile on her face. "Fancy seeing you here."

"Another business trip," I say nonchalantly. "How are you doing?"

"I'm good," she says softly. "Can I get you something to drink? An old-fashioned?"

"That would be great."

She disappears to make my drink, and a few minutes later, she returns with it in hand. "One old-fashioned," she says, setting it on the tray next to me. "Please let me know if I can get you anything else."

"Actually," I say, placing my hand over hers to stop her from leaving, "I've been meaning to ask, did that pilot leave you alone after our conversation?"

Peyton's eyes bounce all over the plane before she nods. "Yeah. Everything is great," she lies straight through her teeth.

"Good. I'm glad I could help."

She forces a smile and then moves on to the next person while I text my brother, asking him to bump Dale to the top of his to-do list.

Matteo: Already done, bro.

I spend the flight going over contracts and working on the plan Matteo and I have in motion to separate Antonov business dealings from the Russos and Rothschilds. Then, when our dad dies and we refuse to follow through with the arranged marriages, Giuseppe and Joseph won't have anything to threaten us with.

Lorenzo is on board, but because his father is still competent, even though he's next in line, he doesn't have the capability of making the executive decisions.

If our fathers didn't have so much of their businesses intertwined, separating everything would be easier. But because they do, it's like playing a deadly game of chess. One wrong move, and we could send up a red flag, alerting them to what we're trying to do, and then it would be checkmate—and not in our favor.

When the plane lands, I don't wait around for Peyton, not wanting to draw any attention to myself. With whatever Matteo has planned, the last thing I want is to lay any breadcrumbs on the ground that would lead to Peyton or me.

I'm out of the terminal and halfway to the exit when I hear my name being called. I turn around and find Peyton speed-walking toward me.

"Everything okay?" I ask once she reaches me.

She glances around and then grabs my wrist in her delicate hand, pulling me into a corner. "I lied," she says softly so nobody can hear. "It's gotten worse. Apparently, your warning messed with his ego, and now, if I don't sleep with him, he's threatening to lie and say I harassed him. I was wondering …" She swallows thickly, and her tear-filled eyes meet mine. "Could you tell him you were just kidding? Maybe if you take it back? I don't even know if that will work, but—"

"Hey"—I turn her until her back is against the wall, so if anyone walks by, they'll only make out the back of me—"I'm taking care of it, I promise. He's never going to bother you again."

"Okay," she breathes. "Thank you. It's just that my mom isn't doing so well, and I really need this job."

"It's okay," I assure her. "You don't have to explain anything to me." *And I can't afford to get to know you more than I already do because it's only going to make me want you that much more*, I think, but don't voice. "You don't know me, but I promise, I am a man of my word."

"Thank you," she murmurs.

"No problem."

Her lips curve into a smile—a real one this time—and her entire face lights up. I'm about to do something stupid, like ask for her number, when my phone rings, breaking the moment.

"I need to take this," I tell her, taking a step back. "But don't worry. It will all work out."

Without waiting for her to respond, I take off toward the exit to answer the call.

It's from Matteo.

"Any news?"

"I think he killed her boyfriend."

"Who?" I ask in confusion since our last conversation was about Peyton and she never mentioned having anything other than an ex-boyfriend.

"Brielle. I think Andrey killed her boyfriend. We searched her apartment and found pictures of her with a guy. I ran his picture through the system, and his name is ... well, *was* Owen Levine. Senior at the same college Brielle attends. Business major. He went missing a few days ago, and this morning, my guys found a dead body that matches his description. It's clear he was murdered. I made sure nothing could be linked back to us or Bri. Since he wasn't killed in Harbor Point, I had to pay off a cop in the jurisdiction where we found him to call it in. We'll know soon if it was him."

"And Brielle? Have you found her?" I hold my breath, praying he has and she's okay.

"No," Matteo says. "And his phone is missing, so I can't check it for texts or calls."

"Dad probably has it."

"Yeah, which could mean he's closer to finding her."

"Fuck, I'm coming back there."

"There's nothing you can do," Matteo says. "I have all my men searching for her, and as soon as we find her, I'll let you know. You coming home won't change a thing. You're a good businessman, but you don't know the streets like we do."

He's right, but I hate feeling helpless.

"Besides, Andrey isn't going to hurt her," he points out. "She's the only daughter he has, so she's his only hope of completing his ludicrous plan."

"We need to take care of him sooner rather than later."

"We will," he promises. "Go to the meeting. I'll let you know if I find anything else out."

"All right," I say after several seconds. "If you need anything …"

"I got this. Get the deal finalized, and I'll see you back at home."

We hang up, and the anger that's been building inside me finally surfaces. Before I can think about what I'm doing, my fist hits the metal beam in an attempt to release a bit of my pent-up aggression.

Fuck!

Brielle just had to hold on a little longer, but instead, she acted in haste, and now, not only did she get her boyfriend killed, but her life is at risk too. She knew better when she chose to fall for someone who wasn't part of our world.

Speaking of which …

My gaze lands on the beautiful, green-eyed beauty standing in the taxi line with her rolling luggage next to her.

I should leave her alone, walk away, and never look back since I know Matteo is going to take care of that asshole for her. But I can't help the way I gravitate toward her.

"Where are you off to?" I ask when I step up behind her.

She jumps and spins, a cute shriek leaving her lips. "Jesus," she breathes when her eyes land on me. "You can't be sneaking up on people like that. I'm headed home."

"Does that mean you won't be serving me my old-fashioned on my flight home later?"

She shakes her head. "I picked up a trip for a crew member. So, unless you're going to the Dominican Republic tomorrow morning, you won't be on my flight."

"That sounds an awful lot like an invitation," I joke, making her eyes bug out.

"What? No," she splutters, shaking her head. "That's not what I—"

I bridge the gap between us and lean in close so only she can hear. "The DR is beautiful this time of year. Maybe I'll have to take a trip there." *And it would be the perfect distraction from the bullshit that has become my life.*

"I've never been," Peyton chokes out. "We have a one-night layover, so I'm hoping to spend tomorrow seeing some of the sights."

"I could show you around," I tell her, lifting her chin so she's forced to look at me. I have a few business associates in the DR, so I've been there several times over the years. "Would you want that?"

"I told you that I have a lot going on and my mom is—"

"I'm not asking you to marry me," I say, placing two fingers against her plump lips. "And whatever is going on will still be there when you are back. I just want one day with you. Could you give me that?"

She swallows thickly, and then after several seconds, she nods. "I need the words."

I need to hear that she wants me the way I want her. That despite neither of us being in a position to see where this could go long-term, neither of us can deny the chemistry sizzling between us. And it would be a waste to not let it burn.

"*If* I were to see you in the DR, I wouldn't be opposed to letting you show me the sights."

I nod and smile, so damn intrigued by this woman. "Well, maybe you'll see me on the plane tomorrow."

The line moves forward, and Peyton's taxi arrives. With a quick glance back at me, she slides into the back seat and takes off.

Since I didn't book a town car—too busy dealing with Peyton and then the phone call from my brother—I grab a taxi to take me to my meeting.

> Me: You think the commercial flight was bad? You should see me inside of a taxi.

> Matteo: Who are you, and what have you done with my brother?

I arrive at my meeting on time, and it goes smoothly. The other investors and I sign the contracts, and it feels good to know that the deal has none of my father's tainted blood on it.

I'm walking out of the meeting, toward the town car that's waiting for me, unsure if I'm going to head to the airport or book a flight to the DR, when a notification catches my eye, alerting me of a new email from Victor Rosa. He's a business associate of ours in the DR. We've been handling his shipments into Harbor Point for years, and our contract with them is due to be renegotiated.

Usually, Victor would make the trip to Harbor Point, and I'd have my brother with me since he recently started handling the port, despite our father's objections.

But my brain goes to a certain red-haired, green-eyed woman who will be flying to the DR tomorrow, and my decision is made.

I shoot a text to my brother, hoping he won't see through my lie, and then tell the driver I'm going to be staying in Coral Bay tonight, so I'll need to be taken to a hotel.

> Me: I have some business I need to attend to in the DR, so I'm going to handle Rosa's contract renegotiation while I'm there.

It shows he read it, but he doesn't respond for several minutes. When he does, I can't help but groan because it's like he's Big Brother.

Matteo: Any chance the flight attendant is accompanying you to the DR?

Me: Focus on handling the fucking pilot.

Matteo: Don't think I haven't noticed that you haven't mentioned her name. But I'll let you keep your little secret for now. Have fun, bro … but not too much.

Since I don't have any clothes with me because it was only supposed to be a day trip, after getting checked in to my hotel, I have Janet order me clothes and a carry-on suitcase to be delivered to my room, and then I spend the rest of the evening working.

Several times, I consider finding a way to contact Peyton to ask her to dinner, but I don't because spending time with her here would feel too personal. This is where she lives, but the DR will be neutral ground. We'll spend some time together, and I'll show her the sights. She'll be a good distraction, and we'll go our separate ways. Then, I can focus on the important shit, like ending the ties between the three families so we'll be free from our father once and for all.

"That's all I need," I tell myself. "One night with Peyton to get her out of my system, and then we can both move on."

PASSPORT

FIVE

Peyton

I'M ALMOST POSITIVE I AGREED TO HAVE A ONE-NIGHT STAND with Dominick Antonov, the gentleman from business class. It wasn't mentioned outright, but I'm pretty sure the *sights* Dominick wants to show me don't include the local museums and parks.

As I shave my legs, I tell myself that he was messing with me. No sane man is going to take a commercial flight to the Dominican Republic with the sole purpose of getting laid. Chances are, I'm going to get on the plane, and he won't be there, but …

I continue to shave, because I'll be damned if, after going through a six-month dry spell, I'm going to be caught with prickly legs, hairy pits, and bushy lady bits.

The man is gorgeous in a suit, and I have very little doubt that he's any less gorgeous without it on. I've met plenty of men like him before—confident, sure of himself, knows his place in this world. Unlike Dale—who I've been told is all dad bod—Dominick doesn't try to flaunt it or throw himself at women because men like Dominick know they can have sex anytime they want, and they don't have to harass or beg or threaten women for it to happen.

After finishing in the shower, I turn the water off and go about drying off and blow-drying my hair. I apply my makeup, laying the red lipstick on thick to match my naturally red hair, fully aware I'm doing it for a certain man I'm hoping will be on the flight.

My results came back, and I'm STD-free—thank God. But I'm

not risking that shit again, so I pack a few condoms I keep on hand. I need to get on birth control, but that's for another day.

I consider what to pack, wondering if it will look presumptuous if I bring lingerie. This past year has been rough, and with Mom's medical expenses, I haven't had the money to buy much for myself, but when a friend of mine from college was getting married a few months ago, she bought her bridesmaids a sexy set of lingerie to wear under our dresses. She said it was so we could be clichés and find a guy to hook up with after her wedding. At the time, I laughed since I wasn't in the right frame of mind to have casual sex, but now, I'm thankful for her little gift.

I grab the bra and panty set from my drawer and toss it into my bag—because who cares? The guy is clearly looking to get laid, and I'd rather be prepared than have him see me in my flowery cotton underwear.

"Peyton, you look beautiful," Mom says when I roll my overnight bag out to the living room, where she's reading a book and drinking her morning coffee.

"I was feeling good this morning," I tell her, not completely lying since the thought of an orgasm that's not self-induced does have me feeling good.

Mom smiles warmly at me, and I lean down to give her a hug and a kiss on her cheek.

"I love you," I tell her, so thankful that she's still here.

After we found out she had hepatitis C—more than likely from a blood transfusion she had received when she gave birth to me, although it can't be proven—I thought I was going to lose her, but she did treatment and was in remission for several years.

Then, we found out that the hep C caused liver cirrhosis, which led to liver cancer. Again, I thought I was going to lose my mom. But after a successful liver transplant, she was back in remission.

Everything was going well until we got the news a few weeks ago that her liver was failing. And we were told that even with dialysis, her liver would only last—in a perfect world—two to three years.

The only option is to do another liver transplant, but Mom will never survive that, nor does she want to go through that again. So, that means she's dying, and there's nothing I can do about it.

"I love you too," she says. "Have a safe trip, and I'll see you in a couple of days."

"You'll see me tomorrow."

Since finding out that her liver is failing, I've started to look for jobs at home. I took the flight attendant job after her transplant because the schedule allowed me to do quick trips, never being gone for more than a night or two, and our neighbor—a sweet elderly woman, who is also a nurse—could check on her while I was away.

But now, with her time limited and her health declining, I don't want to be gone overnight. I've applied to several local jobs, including a few upscale bars and clubs, and my hope is to get one and then go back to school to finish my degree.

When I get to the airport, there's a bunch of chatter, and when I ask Ericka—a colleague and fellow flight attendant—what's going on, she shocks me when she says, "Dale was found dead late last night. Apparently, the guilt from all his infidelity caught up with him, and he killed himself."

"What?" I gasp. "How do you know that?"

"His wife found an apology letter."

"That's insane," I say. "He didn't seem like the type who would feel any remorse for his behavior."

"I guess it just goes to show you that we never truly know what's going on in other people's heads." Ericka shrugs.

I think about Dominick promising that he would handle it.

There's no way he had a hand in this, right?

It's just a coincidence. He said he would handle it, and then Dale killed himself. There's no way Dominick murdered a man and then made it look like he'd committed suicide. He's a businessman, not the head of some criminal organization.

I shake myself from my crazy thoughts. I seriously need to stop watching those true crime documentaries when I can't sleep at night.

"I guess so," I agree.

We go about prepping the flight to the Dominican Republic. Since it's only an hour-long flight, we won't have to serve food, aside from snacks.

"A few of us are going to head to the beach when we get there," Ericka says as we walk to the galley to get situated. "Want to join?"

"I'm not sure," I tell her. "I'm feeling a bit under the weather. Can I let you know?"

"Of course. Are you good to work?"

"Yeah," I say, backtracking. "It's more mental."

She nods. "I get it. Dale was a major dickhead, but knowing he's dead is messing with my head too. And I know he was constantly trying to hit on you. If you need to talk …"

"I'm good," I promise. "I think I just need some time to wrap my head around it."

Since I'll be working in business class, I grab the clipboard with the list of passengers and scan it, looking for a certain name. The chart is done by row and seat number, and after several rows, when I don't see his name, I tell myself it's for the best. And then in the last row in business class is *Dominick Antonov*.

Holy shit. He's on my flight.

The passengers start to walk on board, and I stay busy, helping them with their luggage. I can feel Dominick's presence, but I don't give him any attention, unsure how I feel about what's going to happen once we get off this plane.

In theory, the idea of spending the night with this man sounded great, but the truth is, I've never done this before. I've always been a relationship type of woman.

After the other attendants and I do the final cabin check, the pilot announces that we'll be taking off shortly, and we have a seat in the jump seats for takeoff.

Where I'm sitting, I have the perfect view of Dominick, who is staring at me. His gray eyes are filled with lust, and the way he's eye-fucking me has my thighs clenching in need. If I could orgasm from a look alone, I'd be damn close to screaming his name in pleasure. And if he can cause all this from just a look, I can't even imagine what he might do in the bedroom when he could actually touch me.

Once the plane is in the air, I stand and start to make my rounds, asking everyone what they'd like to drink. It takes a while before I get to Dominick, but when I do, instead of asking him, I bring him an old-fashioned and set it on his armrest. I've noticed that every time he flies, he never has anybody next to him, and when I double-check, I see that he paid for two seats.

"Thank you," he says, taking a sip of his drink, his eyes locked on me. "I didn't see the *pilot* on this flight. Did he finally heed my warning?"

At his words, my heart stills and then kicks into overdrive. I was worried that he'd had something to do with Dale's death, but if he's asking about Dale, that means he doesn't know what happened, right?

"Actually," I say, leaning in so nobody will overhear, "he was found dead last night."

Dominick's brows kiss his forehead.

"Apparently, his guilt caused him to commit suicide."

He nods in understanding. "You don't feel guilty for that, do you?"

When I shrug, unsure how I feel, he adds, "He was married with three children, Peyton. From what you told me, rather than being faithful to the woman he'd made vows to, he used his power to take advantage of women, such as yourself. If his guilt caused his death, that's on him, not you."

He's right. I know he is, and I'll accept that, but it's going to take time.

"Can I get you anything else?" I ask him, standing up straight and changing the subject.

"Not unless you're on the menu," he says, eyeing me up and down with a smirk that has my lady parts tingling in want.

If I wasn't sure what his intentions were regarding showing me the sights, my thoughts have now been confirmed. He wants me. In his bed. For one night. And then we'll go our separate ways. Even though I've never done this before, I am completely on board.

"Unfortunately for you, I'm not on the menu," I tell him, hiding my own smirk as I turn to walk away.

Before I can get too far though, his fingers wrap around my wrist, and he pulls me toward him. I fall into the empty seat next to him, and he leans in, his lips brushing my ear.

"I beg to differ," he murmurs. "I think you're not only on the menu, but when I lay you out on the bed later, I'm also going to find that you're soaking wet and ready for me to feast on your cunt."

I open my mouth to argue, but before I can get a word in edgewise, he continues, "Before you try to deny it, I saw the way your thighs clenched as you watched me while the plane was taking off. You didn't have to say a word for me to know you were imagining me making you come. The only question is, how were you envisioning it? Did I use my tongue, fingers, or cock?" When I don't respond, my labored breathing making it hard to speak, he chuckles darkly. "Don't worry, Peaches. Tonight, I plan to use all three."

He lets go of my wrist, sits back, and goes about typing on his laptop, like he just asked me about the damn weather instead of telling me what he's going to do to me later in detail.

The rest of the flight, I keep busy, trying to avoid Dominick, and by the end, when all the passengers have disembarked, I realize he didn't try to speak to me again and he got off without letting me know where to meet him.

Maybe he was just messing with me.

Since the flight back to Coral Bay doesn't leave until tomorrow morning, the airline booked us rooms at the hotel near the airport.

After finishing up our duties, we head out, and I'm about to tell Ericka that I'll join her and the rest of the crew at the beach when I spot Dominick leaning against the wall, his eyes trained on me, with a small carry-on next to him.

Unlike every other time I've seen him—dressed sharply in a business suit—he's dressed in a pair of khaki shorts and a navy-blue collared shirt, making him look like he's about to dominate the golf course instead of the boardroom. Both looks are different yet equally mouthwatering. He's wearing a chunky, expensive-looking watch, and he's sporting a few-days-old stubble. When I get to his feet, I can't help but smile at his white leather sneakers. They're so clean, and they look new. I wonder if he had to buy clothes since he hadn't planned on coming to the DR.

Wordlessly, I follow him through the airport, customs, and security. It isn't until after I tell Ericka I'm going to do my own thing and she takes off that Dominick approaches me.

"I thought you'd never be alone," he says, threading his fingers through mine and guiding us to a black town car.

"Mr. Antonov?" the gentleman standing outside it says, tipping his hat.

"*Sí, gracias,*" Dominick says, handing him our luggage and then opening the door for me.

I get in, and after he speaks to the driver in Spanish for a few moments, he slides in next to me. He types away on his phone for several minutes, and I start to wonder if this is how it's going to be all day—him working and giving me his leftover time—when he pockets his phone and looks at me, finally giving me his attention.

"I'm sorry," he says. "While I'm here, I have to meet with a business associate to go over some contracts, but once that's out of the way, I'm all yours."

"Okay. If you want to drop me off at the hotel …"

Dominick shakes his head. "I only get you for twenty-four hours," he says, pinching my chin with his thumb and forefinger. "I'm not letting you out of my sight. You will join me for my meeting, and then the rest of the day will be spent seeing the sights. We'll have to stop and get you a bathing suit. The waterfall I'm going to take you to is too beautiful to merely look at from afar."

Shoot. I was so focused on which undergarments to pack that I forgot to pack a bathing suit. I always bring one when I'll be staying overnight, just in case I want to go to the hotel pool. And we're in the DR, which has some of the prettiest beaches in the world.

"Wait," I say, his words hitting me. "We're actually going sightseeing?"

Dominick stares at me for several seconds and then throws his head back with a laugh. The sound momentarily startles me, but once I get myself together, I take him in. Serious, broody Dominick is gorgeous, but when he laughs, his entire face lights up. His gray eyes lighten and twinkle with mirth, and I swear, he looks ten years younger.

When he stops laughing, his smile remains, and I memorize the way he looks for when we part ways and I think about him. This is how I want to remember this man—laughing, smiling, happy. It's clear from the intensity he carries that whatever he does for a living is stressful. When I watch him working on his phone or laptop, he's so serious, his eyes turn dark, and I worry that the stress will eventually give him a heart attack. But right now, he looks young and carefree, like he's a completely different person.

"Of course we're going to see the sights," he says as his eyes scan my body. "Do you have something to change into for brunch?"

I think about what I brought and cringe. "I brought shorts and a shirt to change into when I arrived and one dress in case I went to dinner tonight."

I honestly didn't think he would be on my flight, but just in case, I threw a little black dress and heels into my luggage. It will work for dinner, but not for brunch.

"We'll stop and get you something," Dominick says matter-of-factly.

"I don't want to be a burden," I tell him, but he simply shakes his head.

"I can assure you," he says, his eyes alight with lust, "watching you try on dresses and bikinis will benefit me as much as you."

PASSPORT
15:45
25 DEC 18
HGRB15
IFK
JOHN
New
Lond
gate 35
AI

SIX

Peyton

W HEN DOMINICK SAID WE WOULD GO BY THE STORE TO FIND me a dress and bathing suit, I thought he meant Target or Walmart. So, when we pulled up to the most adorable local boutique, I was pleasantly surprised. But once we walked in, I was in heaven. Beautiful dresses donned the mannequins, and every style swimsuit imaginable hung on the walls. Gorgeous shoes, heels, and wedges were showcased on the shelves. I could've bought one of everything. Until I saw the price tags.

With one look, I stepped back, and that had Dominick insisting that he was paying. And since he clearly makes enough money to—I mean, the guy books two business-class seats just so no one will sit next to him—and the brunch *is* for his business meeting, who am I to say no?

"What do you think?" I ask, doing a quick twirl in a navy-blue-and-white floral dress that is cut low in the front, showcasing my cleavage, and hits just above my knees.

I thought Dominick would tell me to grab something and meet me at the register, so I was shocked when he sat in the seat outside of the dressing room and told me to model each one for him.

I've tried on and shown him two other dresses, and he's looked at both like he wants to rip them off and fuck me against the wall in the changing room.

To be honest, I wouldn't be opposed.

"That's the one," he says, his gaze gleaming with want. "But just to make sure, turn around one more time. I didn't get a good enough look from the back."

I playfully roll my eyes but twirl again. "You know, if you want to check out my ass, all you have to do is—"

Before I make it all the way around or finish my sentence, the front of his body is pressed against my back, and he's pushed me against the wall in the changing room, caging me in. He's so close that I can smell his fresh, masculine scent, and it momentarily distracts me.

Until his hand goes to my hip, and his face nuzzles into the side of my neck.

I gasp at his touch and wait to see what he'll do next.

"Fuck, you smell so good," he murmurs, running his nose along my now-heated flesh.

"It's lavender," I say dumbly.

He inhales deeply, and a shiver visibly races through my body, making him chuckle.

"Tell me I can touch you," he whispers against my ear. "That I can slide my hand under this dress and feel how wet you are. I bet this cunt is drenched."

I tighten my legs and nod.

"You know I need to hear the words," he says, his voice smooth, like he's not anywhere as affected as I am.

"Yes," I breathe, desperate for him. "You can do whatever the hell you want to me," I find myself saying.

He turns me around so my back is against the wall and our fronts are almost flush together. Even while I'm still in my work heels, he's only about six inches taller than me, yet it feels like he towers over me with his dominating presence.

His hand glides down my waist and under my dress while his mouth hovers millimeters above mine. He doesn't make any move to kiss me though as his fingers skate across the hem of my panties and slide underneath, the rough pads just barely grazing the hood of my pussy.

When the tip of his finger lands on my clit, I gasp, and then Dominick's mouth is on me. He kisses exactly how I imagined he would—strong and demanding.

He taps the top of my pussy, and I part my legs slightly, giving him access, as our lips curve around one another.

"Fuck, Peaches, you really are soaked," he murmurs against my lips as he slides his finger through my center, causing warmth to flood through my veins.

The pad of his finger reaches the sensitive bud between my legs, and I release a soft moan at how good it feels.

Dominick deepens the kiss by sliding his tongue into my mouth and stroking mine. With our mouths fused together, our tongues move frantically against one another. One of his hands grips the curve of my hip while the other massages my clit. And in response, I rest my hands on his chest, needing to touch him back.

I'm fully aware this is our first kiss, but it feels like we've done this a million times, and I have to remind myself that what we're doing has an expiration date. Today, I feel like a princess. But tomorrow, I'll turn back into a pumpkin. Dominick will return home—which I'm assuming is Harbor Point since he always flies to and from there—and I'll go to Coral Bay, where I'll focus on my mom as we count down the days she has left.

Just as that morbid thought hits me, Dominick adds pressure to my clit, and my orgasm overtakes me. He swallows my moans of pleasure, and when my orgasm begins to subside and I try to push him away, he lightens his touch as our kiss moves from hard and deep to a soft caress.

"Thank God I have more time with you," he mutters once he breaks the kiss, his forehead pressing against mine. "Otherwise, I'd say fuck the sightseeing and drag your sexy ass to the hotel I booked."

I can't help the giggle that escapes me.

Dominick is a charmer.

"C'mon," he says, pulling his fingers out of my panties and taking a step back. "We're going to be late for brunch."

"I still have to pick out a swimsuit," I remind him, making him groan.

"That can't happen," he says. "If I see you in a bikini, we'll never make it to my meeting. Do you know your size?"

"Yeah," I say with a laugh as I grab my clothes from the floor and he threads our fingers together, guiding us back to the main area of the boutique.

"We're taking this dress," he tells the saleswoman. Then, to me, he says, "Grab a few bikinis, and you can try them on later." His gaze descends to my feet. "And a pair of heels that match the dress."

Dominick pays for the items, and when I thank him for the cute new dress, heels, and swimsuits, he grants me a brief yet toe-curling kiss.

"This meeting needs to be quick," he mutters once we're back in the town car. "I took it as an excuse to come here so I didn't look like a crazy stalker, but now, I'm wishing I hadn't."

"You can't stalk the willing," I tell him, pulling his face to mine for a kiss. "But don't worry. It will be over soon, and then we'll have the rest of the day and night."

"Mmm," he hums against my lips. "I'm not sure that will be enough time for everything I want to do with you."

"Well, it will have to be," I say, pulling back. "Because that's all we have."

While Dominick does his business stuff, I switch out my work heels for the cute boho-style beige wedge sandals I chose. They're both classy and comfortable. Then, I let my hair down and fluff it since it was up for the flight before reapplying my lipstick.

I've just finished making myself presentable when the car pulls up to what looks like a beautiful resort.

"Is this where your meeting is?" I ask as the driver opens the door for us.

"It's also where we're staying," Dominick states.

I whip my head around to look at him in shock. "What do you mean, where we're staying?" I whisper, looking at the resort in a new light. I can't see beyond the main building, but it screams luxury and wealth, and I could be wrong, but I think I saw this resort listed as one that celebrities stay at when they visit the Dominican Republic. "The airline paid for a hotel near the airport. We could stay there for free."

Dominick takes my hand in his, and with nothing more than a swift, incredulous look my way, he heads past the valet and into the entrance of the resort.

"Hey," I say, tugging on his hand. "I spoke to you, which means you respond. Maybe in your business world, people just jump at your command, and you don't have to converse, but with me, it's a requirement."

He stops in place, and for several seconds, he looks at me like I've grown two heads. Then, a smile spreads across his face, confusing the hell out of me.

"If you only knew how my world works." He chuckles. "Keep talking, and I'm going to find a restroom I can fuck you in."

"Dominick," I chide, "I'm serious."

"I know you are, and it's sexy as hell. Aside from my brother, nobody questions anything I do or say." He releases my hand and pulls me toward him. "I appreciate you offering the free hotel, but this one is nicer and safer, and it has amenities I fully plan to take advantage of with you later."

"Like what?"

"For one"—he slides his hand around my backside and tugs me even closer—"our room has a Jacuzzi on the terrace."

"Oh," I breathe, imagining him eating me out on the edge of the Jacuzzi.

As if he knows what I'm thinking, his smile widens, and he nods.

"Exactly." He leans down and kisses me softly. "So, are you okay with staying here? Or are you going to insist we go to the free hotel?"

"Here is good," I say, making him chuckle.

"Good." He kisses me again, this time giving my butt cheek a firm squeeze. "Now, let's get this meeting over with so I can spend the rest of the day focused on you. The only thing getting me through it is knowing when we're done, I'll get to see you in one of those bikinis."

"If you make it quick," I say, running my fingers through the back of his hair, "I'll let you see me in all three."

"Dominick!" an older gentleman says, slapping Dominick on the back with one hand and shaking his hand with the other. "*Que bueno verte, mi hermano.*"

"*Hola, mi amigo,*" Dominick says back, shocking me as he speaks fluent Spanish. With his last name being popular in the Russian community, I didn't peg him for a Spanish speaker. "*Que bueno verte a ti también.*"

"*¿Y por aquí a quien tenemos?*" the gentleman responds, glancing at me.

I have no idea what they're saying, but judging from the way Dominick looks my way as well, I have a feeling they're talking about me.

Damn it, I should've paid better attention in Spanish class.

"*Este es una amiguita especial,*" Dominick says, pulling me into his side like he's staking his claim. "*Le daré un recorrido privado por tu hermosa isla.*"

The gentleman chuckles. "*No te preocupes, mi hermano. Te escuché fuerte y claro.*"

Dominick nods and then switches to English. "Peyton, this is my longtime business associate and friend, Victor Rosa."

"It's nice to meet you," I say in English since that's my only option.

"It's good to meet you," Victor says, his English a bit broken and his accent heavy but still understandable.

He takes my hand and brings it up to his lips for a kiss, and I still in my spot, a little uncomfortable even though I'm not sure why. I barely know Dominick, yet I let him finger me in a dressing room without thought, but this guy kisses my hand in greeting, and I want to take a hot shower.

As if Dominick can sense my unease, he pulls me into his arms and tips my chin to kiss me on the lips. And this time, there's no mistaking him making a claim on me.

Victor chuckles. "Shall we go eat? I'm famished."

The way he says it while looking at me, as if he'd like to eat me for brunch, has me moving closer to Dominick, who doesn't seem fazed by his business associate's blatant flirting.

Brunch is delicious. Because I didn't eat much before work, I'm starved, and I devour my meal while the men discuss business—and Victor thankfully pays no interest in me.

I have no idea what they're talking about, and it doesn't help that they switch back and forth between Spanish and English frequently, but from what I can gather, Victor ships his products from the DR to Harbor Point and pays Dominick to house them. They must come to some kind of agreement because they shake hands, and then Dominick insists on paying the bill.

Once Victor leaves, Dominick goes to the front desk to check in. I'm not sure what is said since they're speaking in Spanish, but it ends with the woman handing Dominick a room key.

"So, we're skipping the sights and going straight for the Jacuzzi?" I half joke as we walk toward the elevator.

Dominick laughs. "No, Peaches. Our luggage and bags are waiting for us in our room. I figured it would be easier for you to change in there instead of somewhere public."

"And what about you?" I ask, eyeing his attire. "Will I get to see you in your swimsuit?"

"Only if you're a good girl and show me all three of the bikinis you chose." He waggles his brows playfully, and I roll my eyes.

When we step into the room, I don't know what I was expecting, but this wasn't it. I knew the rooms were nice, but, holy shit, this place is more extravagant than anything I've seen on TV or in movies. The main room alone is larger than my mom's entire house.

"Come," Dominick says without batting an eyelash.

Taking my hand in his, he brings us into the master suite that screams opulence and wealth while still making me feel warm and cozy. The king-size bed, situated in the center of the room, is covered with fluffy blankets and pillows and looks like a giant cloud.

Our bags are at the end of the bed, and I grab mine so I can get changed into my swimsuit in the bathroom.

From the floor to the ceiling, sleek marble makes up the bathroom, which has a huge freestanding tub that I could fill with bubbles and get lost in for hours and a shower that could probably fit five people comfortably.

It's amazing what money can buy. If I had a home that looked like this, I don't think I'd ever leave.

I grab the first bikini and try it on. It's black with gold hoops holding the bottom pieces together and a single gold hoop in the center of the triangle pieces on the top. It fits perfectly, and when I turn around, my ass looks good in it.

With all the stress between dropping out of school, my mom being sick, and my ex cheating on me, I started taking kickboxing classes at the local gym to blow off some steam, and I must admit, it's doing wonders for my figure.

I'm about to throw on my jean shorts and tank top when I remember I'm supposed to show Dominick my bikini. I consider messing with him and covering it up so he won't see it until we get to wherever we're going, but honestly, it's been nice, having a man show his attraction toward me. My ex cheating on me was a huge hit to my ego, so having Dominick drooling all over me and marking me as his territory in front of that creepy guy was kind of refreshing.

When I step out of the bathroom, Dominick is nowhere to be found. I check the living room and kitchen and the second bedroom and bathroom, which are almost as beautiful as the master. I'm about to give up when I notice the French doors leading out to what I assume is the terrace are open, the warm breeze hitting the lace curtains and blowing them inside.

He's standing against the railing with his back to me, sporting a pair of black board shorts, sans shirt. His skin is tanned, his waist trim, and his back muscles are prominent. I knew, under that suit, he was fit, but I'm not sure there's even an inch of fat anywhere on him.

As if he can sense me, he turns around, pocketing his phone he must've been on, and drags his gaze down my body, his gray eyes turning molten with lust.

"Turn around," he says, his voice smooth and commanding.

I twirl in my spot, nice and slow, to give him a good look, and even from here, I can hear him groan.

"Come here," he murmurs with a slight nod.

Like a moth to a flame, I go without argument, sauntering over to him. The heat envelops me the moment I step outside, and since it's been cool in Florida, I welcome it, basking in the warmth and sun.

Once I'm within reaching distance, he hooks his arm around my waist and pulls me into his chest. His other hand cups my face and lifts it so he can easily press his mouth to mine. He kisses me with fervor while his hands roam my body—gripping the curve of my hip, palming one of my breasts, tweaking my nipple through the material. When he gets to my ass, he gives both cheeks a hard squeeze, and then he lifts me into his arms without breaking our kiss.

I wrap my legs around his torso, and my hands go to his nape, toying with the hair, tickling his neck as Dominick grinds his hard length against my center.

"Fuck," he hisses, breaking our kiss and leaning his forehead against mine as we both attempt to catch our breath. "I really do want to show you the sights."

"I think you're doing a great job of showing me them," I say coyly, reaching down and cupping his cock. "The only thing better than sex is sex with a view."

I nod toward the ocean right in front of us. Thanks to the privacy walls, we could literally have sex out here, and nobody would see us. I glance at the Jacuzzi in the corner and note that we will definitely be using it later.

"I'm serious." He chuckles, setting me down. "We have all night to get to know each other on an intimate level, but first, I want you to see something."

PASSPORT

SEVEN

Peyton

"OH MY GOD, THIS VIEW."

As we stand in front of the most breathtaking waterfall, I wish I had brought my phone so I could take pictures because my memory will never do it justice. Three different streams of water fall smoothly into a natural pool of water. Because it's surrounded by nothing but lush vegetation, it creates an illusion of us being in the middle of nowhere rather than only a short drive from where we're staying.

"It's really something, huh?" Dominick says, never taking his eyes off me.

"Thank you for sharing this with me. I've never seen anything like this."

"Well, it's not just for looks," he says, peeling his shirt off and tossing it onto the ground. "Let's go swimming."

I strip out of my shorts and shirt, toe off my flip-flops, and then take his hand in mine. We make our way into the crystal-clear water. Because it's March, it's in the mid-eighties, making the temperature of the water perfect. Once we're almost to the middle, Dominick lifts me into his arms, and I wrap my thighs around his waist, holding on to him while he walks us closer to the waterfalls.

"This is stunning," I tell him, watching as the streams fall into the plunge pool, the sound creating the perfect, soothing background noise.

"It is," he agrees. "But it's got nothing on you."

I roll my eyes and scoff at his flirting. "Okay, cheesy much?"

Dominick shrugs. "Maybe, but it's the truth."

He moves us toward the side and leans against the rocks so he can get comfortable. Since he makes no move to release me, I stay in his arms while we watch the waterfall for several minutes in comfortable silence. Surprisingly, there's nobody but us here right now, and it makes it feel like it's our own personal paradise.

"So, I know you are a flight attendant based in Coral Bay, and your ex is a cheating asshole, but that's all you've given me," Dominick says after a while. "Tell me something about you."

I consider his request for a few seconds. I've made it a point not to let him in because it would only make things harder. We don't live near each other, so we couldn't have a future together, unless he was willing to move to Coral Bay. And even if he did move, I'm not sure I would want to start something serious with anyone, even him, while my focus needs to be on my mom.

At the same time, I feel like I've been isolating myself from everyone since I moved home and my boyfriend and best friend broke my heart. So, maybe, just for today, I'll let Dominick in a little. I'll pretend like tomorrow doesn't exist and make the most of our time in the DR. Because once I return home, reality will hit, and all I'll have are the memories from our time together.

"This is the best non-date I've ever been on," I blurt out, feeling my cheeks heat at my admission. "I mean …" I try to backtrack, but really, there is no coming back from that, so I just go with it. "Every date I've been on was kind of lame. Dinner, drinks, sometimes a movie. Wash, rinse, repeat. But this? This is amazing. Thank you for bringing me here. We both know I would've slept with you, even without the sightseeing."

Dominick barks out a laugh. "I'm glad you like it. I'm not an expert on dating, so dinner and drinks sound like a normal date to me. Though I haven't seen a movie in an actual theater in … well, ever." He chuckles.

"What? You've never been to the movies?"

"Nope. And I honestly haven't thought about watching a movie in years," he admits. "I can't even remember the last movie I saw."

"Yeah, same," I agree. "Between school and work and taking care of my mom, I don't have time for much else."

Dominick smiles softly and tightens his hold on me. "Clearly, your date expectations are high. No dinner or drinks or movies. So, what are we talking here? Trip to London? Paris?"

"No." I laugh, slapping his chest playfully. "I'm not that high maintenance, I swear. I just feel like every guy I've ever gone out with was lazy when it came to courting a woman."

"Okay." He nods with a smirk. "If you could go on a date any-where, where would you want to go?"

I think for a moment and then say, "It's not about the perfect date. It's about knowing me. I dated this guy for years. I would con-stantly talk about my love of books and poetry and art. When an art show came around, I got us tickets, and he looked at me and said, 'You like art?'"

I look at Dominick, deadpan, and he laughs.

"Dinner and drinks are unoriginal. I want a partner to experi-ence the world with. I want to visit museums and wineries and art galleries. Every night before bed, I read, yet I'd mention going to the bookstore, and he'd get annoyed."

I shake my head. "Looking back, I've dated some clueless guys, and I was starting to wonder if all guys were like that, but you're giving me renewed hope." I slide my arms around his neck. "So, thank you."

"Great," he growls. "I'm glad I could renew your faith in men so you can leave here tomorrow and find someone else."

I laugh at his words. "Well, I don't know about that. But I will be holding men to a higher standard. If their first choice of a date— or non-date—isn't taking me to see the beautiful waterfalls in the Dominican Republic, then I'm saying no."

Dominick chuckles. "Good girl. So, books, art, museums, and wine. What else do you love?"

"The beach. When I have free time, I pack a basket and my current read and go to the beach to have a picnic. I love sports—mostly football and hockey—but I've never been to a game. What about you?"

"Truthfully, you make me feel rather boring. I run my family's business and travel for work quite a bit, but I rarely sightsee."

"Okay, so I'm throwing your question back at you," I tell him. "If you could go on a date anywhere, where would you go?"

He thinks for a moment and then says, "I wouldn't care where I was as long as I was with you."

"Oh my God!" I splash him with water. "You are such a flirt. I'm being serious."

"I don't know." He shrugs. "I've been so busy. I can't even remember the last time I went on a date."

"Ahh." I nod in understanding. "You're one of those guys. No strings or commitments. Catch and release." I waggle my brows, and he shakes his head. "I get it."

"It's not that," he says with a grin. "I'm not opposed to dating. I just haven't found anyone worth spending time with. For the record, it's been a long-ass time since I had sex."

His eyes lock with mine, and even though I don't know him well, I sense the honesty in them.

"So, school, huh?" he asks, changing the subject. "What's your major?"

"I *was* double-majoring in business administration and hospitality at the University of Florida."

"Gainesville," he says with a nod. "That's a good school."

"I was a good student."

"And now?"

"I dropped out to take care of my mom. I thought I'd go back after she recovered, but before I made it that far, we found out that she was dying."

"And what would you have done with your degree?" he asks, focusing on school instead of my dying mom, for which I'm grateful because the last thing I want to do is taint this magical place with my depressing life.

"I'm not sure. I thought about going to work in the hospitality industry, maybe for a hotel or a restaurant."

Dominick grins. "I own a few. I could get you a job."

I laugh and shake my head. "In Coral Bay?"

"Soon. Give me your number, and I'll let you know once we're hiring."

"You're so ridiculous." I playfully slap his wet chest and push away from him.

Instead of letting me go, he pulls me closer to him. "Tell me something about you that nobody else knows. A secret, a fear, anything."

I swallow thickly at his sudden intensity. "You go first."

He nods once and releases a harsh breath, then looks past me as he thinks about what to say. I start to think he's not going to answer his own question when he finally speaks. "I'm terrified of failing."

"Aren't we all?"

"Probably," he agrees. "But in my world, failure can mean ..." His jaw tics. "In my world, failure isn't an option."

"I'm not sure I like your world."

"It's the only world I know," he says, his tone filled with a darkness that sends a chill racing up my spine.

Before I can ask him more on the subject, he captures my mouth with his, kissing me with an intensity I've never felt before. My hands delve into his hair, and his hold on me tightens, like he's afraid to let me go. This kiss feels different ... deeper, darker. His mood has shifted, and I'm not sure what to make of it.

But before I can think too hard on it, Dominick ends the kiss and says, "Your turn."

When I groan, he chuckles. "Oh, c'mon. I just dug deep into

the pits of my soul for my answer. The least you can do is give me something … *anything.*"

"Fine." I sigh. "I'm afraid of … spiders."

Dominick glares, but I keep going. "Seriously! They're hairy, and they have, like, a million legs. I once read that the average person swallows, like, four spiders in their sleep every year!" I mock shiver. "It's a valid fear."

"I'm about to show you a valid fear."

Dominick grabs ahold of me and starts tickling my sides, making me scream.

"That doesn't even make sense!" I screech while I try to get away from him.

"Oh, it will. I'm about to tickle you to the point where you fear peeing in your pants."

"Stop!" I yell through my laughter, kicking and flailing about.

"Give me a real secret, and I'll stop."

"Fine, fine!"

He quits torturing me and raises a brow while I catch my breath.

"I'm afraid of the cycle repeating itself."

"What cycle?"

"The cycle of abuse. I read—"

"In the same place you read about people swallowing spiders?"

"No." I roll my eyes. "I read that daughters of mothers who were in abusive relationships are thirty percent more likely to end up in one as well."

"You need to stop reading," he deadpans.

"I'm serious," I tell him. "My mom was in an abusive relationship for years before she found the courage to get out. And I'm scared I'm going to follow in her footsteps."

"You won't," he says, reaching out and pulling me into his arms. "You're too strong for that. And if any guy ever lays a hand on you, you come find me, and I'll kill him myself."

The seriousness in his tone causes goose bumps to prickle my skin, and I wonder if it really is possible that he killed Dale.

No, I tell myself. *He's just speaking metaphorically.*

And then his words hit me. *"… if any guy ever lays a hand on you, you come find me …"*

Come find him. Because I won't be with him. Because after tomorrow morning, whatever this is between us will be over.

The thought of never seeing Dominick again is sad, so I push it aside and focus on the now.

"You're not killing anyone," I scoff. "Now, enough of this deep shit. Let's go swimming. I bet I can make it to the waterfalls before you."

Without waiting for him to agree, I push out of his arms and take off toward the waterfall. Of course, Dominick quickly catches up and then passes me, making it to the waterfall a few seconds before me.

"I win," he says once I arrive. "What's my prize?"

"Me," I tell him, swimming straight into his arms. "You win roughly eighteen more hours with me."

"Now, that," he says, pulling my face toward his, "is the best damn prize I've ever won."

His mouth crashes over mine, and as we kiss, I say a prayer to the gods above that I don't fall for this man. I've already had my heart broken once in the past year, and I don't need to experience that again.

PASSPORT

EIGHT

I CAN'T REMEMBER THE LAST TIME I SPENT THE ENTIRE DAY sightseeing. Aside from the occasional texts with Matteo—him telling me he thinks he's getting closer to finding Brielle and me letting him know the contract with Victor was a done deal—I didn't handle any other business. My only focus was on the fiery redhead that I'd quickly become obsessed with.

After we visited the waterfall, I took her to see a few other sights that the concierge had confirmed were the perfect spots to show a woman I was trying to impress. The truth is, while I've been to the DR several times over the years, I've never taken the time to explore the island. My trips have always been business-oriented … until now.

Until her.

We came back to the hotel to take showers and get ready for dinner, but as I watch Peyton step out of the room in a tiny black dress, the only thing I want to do is stay in and rip that fucking dress off her.

"I hope this is okay," she murmurs, running her hands down the front of her formfitting dress while eyeing the suit that I had brought over since this trip was unexpected.

"It's more than okay," I say, taking in her black fuck-me heels that I can imagine digging into my back as I fuck her on the terrace under the stars. "Let's go before I change my mind and make you my meal instead."

Peyton smirks. "I wouldn't mind." She saunters over and slides her hand down my chest and torso, landing on my groin. "Especially if it means I get to make *you* my meal."

She squeezes my cock—which is stirring to life, thanks to her—and I back away, groaning in frustration.

"We're going to dinner," I insist, making her pout in response.

As much as I want to lay her out on the table and spend the night inside her, I also want to do this right since I only have one night with her, and that starts with wining and dining her.

The upscale restaurant I take her to is located on the water and serves authentic Spanish cuisine. Since she isn't sure about what she wants, I order several items from the menu for us to split. The conversation is light, and she lets me in a bit more when she tells me about her time at college. It doesn't surprise me that she was in a sorority, but it's a reminder of how different our lives are.

I tell her a little about my business, keeping it PG, and she's in awe of how many businesses Antonov Enterprises owns. We discuss the possibility of her going back to school, and when she mentions that she's not sure if the loans will be worth it, I note to have Janet put together an anonymous scholarship that will cover the cost of Peyton's schooling.

I hate that I won't be able to see her follow her dreams, but at least I know she'll be given the opportunity.

"I'm so full. I think you're going to have to roll me out of here," she jokes after taking the last bite of dessert.

"How about a walk instead?"

"That sounds nice."

I pay the bill, and then we head out the side entrance, which leads to a sidewalk that will take us back to the hotel.

We walk hand in hand, and I can't help but note how natural it feels with Peyton. The talking, the flirting, the kissing. Everything with her just feels right. As she smiles up at me, I consider telling her about the arranged marriage and asking her to wait for me to figure it out. But it wouldn't be fair. I didn't choose this life. I was born into it, and I've embraced it, accepted it—hell, most days, I fucking thrive on it—but she deserves better than this. Better than what I'm capable of giving her.

"Thank you for today," Peyton says, not for the first time.

We stop just before the entrance to the hotel, and she rolls onto her tiptoes to give me a kiss. Her lips are smooth and sweet and perfect. When I'm back home, I know one of the things I'll miss the most is this connection. Aside from my brother, I've always had to keep people at a distance. But with her, I let my guard down, and it feels good.

"I will always remember this trip," she murmurs against my lips. "And I was wondering …"

In the lights shining down on us, her cheeks turn a beautiful shade of peach, and I quirk a brow, silently willing for her to continue, unsure what she wants to say that has her blushing.

"I was wondering if we could take a picture. I won't post it or tag you or anything like that. I just want it so I have a memory of us to—"

"Peyton, breathe." I chuckle, and her shoulders sag. "I'd love to take a picture with you."

I'm usually a private person. We even have an entire IT team on standby to wipe out anything we don't want online. I've never had a social media account, and my family knows better than to post pictures on any of the platforms. But if it means Peyton has this memory, I'll gladly go against my norm.

I spot a couple with two small kids walking down the sidewalk and ask the gentleman if he can take our picture.

"My wife would probably be the better option," he says with a light laugh. "She's the photographer in our family."

He looks over at her lovingly, and she smiles. "I'd love to."

Peyton hands her the phone, and we pose in front of the water— me holding her in my arms and her resting her hand on my chest.

After thanking them for taking the picture, Peyton watches as the family continues to walk away.

When I eye her in confusion, she answers my unspoken question.

"That's what I want," she says with watery eyes. "A loving husband and two, maybe three kids. All close in age so they're not lonely, like I was as an only child. I want family vacations and romantic getaways."

"You'll have that one day."

"It's what my mom wanted," she says, her tone somber. "Instead, she got an abusive husband, years of heartache, and one daughter she struggled to care for."

"You're not going to be her," I say. "You'll break that cycle."

She nods in agreement and then looks down at the photo of us as I eye it over her shoulder. I already knew she was the sliver of good in my otherwise corrupt world, but as she stands next to me, I can't help but be reminded of it. She's all smiles and innocence and softness in contrast to my stoic expression, which hides all the shit I've been through that hardens a person.

But even with our differences, I could envision a life with this woman in another world. Date nights and vacations. Asking her to be my wife. Creating a family together, just like she wants.

Fuck, the thought of her swollen with my child has me instantly hard. Would they have her fiery-red hair with my gray eyes?

I would run the real estate company with my brother and sister by my side, and after Peyton was done getting the degree she wanted so badly, I'd teach her the hospitality industry so she could run it along with me, if that was what she wanted.

But that's not my reality because real estate is only the tip of the iceberg. It's the legal business that helps us wash our illegal money.

I try to picture Peyton in my world, filled with drugs and prostitutes and weapons. She'd have to have a guard everywhere she went. Our children would always be a target. Every day, her life would be at risk.

No, Peyton doesn't belong anywhere near my world. She's too good, too innocent. She deserves to stay in the light, not be sentenced to a life shrouded in the darkness.

We only have tonight. The hours are dwindling down until we

get on the plane and fly back to Coral Bay, where we'll part ways and I'll stop stalking the gorgeous woman who can never be mine.

The ride in the elevator is quiet, and I wonder if she's getting cold feet. Maybe it was all too much, too quick, and she's having second thoughts about spending the night together.

As we step into the suite, my phone rings with a call from my assistant, Janet, who texted me earlier to say she would be calling with a couple of time-sensitive questions.

"I need to take this," I tell Peyton.

"Of course. I'm going to step out onto the terrace and get some fresh air."

I nod and answer the call, then head into the second bedroom for a little privacy.

Janet and I go over a few things she needs for an upcoming project, and once we're done, I let her know that I won't be reachable until tomorrow.

I put my phone on Do Not Disturb—with exceptions set for Matteo, Mom, and Brielle—and then head into the bedroom to get changed. After throwing on a pair of sweats, I grab my shirt and bring it with me into the bathroom so I can brush my teeth before I put it on.

I assumed Peyton was still on the terrace, so I'm momentarily taken aback when I find her standing in the bathroom—in only a white lace-and-satin bra and matching panties set.

She's leaning over the sink, reapplying her lip gloss, and her breasts are hanging like perfect raindrops, begging to be released from their confines. Her ass, which is as creamy and smooth as the rest of her, is popped out, the tiny thong leaving nothing to the imagination.

"Dominick," she breathes when she spots me in the doorway.

Needing to be closer to her, I cut across the bathroom and come up behind her, both of us standing in front of the mirror.

"Do you have any idea how enticing you are?" I tell her, running my hand over the curve of her shapely ass. "Standing over the sink in your virginal white bra and panties set?"

"I was hoping you'd like them. I hate to break it to you … but I'm no virgin," she murmurs, her emerald eyes meeting mine in our reflection.

The thought of her being with another man has me wanting to find every guy she's been with so I can punish them for having touched what's mine.

I reach around and pull her bra cup down, exposing the swell of her breast and her rose-dusted nipple. I tug the other side down and then pinch both nipples, eliciting a moan from her.

Fuck, I can't wait to have her screaming my name as she comes on my cock.

"Dominick, I need you to fuck me right now," she begs as I tweak and pluck her nipples.

I ignore her, focusing on her breasts, and the vixen pushes her ass back into my groin.

"Did you hear me?" She glares. "I need you to—"

Crack!

Her words are cut off when my hand hits her luscious ass, making it jiggle and turn a beautiful shade of pink.

"I'll fuck you when I'm good and ready," I tell her, rubbing the area I just smacked. "Now, be a good girl and put your hands on the vanity and spread those thighs so I can get a good look at what's mine."

With a huff, she does as I said, and once she's in position, I slide my hands down her smooth flesh, along her back, and then hook my index fingers into her thong, tearing it off her body and leaving her in only her bra.

"You're such a caveman," she says smartly. "Now, you owe me a pair of underwear."

I'm about to tell her I'll buy her as many as she wants, but then I remember this is only one night and I won't be around her again to buy her anything. Instead, I shake the thought from my head and focus on the beautiful woman in front of me.

"The first time you landed in my lap, I wondered what it would be like to fuck you," I say, rubbing circles on her creamy ass before I part her thighs further.

"Well, you would know if you just did it already," she grumbles, earning herself another hard slap on her ass, this time on the other cheek.

She sucks in a harsh breath and then moans, and I wonder if she's being sassy in hopes that I'll keep spanking her ass.

"I don't know what men you've been with, but I have no intention of rushing with you."

I rub her reddened asscheek for a few seconds and then glide my hand between her ass cheeks, working my way down until I get to her dripping wet cunt.

"You're soaked, Peaches," I murmur, leaning over her arched back so my lips are next to her ear and my cock, begging to be released, is pushing against the crack of her ass. "Do you like me spanking you?"

I lick the shell of her ear, and she groans, shaking her ass against my cock.

"Please," she whines. "I get that you're in control and not as affected as I am, but I'm ready to burst at the seams."

"Not affected?" I scoff. Grabbing her hips, I step back and spin her around so her back is pressed against the counter. "You don't think I'm affected by your perfect tits"—I tweak her nipple—"or this luscious ass"—I reach around and give her cheek a light tap—"or your sweet cunt?" I swipe a finger up her center and then bring it to my lips, sucking her juices off my flesh. "Fuck, baby, you taste so good."

I tug my sweatpants down, and since I'm not wearing anything under them, my cock springs out, hard as granite and needing to be inside Peyton.

Her gaze descends, and her tongue glides across her lips, like she's eyeing a dessert she wants to eat. Her reaction only makes me that much harder as I imagine all the noises she'll make when I fuck her face and then come down her slender throat.

"Tell me again that I'm unaffected by—"

Before I can finish my sentence, she drops to her knees, wraps her delicate, manicured fingers around my shaft, and kisses the tip with her glossy red lips.

"I get it—you're affected," she says just before she parts her plump lips and takes me all the way down her throat.

I have nothing to hold on to, so I grab ahold of her head, fisting her hair, and release a guttural moan as she slides her warm, wet mouth up and down my shaft.

"Fuck," I groan, knowing I need to stop her soon or I'll blow my load in her mouth instead of her cunt, which I've been dreaming about fucking for weeks.

Her fingers move to my ball sack, and she tugs on them as she continues to deep-throat me. After God knows how long, my balls start to seize up, and just before I coat her mouth with my cum, I pull her head back.

Peyton looks up at me, and I swear, seeing her like this—with mascara running down her cheeks, her lips swollen, and drool dripping down the corners of her mouth—it's the second most beautiful sight I've ever seen. The first being the dreamy look in her eyes when she came all over my fingers earlier today.

I wipe a bit of the black from under her eyes and wonder how I'm going to let this woman go tomorrow.

"C'mere," I tell her, helping her to her feet. "Turn around and put your hands back on the sink and hold on tight."

She spins around, and her hands grasp the counter while I pull a foil packet out of my pocket, rip it open, and roll the condom onto my shaft.

I lift her leg, hooking it in the crook of my arm, and then guide my cock into her. Because she's so wet, I slide in easily, and once I'm balls deep, I grab her breast.

"You good?" I ask, wanting to make sure she's comfortable.

"Yes," she croaks. "Please fuck me."

I slide out and then back in a few times, not wanting to hurt her. She's obviously not a virgin, but the way she's choking my cock like a vise, despite her juices dripping down and all over my shaft, tells me it's either been a while or she hasn't been with anyone worthy of being inside her.

"Dominick," she pants, "harder, please. I promise I won't break."

"You got it, baby."

I reach around her and grip the edge of the counter, caging her in, and then I start to fuck her how she wants. The first few thrusts damn near send her into the sink, but I hold on to her tightly so she can't go anywhere while I fuck her with everything I have.

Peyton's eyes meet mine, and she screams out in pleasure as I continue to ram my cock in and out of her, watching as I hit her in the perfect spot that has her orgasm creeping up on her.

"Oh my God, more!" she moans, turning slightly so I can tilt her face toward me and kiss her the way I'm fucking her—like I need her to survive.

My balls start to tighten, but I'm not done with her yet, so I pull out and lift her onto the vanity. She wraps her legs around my waist, and I go back to fucking her so deep that I'm not sure where she begins and I end.

"I'm so close," she chokes out, pulling my face toward hers.

As I fuck her with deep, sensual thrusts, we kiss one another with the desperation of two people who know their time is running out.

I try to hold back, not wanting it to end, but all too soon, Peyton flies over the edge, and I have no choice but to go with her—which makes sense because, even though I've only known this woman for a short time, I'd follow her anywhere.

"Holy shit," she murmurs, pushing her sweaty hair out of her face as we catch our breath. "That was …"

"Only the fucking beginning."

PASSPORT

NINE

Peyton

I'M NOT SURE HOW EARLY IT IS, BUT AS I ROLL OVER, I LET OUT a groan, my body deliciously sore. My alarm hasn't gone off yet, so it must be early. Instead of checking the time, I lie where I am, recalling the events from last night and earlier this morning.

Sweaty bodies.

Tangled limbs.

Too many orgasms to count.

Sex on damn near every surface of the suite.

Laughing, kissing, foreplay.

Dominick devouring my pussy while I sat on the edge of the Jacuzzi and then fucking me in it.

I should be satiated for the next year based on the number of times he made me come, but the thought of not seeing or kissing or fucking him after today has me reaching for him in hopes that I can convince him of one more round of amazing sex before we have to shower and then head to the airport.

But when my hand lands on the cold sheets and my eyes fly open, I realize I'm alone.

I sit up, and for a moment, I wonder if this was all a dream.

Did I imagine my time with Dominick?

I grab my phone from the nightstand and click on my photos. And right there, in color, is a picture of Dominick and me standing in front of the water. Him in a sharp black suit and me in my little black dress.

I swipe out of my photos and turn off my alarm since I'm awake. Then, I pad into the bathroom. I'm butt naked, having fallen asleep with Dominick's body wrapped around mine, so I grab a robe that's hanging from the door.

With every step I take, my muscles ache from the numerous ways Dominick fucked me, further proving that it wasn't a dream.

When I turn the light on, I'm met with several bite marks and hickeys. At the time, I didn't think about how it would look. I was too enraptured by Dominick's need to mark me and make me his.

Now, I have to hope my concealer will cover it all before I get on the plane.

The plane …

We were supposed to take a car to the airport and fly back to Coral Bay together. He asked if we could have lunch before he went home.

Yet he's gone.

I quickly pee and then go in search of him. The suite is big. He could've gotten up to take a phone call and didn't want to wake me.

But even as I think it, I know it's not true.

I can feel it. He's gone.

His suitcase is nowhere to be found. His briefcase is missing. There aren't any men's clothes in sight.

I look for a note, but there isn't one.

Tears sting my eyes, and I try to hold them back. But finally, I give in and let them fall.

I knew what we had was only for one night. He told me that was all he could give me. But for some reason, as we lay in bed, both of us sweaty and sleepy, and he asked if he could see me after the flight, I thought maybe he'd changed his mind.

By the time I fell asleep in his arms, I had convinced myself that, even though it was a bad idea due to the distance, I wanted to see where this would go because I had fallen for him. For his charm, for his smiles that were few and far between, for the laughter that he seemed to reserve for me. During the short time I had been around him, I fell for his touches and kisses and words.

Fuck, even though I knew the score, it still hurts.

After my tears have dried, I take a shower, wanting to get his scent off me. I get dressed and call for a cab to take me to the airport.

I go about our preflight routine, and the entire time, I keep looking for him. I'm not even sure what I'd say to him. But it doesn't matter because he doesn't check in and he never gets on the plane.

Two seats, both assigned to him, are empty, and if I'm honest, so is my heart.

TEN

"**T**HIS IS BULLSHIT, AND YOU KNOW IT!" ANTHONY BARKS from where he's sitting in a metal chair, his hands bound behind his back.

We're in the middle of an empty room in the warehouse where Matteo brings the people we need to interrogate when we know shit's gonna get messy.

"No," I tell him, pulling his pretty-boy hair and yanking his head back.

He's already sporting a busted lip and swollen eye from fighting Matteo instead of coming willingly.

"What's bullshit is that our father's dead at the hands of yours, and somehow, the cameras got wiped. Now, I'm going to ask you one more goddamn time, and if you give me another bullshit answer, I'm going to be forced to pry the truth out of you. What the fuck happened?"

"I don't know!" he cries, earning himself a punch to his face, courtesy of Matteo.

Blood, with a mixture of saliva, flies from his mouth, and he's momentarily knocked unconscious.

"Sorry," Matteo mutters. "I couldn't stand listening to his voice for another second."

"When's your next fight?" I ask, noticing the way his shoulders tense.

"Next month," he says. "With everything going on, I haven't been to the gym in a few days."

Since we were little, Matteo has been filled with an anger that couldn't be contained, most of it directed at our father. It wasn't until he started training at a gym in South Harbor Point—with a guy named Lucian, who took him under his wing when he saw the fury brewing in Matteo's eyes—that he was able to find a way to release some of it.

The training eventually led to underground fighting, and now, Matteo's one of the most notorious underground fighters in the circuit. Guys come from all over, hoping to take him down, but he's never lost a fight.

"You need to get back in there soon," I tell him, leaning against the wall while we wait for Anthony to wake up so we can continue questioning him.

After a few minutes of silence, I say, "None of this makes any sense."

When I woke up to my phone ringing this morning, I thought it would be Matteo telling me he'd found Brielle. Instead, he told me our father was dead.

From what he could gather, our father had found Brielle and brought her home, and then he took off for a meeting with Joseph, Giuseppe, and Anthony.

Shit went down, and Joseph shot our father. After taking him out, Joseph went after Giuseppe, but he was able to get away unscathed. Giuseppe is now looking for Joseph, and Matteo was able to grab Anthony.

When I spoke to Giuseppe after arriving back in Harbor Point, he said he'd walked in on the tail end of the conversation between Joseph, Anthony, and our father and had no idea what had been said. When I had my security guy, Eddy, pull the footage, he discovered the cameras had conveniently been wiped clean.

"Hello?" Matteo answers his phone.

He mouths to me, *It's Giuseppe.*

He listens for a moment and then says, "Okay," before hanging up.

"Joseph is dead."

"Are you fucking kidding me?" Anthony groans, obviously having woken up and heard the news.

"What are you so mad about?" I ask him. "You couldn't stand the man."

While Matteo and I were smart about keeping our hatred toward our father a secret, Anthony did little to hide the animosity he felt toward his old man.

"Doesn't mean I wanted him dead," he mutters.

"I'm bored of this," Matteo says, pointing a gun at Anthony. "Talk, or you'll be buried right alongside your dad."

"Fuck," Anthony cries out. "I don't know what happened!"

Matteo pushes the gun against Anthony's temple, and he whimpers like a little bitch.

"I swear! I was with my dad when Andrey called for a meeting, so I went with him. We got there, and they argued about the arranged marriage. Giuseppe walked in and then shit went down. My dad shot yours and then we took off. We got to the house, and my dad said he needed to handle some shit and left. I stayed at the house with my mom until Matteo showed up and dragged me out. That's all I know."

I glance at Matteo, and we exchange a look. Something is missing from the story, but without the footage, we can't prove shit. If we kill him now, with his dad and ours dead, we might never know what really happened in that meeting.

I nod at Matteo, silently telling him to let Anthony go, and he glares my way.

I give him another look, conveying that I'm not playing, and he sighs. Then, like the asshole he is, he punches Anthony in the stomach, making him double over in pain.

"Fuck!" Anthony groans. "Stop … please."

"Well, since you asked so nicely"—Matteo pulls a knife out and cuts his binds—"you're free to go … for now."

Anthony widens his eyes, momentarily stunned, and then stands. "What about the marriage?" he says, looking at Matteo, then me.

"What about it?" I ask.

"It's still happening, right?"

He juts out his chin, and I stifle a laugh because this is precisely why his father didn't let him run the business. The guy could've been killed—hell, I wouldn't put it past Matteo to still do it despite me making it clear he's to let Anthony live—and instead of running, like a smart person would, he's poking the beast.

"Is he fucking serious right now?" Matteo barks out a laugh, glancing from Anthony to me. "He's clearly nuts. C'mon, Dominick. Let me kill him. I'll even clean up the mess myself."

"No," I tell Anthony, ignoring my brother's antics, "the deal is off."

"That's bullshit!" Anthony barks. "I want what's owed to me."

Before I can stop him, Matteo punches Anthony in the mouth, and he flies backward. I know Matteo went easy on him because if he had hit Anthony with his full strength, he'd have sent Anthony into a coma.

"Not my problem." I shrug as he crawls toward the wall so he can use it to help himself stand. "A deal is only as good as the men who make it, and the men who made that deal are both dead."

"You don't understand," he whines, standing and hobbling over to us.

He's dripping blood all over the floor, and I'm almost positive a tooth is missing, but he isn't giving up.

"Without her, I'm fucked," he says. "My dad said the only way he'd consider letting me take over the business was if I married her."

"Then, you're fucked." I step into his space and pull out my 9mm. "The deal is as dead as our fathers, and as far as I'm concerned, so is any business Antonov Enterprises had with Rothschild International. I'm going to give you two choices. You take the loss and walk away. Or I put a bullet in your chest and you go away permanently. The call is yours. Either way, this is over."

"This is fucking bullshit," he hisses.

I raise my gun, ready to kill him. But before I'm forced to do so, he puts his hands up and leaves.

"You know he's going to be a problem," Matteo says once Anthony is gone.

"There's nothing he can do. You heard what he said. His dad didn't even leave him the company. If he does cause problems, then we'll put him down. But with our father's and Joseph's deaths, all eyes will be on us, and the last thing we need is more attention drawn to us if Anthony goes missing."

We might have several cops in our pockets, but we also have a legitimate business to run, and with Andrey's and Joseph's deaths, people are going to talk. If Anthony comes up missing or dead, fingers will point straight at us, which will be bad for business.

Before Andrey's, Giuseppe's, and Joseph's fathers got ahold of this city, it was filled with poverty that nobody wanted to touch. But they cleaned up the streets, secured employment, and helped protect businesses. And then Andrey, Giuseppe, and Joseph took over—taking what their father's did to the next level.

The city might be corrupt, but it's thriving, thanks to our families. When people see us, they both respect and fear us, but most importantly, they trust us. But trust can be taken away as easily as it is given. And if we start killing each other off, we're going to lose their trust.

"This whole thing is a fucking mess," Matteo mutters.

"Nah, it's really not. Our father and Joseph were both loose cannons, and now, they've been removed from the equation. The arranged marriages are done, which is a win for Brielle and me. Giuseppe will either cooperate or we'll cut him out too. The fact is, our father has been carrying them on his back all these years. Joseph was dead weight, and if Giuseppe is smart, he'll get on board."

"Holy shit." Matteo barks out a laugh. "It's really fucking

happening. Andrey's dead, and we're taking over. And we didn't even have to lift a finger for it to happen."

I chuckle. "It's really happening. If Joseph wasn't dead, I'd send him a fruit basket as a thank-you. Maybe I'll send his wife one."

"Speaking of Maria, do you think she's going to take over Rothschild International?"

"I don't know, but it doesn't matter," I tell him as we walk out. "Our business with them is over. I'm going to meet with our legal team to ensure all ties are cut. And if Giuseppe gives me shit about the way we plan to run the business, we'll cut him out too. I've been playing our father's game for too long, and I'm done."

"What the hell do you mean, Brielle is on her way to Russia?" I bark, making my mom jump. "We were gone for a few damn hours, and you shipped her off to another country?"

"I didn't ship her anywhere," Mom says, glaring at me. "And don't you take that tone with me. She wanted to go, and I agreed."

"And who gave you the right to make that decision?" Matteo cuts in.

"I'm her mother," Mom says, redirecting her glare at Matteo. "I might have messed up while your father was alive, cowering to that piece of shit, but he's gone now, and I'll be damned if, even in his death, he continues to hurt her. She lost her boyfriend and was terrified of having to marry that horrible man, and I wasn't going to let it happen." She steps into my face, and even in heels, she only comes up to my chest, but fuck if I'm not proud of my mom for finally standing up for herself. "I'm not going to let it happen."

"It's not happening," I tell her. "I already told Anthony that the deal was off. I appreciate you trying to protect Brielle, but I was never going to let that deal go through."

Mom's blue eyes soften, and tears form in her lids. "Is he really gone?" she chokes out.

"He's really gone." I open my arms, and she falls into them, letting out a guttural cry. "He's never going to hurt you again." I lean over and kiss the crown of her golden-blonde hair. "I'm so fucking sorry we couldn't stop him sooner."

"There's nothing you could've done," she says through her cries. "The only way was to kill him, and up until last year, had he died, we would've lost everything. He made sure of that."

What she means is, up until last year, our father's will stated that if he died, Giuseppe would take over the company and make the decisions as he saw fit. It was Andrey's way of controlling me. But after his Alzheimer's diagnosis, he gave in and changed his will to state that if he died, everything would go to me. Which was why Matteo and I were working on figuring out a way to kill him, but we wanted to do it right because of the three companies being tangled with one another.

But with Joseph's death, it will force Giuseppe to take a side—us or the Rothschilds—and we all know he'd rather get in bed with the one he knows than the one he loathes.

"You and Brielle are safe now," Matteo says. "She doesn't need to go to Russia."

"But she does," Mom says with a frown. "She needs a break from this life. She's going to finish her classes online and spend time with your grandparents. Polina and Boris are excited for her to join them."

"And that's what she said she wants?" I ask.

"She was extremely distraught. Wouldn't stop crying and begging to leave. When I suggested she go visit your *babushka* and *dedushka*, she agreed."

While our grandparents lived in Harbor Point while we were growing up, after our grandfather and our dad got into a huge fight over their differences in the way they wanted to run the business, our grandfather walked away, and he and our grandmother moved back to Russia where he started a gas company that's now worth billions.

The only time we see them is when we visit. Brielle has always been close to them, so I know she'll be in good hands.

"I want to talk to her when she lands," I say, and then it hits me. "Did she take the company jet?"

With Anthony pissed that the marriage has been called off, the last thing we need is him tracking her down.

"No, I didn't want to risk anyone knowing she was leaving. I assumed you were going to force her to hold up your father's end of the deal, so Boris chartered a private jet under a dummy name."

"That was smart," I tell her. "Shit's going to be different around here now that Dad is gone, but you need to understand that our world is still dangerous, and while I like that you've grown a backbone, you can't be doing that shit outside of this house. Someone might mistake it for disrespect."

"I know," she says with a sad smile. "Which is why I was thinking of taking a trip after the funeral."

"Alone?" Matteo asks.

She nods. "After thirty-three years of being stuck in this prison, I'd like to finally see the world," she chokes out.

"Then, you should see the world," I tell her. "As long as you bring security."

PASSPORT

ELEVEN

Dominick

"**D**ominick, be reasonable," Carlos Santiago, my father's former business associate, says, hitting me with a glare that would scare other people. "Your father—"

"Is dead," I say for what feels like the millionth time in the last several weeks.

When my father died, I knew I'd have to clean up a few messes, but what I didn't know was just how shady Andrey Antonov was. When he allowed me to run Antonov Enterprises, I assumed he'd handed me all the reins, but the truth is, he only handed over the ones that made him look good—the property development company, import and export of legal goods, the hotels. What I didn't see was the shit he did behind my back, like the deal he had with Carlos. And I say it in the past tense because it's over whether he likes it or not.

"I don't give a shit how much money you're offering," I tell him, leaning forward in my seat and locking eyes with him. "If it has a heartbeat, it's not coming in or out of my port."

How my father was able to juggle all the deals he made right under our noses will forever be a mystery. And if I wasn't so pissed at him and he wasn't six feet under, I'd pat him on the back because he was smarter than I gave him credit for. I didn't know why he had thrown a fit when I insisted Matteo take over the port last year, but now, I know. Matteo running the port made it harder for our father to go behind our backs.

"Your father took you under his wing," Carlos says slowly, "so he must've taught you about the importance of making friends instead of enemies."

"I never was one to get along with the other kids in school." I shrug, and Matteo snorts out a laugh, reminding Mr. Santiago of his presence.

Carlos sighs and shakes his head. "Don't say I didn't warn you."

His intention is clear. I know I should let Matteo handle it, but the pent-up aggression simmering in my veins bubbles over, and before Carlos is all the way to his feet, I've rounded my desk, and I have my fingers wrapped around his throat. I shove him back until he's against the wall, and his eyes widen with fear.

"My father might've forgotten to teach me about making friends," I spit. "But there's one lesson he instilled in me at a young age." I tighten my hold against his windpipe, and he struggles to breathe. "If someone is bold enough to threaten you, they're willing to act on it. And if you knew my father the way you say you did, then you know what he did to anyone who threatened him."

"I-I ..."

I apply pressure to his windpipe—knowing from experience that if I squeeze a little more, I'll crush it, and it will be game over—while warring with myself. I can kill him and make an example out of him, or I can let him live and risk him making good on his threat.

My conversation with Peyton comes to the forefront of my mind—something that's been happening since I left her in the hotel room, in shock from my father's death and not thinking clearly.

"I'm terrified of failing."

"Aren't we all?"

"Probably. But in my world ... failure isn't an option."

"I'm not sure I like your world."

Over the past several weeks, I've considered going in search of her, but it's moments like this—when I'm about to kill a man because he wants to harm me and my family—that remind me why I can't be with her.

She's sunshine and waterfalls, laughter and happiness. And pulling her into my fold would only snuff out her light.

I watch as the life in Carlos's eyes dims, and then I wait a few more seconds, just to ensure he's dead. Then, using the hand not holding him up, I lower his lids and then let go, so he slumps to the ground.

This is my world.

Darkness.

Decay.

Death.

And Peyton doesn't belong anywhere near it.

"He's dead," Matteo says. "I'll call the cleaners. Why don't you take off? Go blow off some steam?"

I look at him and scoff.

He's one to talk.

"It wouldn't kill you to get laid." He shrugs.

My brother thinks the answers to life's problems can be found in between a woman's legs. I, on the other hand, find that women only complicate shit.

Except ...

No.

I mentally shake the thought off.

"I don't need to get laid."

"Really? When was the last time you were with a woman?" He quirks a knowing brow. "It's been over a month since your little rendezvous with ... what's her name?"

"It doesn't matter." I refuse to speak her name, not wanting the filth from my life to ever touch her, even metaphorically. "It was a onetime thing."

"Well, maybe you should make it a two-time thing."

"It's not happening, so drop it."

"I'm just saying, maybe—"

"I left her. When you called to tell me about Andrey's death, I left her in the fucking hotel room without even a note."

Matteo chuckles. "Well, maybe that's the problem. You guys have unfinished business. You know where she works. Go to her. Apologize. See where shit goes. You seemed really into her, and now that you don't have the arranged-marriage bullshit hanging over your head …" He shrugs.

"What are you, Cupid? You don't even believe in relationships."

"Whoa," he says, holding his hand up. "One"—he puts four fingers down, leaving only his index finger up—"I didn't say anything about a relationship." He laughs. "I just meant maybe you guys could have a repeat of whatever you had in the Dominican Republic. And two"—he lifts his middle finger—"I have nothing against relationships."

"So, you're telling me if you met a woman and liked her, you'd consider being in a relationship with her?"

"Now, you're just talking crazy." He grins. "I said I have nothing against them, not that I'd ever want to experience one. And not for the reason you're thinking."

"What reason am I thinking?"

"Pussy." He rolls his eyes. "You think I couldn't handle being with only one pussy for the rest of my life. But that's not true. Pussy is pussy. Once you've had one, they're all the same."

I think back to the way Peyton's cunt felt while wrapped around my cock, and I disagree. Maybe pussy is pussy … until you've been with someone who means more.

"You're thinking about that woman's pussy, aren't you?" Matteo laughs.

"Don't fucking worry about what I'm thinking about." I glare his way, and it only has him laughing harder.

"So, if it's not pussy," I say, getting back to the point of this conversation, "what's your reason for not wanting to be in a relationship?"

"The same as yours," he says simply, sobering up. "I watched what Mom went through … what Brielle went through. And I wouldn't want someone I cared about to be within a hundred miles of this life. We might have to be a part of this world, but that doesn't mean I would bring someone else into it. And add in the fact that I'm not exactly husband material." He laughs humorlessly. "What kind of life could I even give a woman?"

Well, shit. I guess I got him all wrong.

"Matteo …" I start.

My brother might be rough around the edges, but I know how far he'll go to protect the people he loves. I have no doubt, if he had a woman he cared about, he'd stop at nothing to make sure she was safe and protected.

"Besides," he says with a smirk, not letting me finish my thought, "relationships come with expectations. Sex would turn into dates and trips and jewelry." He mock shivers. "One night, no expectations—besides the promise of multiple orgasms—that's what's best for me and my bank account."

"You say this like you're not worth fucking millions."

"And I plan to stay that way."

He's deflecting, avoiding the heavy conversation, and I let him because now isn't the time or place to have a heart-to-heart.

"You got this?" I say, nodding toward the dead body.

"You already know I do."

Since I drove into the office today, I head down to the private garage and unlock my Aston Martin. It's not often I drive myself, but I knew I'd be meeting with Carlos this evening, and I wasn't sure how it would go, so I sent Janet home early and told Fernando he had the day off.

I slide into the leather seat and push Start. I had the car customized, so it has B6-level armor, making it completely bulletproof.

I pull out of the garage, but instead of going left, which would take me in the direction of home, I go right, refusing to think about why. Until I get to the airport and park in short-term parking.

I'm just going to apologize, I tell myself.

The way I left things was fucked up. Maybe Matteo's right, and Peyton and I have unfinished business. Once I explain, she'll forgive me, and then we'll go our separate ways. Hell, she might not even be here. This isn't even where she's based out of.

Since I can't get into the terminal without having a ticket, I book one that's leaving in a few hours and then go through security.

When I get to the right terminal, I go in search of her. It's been weeks, so she might even be on a different route, but I won't know unless I try.

"Excuse me," I say to the woman standing at the counter. "I was wondering if you know where I can find Peyton. She works for this airline. Red hair, green eyes. We're friends, and I'm hoping to get in touch with her."

She looks at me in confusion, but her coworker next to her says, "I know her."

I recognize her from the flight to the DR.

"I'm Ericka." She extends her hand. "Peyton and I used to be on the same crew."

Shit. "Used to be?"

"She quit. A couple of weeks ago. Something about her mom being sick and her needing to stay close to home." She frowns sympathetically. "Sorry."

"Any chance you have her number?"

"I do."

"You're just going to give it to him?" the other woman says.

"I know who he is." Then, to me, she says, "Peyton spent that night with you in the Dominican Republic, and then you left her without a word."

Fuck.

"It's not like that," I say. "It's actually why I was hoping to get her number. I wanted to explain."

"Tell you what …"

"Dominick."

"Dominick," Ericka says with a smile. "You give me your number, and I'll pass it along. If she wants to talk to you, she'll call."

The woman next to her grins smugly, and I internally roll my eyes.

"Fine." I sigh.

I rattle off my number, and she types it into her phone, then hits Send.

Almost instantly, her phone dings with a text.

"What did she say?"

"She wants to know if I'm with you." She types something back, and a few seconds later, it goes off again.

"Sorry," she says. "She said not to give you her number and asked that you please leave her alone."

Fuckin' A. Hell hath no fury like a woman scorned.

"I know she's probably pissed about how things ended, but if you can call her so I can talk to her, I can explain what happened."

Ericka sighs. "Fine."

She hits Call, and the phone rings several times before Peyton's voice comes through the speaker.

"Ericka!" Peyton hisses. "Please tell me you didn't give him my number."

"She didn't," I say, plucking the phone out of Ericka's hand and taking it off speaker.

"Dominick," Peyton breathes, and with my name on her lips, somehow, all the stress from the past several weeks evaporates.

"I need to talk to you," I tell her. "I need to explain."

"No, you don't," she says, her tone devoid of all emotion. "There's nothing to say. I need you to leave me alone."

"I know I fucked up, but—"

"I've moved on."

"If you could just—" *Wait, what the fuck did she just say?* "What?" I ask because there's no way I heard her right.

"I've moved on," she repeats. "I met someone else, and I need you to please leave me alone."

Well, fuck …

"Okay," I tell her since there's nothing else to say. "But—"

I pull the phone from my ear, and the display is showing.

She hung up on me.

"Sorry," Ericka says, reaching over and taking her phone from my hand. "I tried."

The entire way back to my car, I replay Peyton's words.

She's moved on.

She met someone else.

She needs me to leave her alone.

My phone buzzes in my pocket, and I pull it out, answering it without checking who it is.

"It's done," Matteo says, getting straight to the point.

"Thanks."

"But there was a little problem. Apparently, there was some miscommunication with the building security, and a woman made it up the elevator and onto the floor where your office is located. I don't know who she was looking for, but after a few minutes, when Janet didn't appear, she left."

"Is it possible she heard anything?"

"I'm not sure."

"Find out who she was and make sure she doesn't know anything."

"And if she does?"

"Then, we'll take it from there. Let's hope she doesn't. I'm on my way home from the airport now, so if you need anything, let me know."

"That was a quick trip."

"She's moved on."

Matteo is silent for several seconds before he says, "Maybe it's for the best."

"Yeah," I agree, even though it feels like it really fucking isn't.

"I was thinking about hitting up Kings Point tonight. You down?"

Kings Point is a club downtown. Because cell phones aren't allowed inside—a rule that doesn't apply to us since we own the club—it's where the elite go to drink, party, and oftentimes fuck, knowing anything that goes on there stays within those walls.

"Yeah," I tell him. "It's time to move on."

The same way she did.

PASSPORT
HGK815
25 DEC 18
15:45
JFK
JOHN
New
to London
gate 35

TWELVE

Dominick

Four and a Half Years Later

"A NTHONY'S BEEN APPROVED TO BID AT THE CITY AUCTION." Lorenzo walks into my office and has a seat. "The little fucking snake is going to be a problem."

"I should've taken him out when I had the chance," Matteo says, sitting in the visitor seat next to his best friend and glaring at me.

"There's no way he has the funds." I lean back and steeple my fingers. "Nobody in this city would give him a loan or back him. We made sure of it."

It took about a year to cut ties with Rothschild International, but the CEO who bought out the company was agreeable, not wanting to spend time or money caught up in court.

When Anthony and his mom, Maria, found out Joseph had sold the company instead of passing it down to either of them, Maria used his life insurance to buy a new house just outside the city, wanting to start fresh, while Anthony lost his shit and took off. We haven't heard from him in years, but apparently, he's back, and he wants to play games.

"Well, someone didn't get the memo," Lorenzo says, throwing a file onto my desk.

I open it up, and sure enough, his name is on the list of bidders who are planning to attend the property auction this week.

Several months ago, a hurricane came through and fucked up hundreds of acres in South Harbor Point. The area was old, taken up by homeless and drug addicts, bringing the value of the city down, so they decided rather than try to restore it, they'd sell off the lots to the highest bidder.

With the development having taken off in Coral Bay, when I saw how many parcels were available, I brought my idea to Matteo and Lorenzo, suggesting we buy up the lots and replicate what we had done in Coral Bay—which was a success and has taken our level of wealth from nine to ten figures.

With the city auctioning off over two hundred acres, if we play our cards right, we could purchase enough to create a gold mine in our city. A high-end shopping mall, residential buildings, condominium development, a private golf course, a luxurious new hotel—everything North Harbor Point has, but shinier and newer.

"We need to find out who's backing him," I tell Matteo and Lorenzo, who both nod in agreement. "With the auction this week, we can't risk anything going wrong."

"The schedule showed you're heading to Coral Bay this weekend. Think I can catch a ride with you?" Lorenzo asks. "It's family weekend at Coral Bay University, and I was thinking about going since our parents went every year ..."

His words hang in the air as we all take a moment to remember how fucking crazy the past few years have been. After Andrey and Joseph died, we created a new business relationship with Giuseppe, who was smart enough to see that he was outnumbered, and it would be better to work with us rather than against us.

He started stepping up, training Lorenzo to eventually take over Russo Property Group, and everything was going smoothly until a few months ago, when Lorenzo was awoken in the middle of the night to learn his family home had been burned to the ground. Both his parents were asleep and died in the fire.

An investigation proved it had been arson, but we haven't been able to get a lead on who's responsible or why they did it. The only thing that was gained by their deaths was Lorenzo inheriting the company. He was given fifty-one percent of Russo Property Group and appointed the CEO while his sister was given the other forty-nine percent. Once she graduates, she's planning to move home and help him run the company.

So, the fire was either a successful suicide attempt or someone had it out for Giuseppe.

We spoke to Maria since he had killed her husband, and she admitted that there was no love lost when Joseph died. We've considered Anthony as a suspect, but until we can catch his slimy ass, we have no way of proving it.

"You should go," I tell Lorenzo. "Daniella might say she doesn't care if you do or don't, but she wouldn't mean it."

"Speaking of which," Lorenzo says, "how's Brielle?"

"She's coming home."

Matteo glances at me in confusion since this is the first he's heard of this. "Does she know this?"

"No, but she doesn't have a choice. With our grandparents both having passed away, she can't be in Russia alone. She's been hiding out long enough. I get that she lost somebody she loved, but it's time for her to move forward. After I attend Jaimie's wedding, I'll be taking the jet to Russia to get her."

"Oh shit." Matteo snorts. "This is going to be interesting."

Over the past four and a half years, we've only seen Brielle when we went to visit her, and every time, she was frosty toward us. I tried to talk to her, to find out what we had done for her to behave this way, but every time, our grandmother would intercept and tell me that she needed time to heal. With Mom traveling, I let it go. But then our grandfather died from a heart attack, and shortly after, our grandmother passed in her sleep, leaving Brielle alone in Russia.

Our mom has been home for the past few months and agrees it's time for Brielle to come home.

"It will be fine," I tell him. "Brielle isn't a child. Surely, she'll be reasonable."

This time, it's Lorenzo who snorts out a laugh. "Name a woman who's reasonable."

"My mother," I say with a shrug.

"The woman who arrived home after being gone for three years and proceeded to burn everything Andrey had bought in the backyard, so the fire department had to be called out?" Matteo laughs. "Oh, yeah, she's full of reason."

"She was going through one of the stages of grieving," I point out.

"Face it," Lorenzo says. "We're surrounded by crazy-ass women in this city, and it's why we're all in our thirties and still single."

Ignoring Lorenzo's comment, I get back to his original question. "You can come with me, but you'll have to charter a flight home since I'm heading to Russia after the wedding."

"Hey, maybe you'll find a bridesmaid to hook up with." Matteo waggles his brows. "Need a plus-one? It'd be nice to dip my pole into some new waters."

"No," I deadpan. "While I'm gone, I need you to handle shit. But first, we need to figure out this Anthony bullshit. We didn't do all this work for him to slither in and bite us when we aren't looking."

"Are you fucking kidding me?" Anthony barks, stomping over to me.

It's been over four years since I last saw him, and time has not been good to him. With greasy blond hair, pale skin, and a beer gut nobody our age should have, he looks like he's spent the past several years sitting in front of the television instead of getting his act together.

Sure, his dad didn't leave him shit, but if I were in his shoes, that would've motivated me to prove my old man wrong and make my way in this world without his fucking money.

"Hello to you too," I tell him, glancing around for Matteo.

We're in public, surrounded by city officials, investors, and the management company that's running the auction, so as much as I'd like to take this fool out, I need to be careful. I might have most of the city's police force in my pocket, but there's only so much they could do if I killed the guy in front of everyone—or if he ended up dead shortly after our encounter.

"They fucking denied me because of you," Anthony spits.

The auction has ended, and between Russo Property Group and Antonov Enterprises, we've scooped up over one hundred and fifty acres in land.

We were hoping to get a few other parcels, but they went to a couple of different bidders. We'll figure it out though. With the land we have, there's only so much they can do with the parcels they bought. We'll contact them and offer them a number they can't refuse, and then we'll be set to put our real estate development plan into motion.

"No, they denied you because you're unstable, and if you default on your loan, they'll lose their ass. How did you get preapproved anyway?"

"Eric Vanderbilt vouched for me."

Mayor Vanderbilt? Hmm, that's interesting.

We've been butting heads with the newly appointed mayor since he was sworn into office.

We'd had a great relationship with Paul Astor, the previous mayor, who unfortunately reached the last term allowed. Everything was set for his son, Paul Jr., to become the new mayor, when he was in a car accident that forced him to drop out of the running and allowed Eric Vanderbilt to slide in and win. Something about it always felt shady to me, but now that I know Eric vouched for Anthony, my interest is piqued.

We don't know much about Eric, aside from him being a conservative family man. He has a wife and daughter, and every Sunday, you can find him at church, sitting in the first row.

"How do you know Mayor Vanderbilt?" I ask casually, watching closely to see how he reacts.

Just as I suspected, he flinches, showing his cards.

"First, you guys took what belonged to me, and then you killed my father," Anthony hisses, avoiding my question. "You'd better watch your back because, thanks to you, I have nothing left to lose."

I wait until he's gone before I pull out my phone and send Matteo a text.

Dominick: I need you to take out the trash.

He doesn't text back, but I know he'll handle it. We discussed this when we found out there was a chance Anthony would be showing up today.

Only now, we have one more person on our hit list—Mayor Eric Vanderbilt.

With the auction out of the way, I head home to finish packing for Jaimie's wedding. Despite the distance, we've become close these past few years. I don't have many friends—in my line of work, it's hard to trust anyone—but he's one of the few I consider an ally. So, when he invited me to attend his wedding, I accepted.

The flight to Coral Bay is quick, and the ride from the airport is long, thanks to the city traffic. They're getting married downtown, in one of the hotels we built, and everyone is staying there as well.

As the driver heads toward the hotel, I can't help but look out the window for the fiery redhead who, to this day, still crosses my mind. I could've looked her up—especially since I had Janet follow through with the scholarship for her, so it would've been easy to get her info—but when Peyton told me she'd moved on, I took it as a sign to let her go. But that doesn't stop me from thinking about her from time to time, especially when I'm in the city.

"Dominick," Jaimie says when I see him after the wedding at the reception, "thanks for coming, man."

"Of course." I give him a one-armed hug, then hug his wife, Beatrice. "Congratulations."

We spend a few minutes talking about where they'll be honeymooning and what Jaimie's plans are for expansion when they get home and he's back to business, which leads to the topic of the real estate development project we've secured in Harbor Point.

I'm going through our plans when my phone vibrates in my pocket. With Anthony on the loose—thanks to my brother being held up and not seeing my text until almost an hour later—and disappearing underground, like the snake that he is, we're all on alert, unsure how serious his threats were.

"Excuse me for a second," I tell Jaimie and Beatrice, clicking on my email from the management company who handles our private jet.

"Dammit." I shake my head when I read the email.

During their routine check, they found an issue with the engine and have to park it to fix it, which means it will be unavailable for my trip tomorrow. They can procure a replacement, but it's going to take a few days.

I send a text to Lorenzo to let him know he'll be able to use the company jet once it's available since I'm going to have to find another plane to take to Russia, and then I pocket my phone.

"Everything okay?" Beatrice asks, concern etched in her features.

Jaimie is one lucky bastard to snag a woman like her. Genuine women are hard to come by. They're either after you for your power or money—or in Matteo's case, they just want a night with a bad boy, but they could never handle the life we live.

"I was supposed to head to Russia to pick up my sister tomorrow, but our plane is down with an engine issue."

"Take mine," Jaimie offers. "We're not leaving for our honeymoon for a few days because Beatrice's family is in town."

He wraps his arm around his wife and kisses her temple, and not for the first time, a small part of me thinks about Peyton, wondering if I hadn't fucked shit up, maybe I could've had what he has. I immediately shove the thought away. Even if I hadn't walked out and pushed Peyton away, I wouldn't have wanted to bring her into my world.

At least with Jaimie, he's a legitimate businessman, so he doesn't have to worry about keeping the people close to him safe.

"I appreciate that," I tell him. "If all goes well, I should only be there for a couple of days."

"It's all good," Jaimie says with a smirk. "Having an Antonov owe me a favor might come in handy one day."

"Good afternoon, Mr. Antonov. My name is Sonia, and I'll be one of your flight attendants today."

I glance up from my phone at the black-haired woman and smile. "Thank you."

"Since this is your first time on Mr. Sanchez's plane, please allow me to show you around."

I nod and follow her around the plane. It has a bedroom, bathroom, and lounge. Since it's a twelve-hour flight, I plan to use the time to get some work done and get some sleep since there's an eight-hour time difference and we'll be arriving in Russia in the morning.

The bedroom will also come in handy on the way back to Harbor Point. I'm betting that Brielle is going to be pissed that I'm forcing her to come home, and she'll need a place to hide out—or vice versa. Eleven hours in a confined space with my pissed-off sister will not be—

"I am so sorry I'm late!" a feminine voice hisses, cutting off my thoughts. "Damien was having a rough day and—"

I glance back, and emerald eyes—the same color I've seen in damn near every one of my fantasies over the past four and a half years—collide with mine. Fiery-red hair, porcelain skin. She's put on a little bit of weight since the last time I saw her, but her curves only add to her beauty. She's dressed in the same outfit as Sonia—a black-and-gold blazer with a matching skirt—but unlike Sonia's chunky boots, she's sporting a pair of heels, reminding me of our night together.

She halts, and with her wide eyes trained on me, she swallows thickly and then glances around, like she's trying to think of a way to bolt.

Before she can, Sonia greets her.

"Hey, it's okay," she tells Peyton. "I was just showing Mr. Antonov around." She smiles warmly at me. "Would you like something to drink?"

"Peyton knows what I like," I say, having a seat on the leather sofa and glancing at the woman who's standing in the same place, looking like she's seen a ghost.

"Oh, okay," Sonia says, her brows furrowing in confusion. "Well then, Peyton, please grab Mr. Antonov a drink. And here's the menu."

She hands me a leather-bound booklet and then looks at Peyton, who's still frozen in her spot. I can't help but smirk because even though it's been over four years, the woman clearly remembers me and is affected. But then I remember how we left shit—with me leaving without a note and her moving on less than a month later—and my mood darkens at the thought of her being with someone shortly after me. Of some other guy putting his hands on her. Fucking her.

I glance at her left hand, but there's no ring on it, and my mood slightly improves.

"Peyton," Sonia hisses, snapping Peyton out of her current trance. "Get Mr. Antonov his drink, please."

Peyton nods and then scurries away while Sonia starts to go over the flight safety protocol with me—a standard procedure that's required on every flight, even private.

She's just finishing up when Peyton comes out with my drink of choice in hand. With a forced smile, she places the napkin on the table next to me.

"They didn't have Kingston," she murmurs. "But they had Woodford Reserve, which is almost as good."

I stifle my smirk at the fact that she not only remembered which whiskey I preferred, but despite the way shit ended, she cared enough to find me a decent replacement since Jaimie doesn't keep Kingston stocked.

As she sets my drink down, her lavender scent permeates the air, giving me the best damn high, and like an addict, I lean in, needing more.

"What are you doing?" she accuses, glancing up at me, our faces only inches apart.

"Smelling you," I say, not giving a shit that she caught me. "You smell the same as you did in the Dominican Republic."

"Well, I might smell the same"—she snaps her body up and glares down at me—"but nothing else about me is the same. So, before you get any ideas, don't."

She turns to stalk away, but before she can, I grab ahold of her wrist, forcing her to fall back into my lap. She scrambles to get off me, and I let her.

"Stop it!" she hisses. "This is beyond inappropriate. I am working, and you're … you're … just leave me alone!"

"Peyton!" Sonia squeaks out when she finds Peyton sitting on the sofa and yelling at me. "I'm so sorry, Mr. Antonov," Sonia apologizes, the tone in her voice telling me, unlike Peyton, she knows exactly who I am.

"It's okay, Sonia," I tell her. "Ms. ..." I glance at Peyton and leave my sentence hanging, hoping I'll get her last name, and Sonia doesn't disappoint.

"Wright," Sonia answers, earning a glare from Peyton.

"Ms. Wright and I were just chatting. If you wouldn't mind, I'd actually like to finish our conversation."

Sonia's eyes go wide, bouncing between Peyton and me, but then she nods and makes herself scarce.

"Now, where were we?" I say, turning my attention back to the beautiful, fiery woman glaring daggers my way.

"I was telling you to leave me the hell alone, and you were about to oblige."

I bark out a laugh.

Fuck, I've missed this woman.

Nobody, aside from my family, would ever speak to me the way she does.

"How have you been?" I ask, trying to keep our conversation surface level when the truth is that I want to know everything about this woman.

I let her go once, but it's like fate intervened, and now that she's back in my life, I have no intention of letting her go again.

"I've been fine," she says in a short tone, her gaze hard.

"And your mom?"

This time, her eyes soften. "She died ... a couple of years ago."

"I'm sorry," I tell her, reaching out and squeezing her hand, shocked when she lets me.

"I got two more years with her," she says with a sad smile. "And Damien—" She cuts herself off and scrambles off the couch. "I really need to get to work. If you need anything, please let—"

"Who's Damien?" I ask.

Her eyes widen, and I could be wrong, but it looks like they're filled with fear. "I-I don't—"

"Don't lie to me," I tell her. "You've said that name twice since getting on this plane. So, if you try to tell me he's nobody, I'll hunt him down and make that statement true."

She opens her mouth to speak, but before she gets a word out, I add, "Before you consider lying, just know that people who lie to me are always punished." I smirk. "And I'm not talking about the spankings you enjoyed while I was fucking you from behind in the DR."

I wasn't planning on showing my cards this quickly, but she'll learn who I am soon enough.

"You want to talk truths?" She nails me with a glare. "How about you start with what really happened to Dale? You killed him, didn't you?"

"No."

Her shoulders visibly sag, and I wait a few seconds before I rock her world.

"My brother did."

PASSPORT

THIRTEEN

Peyton

"**M**Y BROTHER DID."

I take a step back, even though there's nowhere to go on this plane.

"My brother did."

I knew what Dominick was capable of. I'd learned it the hard way four and a half years ago. But the fact that he's outright admitting it instead of denying it tells me more than when I thought he was responsible for Dale's death.

"You—"

"Never lied," he finishes. "I asked if he was giving you any more issues, and you said he was dead."

He shrugs.

The motherfucker shrugs!

"You knew and didn't say anything!"

"Who's Damien?" he asks nonchalantly, changing the subject like he didn't just admit to playing a vital part in a man's death.

"None of your damn business," I hiss, refusing to answer his question.

He reaches out to stop me, but I'm prepared this time and duck out of his hold, practically running to the front of the plane.

"What the hell was that?" Sonia asks once we're out of earshot of Dominick. "You know who he is, right?" she says, her voice shaking.

I do know who he is. Dominick Antonov. The son of Andrey

and Larisa, brother to Matteo and Brielle. His father was worth millions, but after he passed away four and a half years ago, Dominick took over the company and has expanded it tenfold. He's taken the real estate market by storm, investing in dozens of commercial and residential properties, making him one of the youngest billionaires in the country.

The online articles paint him as Harbor Point's most eligible bachelor. Women flock from all over to try to catch the beautiful business mogul. He donates to charities, and his latest project will create housing for hundreds of lower-income families.

But below the surface, there's more to the Antonov family. It's what you won't find online because they make sure to have it all wiped from the internet. But I asked around and learned they were dangerous, violent, and above the law. It was hard to get anyone to talk. From what I've gathered, they own the entire city—drugs, weapons, underground gambling, you name it—nothing in Harbor Point happens without their say.

"Yeah," I tell Sonia, "I know exactly who Dominick Antonov is."

And I'll be damned if he gets anywhere near me or my life again.

The rest of the flight is spent with Dominick working and me avoiding him. Sonia brings him his meals, and I handle things from the galley until he finally calls it a night and retreats to the back bedroom to get some sleep, allowing us to take turns doing the same.

When we arrive at the airport in Moscow, I hide while Sonia sees Dominick off, and then we head through security and go straight to the hotel since it's not even noon yet and we're not leaving until tomorrow morning.

Usually, when we fly to somewhere I haven't been to, I'll explore the city, but from what I could find, Russia isn't the safest, so I decide to stay at the hotel until I need to report back to the plane.

Generally, I try to only fly local, not wanting to be gone overnight, but I'm filling in for a colleague of mine who had a family emergency, and I owed her one.

And it's just my luck that I was stuck on a flight with Dominick Antonov.

Once I'm situated in my room, I text my babysitter, Lisa, to check on Damien, despite it being one a.m. there and she won't see it until the morning when she takes Damien to school.

After my mom died, since I was struggling to pay the bills and had to give up the house we were renting, I moved Damien and me into a small apartment, where I met Lisa. She's a sweet older woman, who immediately took a liking to Damien, saying he reminded her of her grandbabies she didn't get to see because her son was in the military and lived overseas. The woman has been a godsend, watching Damien when I need to work and he's not in school.

The plan was to live in the apartment until I finished school. Thanks to a scholarship I'd received that covered my entire tuition and books, I walked across the stage with my degrees in business administration and hospitality last month, and I've started to apply to companies so I can get a better-paying job and move us somewhere nicer with two bedrooms. I haven't gotten any calls for an interview yet, but I'm hoping something will pop up.

I spend some time reading, order room service for dinner, and fall asleep before the sun goes down, both mentally and physically exhausted.

Before I know it, my alarm is going off to let me know it's time to report back to the plane, and I'm reminded of who I'm going to see on board.

"You've got this," I tell myself in the mirror as I apply my makeup. "One more flight, and then you'll never have to see Dominick Antonov again."

PASSPORT

FOURTEEN

Dominick

"**D**OMINICK," BRIELLE SAYS, HER TONE ICE-COLD, "I THOUGHT we talked about this."

I step into our grandparents' house—which Brielle owns since they left it to her—and close the door behind me, setting my overnight bag on the ground.

"No, I told you that it was time to come home, and you hung up on me."

"I thought my hanging up made it clear that this *is* my home."

She juts out her chin, and I can't help but grin at her defiance.

"Bri, I flew twelve hours. How about you give me a hug, and then we can talk?"

I open my arms, but she stays where she is.

Stubborn fucking woman.

"Talk?" She scoffs. "Fuck you and your talking. I have nothing to say to you. I told you I wasn't going back to Harbor Point, and I meant it. It's not my fault you didn't listen."

I drop my arms, confused as to where all this hostility is coming from. If anyone else spoke to me like this, they'd already have a bullet between their eyes. But my sister isn't anyone else, and I'm starting to see a pattern with the women in my life. My mom, Peyton, Brielle—all of them are strong and tenacious and not the least bit scared of me.

"Apparently, we have a lot to say." I walk past her and into the sitting room.

The place is exactly like it was the last time I visited after our grandmother passed away. It's as if Brielle barely even lives here.

"For starters, why the hell are you so pissed at Matteo and me? You wanted to live here, so we let you go. But, shit, Bri, it's been over four years. Our grandparents are gone, and you're all alone here. Don't you think it's time to come home?"

It's taking everything in me not to pick her ass up and haul her out the door, but the businessman in me knows if I can make it seem like it's her idea, she'll go easier.

"That place isn't my home," she says, crossing her arms over her chest. "And I'd rather be alone here than anywhere near you."

"What the fuck did I do?" I bark, losing my patience.

"Don't yell at me!"

"Then, stop speaking in goddamn riddles and tell me what your fucking problem is."

"My problem is that I've watched both you and Matteo kill men for something as stupid as speaking to you wrong, yet I was raped, and instead of killing him, you merely cut ties with him and let him go about his merry way. I just don't fucking understand, Dominick. Make me understand!"

I watch as tears fill Brielle's eyes and then spill down her cheeks while I try to wrap my head around what the hell she's talking about.

Raped? "Who the fuck raped you?"

I would know if someone raped her. Nobody does anything in our city without me knowing. Even if I didn't know, if it somehow got past me, Matteo runs the fucking streets. He would've heard something.

"Brielle!" I bark when she doesn't answer me. "Who fucking raped you?"

Brielle's eyes go wide. "What do you mean, who raped me? You know—"

"No, I fucking don't." I step toward her, but then stop myself.

My heart is beating rapidly, and my blood is boiling in my veins. "Who. The fuck. Raped. You?"

"Anthony," she whispers. "Anthony raped me. I … I thought you knew."

"Anthony was here?"

I glance around, as if he could suddenly pop out, even though there's no way he could possibly know where our grandparents lived. They made sure nobody knew, which was why we let Brielle live with them. We knew she'd be safe.

"No." She shakes her head as more tears slide down her face. "In the States. I … oh my God, Dominick, are you telling me you didn't know?"

"Know what?" I bark. "When the fuck did he rape you?"

I clench my fists, trying to contain my fury, when all I want to do is destroy everything in my sight. Because what the fuck?

"A month before Dad died. Anthony was pissed that the wedding was taking so long. He showed up at my school and saw me with Owen. I'd thought I was being careful, but I hadn't known he was following me. He waited until I was alone in my apartment, studying, and then he broke in and raped me." She sobs. "I begged him not to, but he was so mad, saying that I gave Owen what was promised to him."

Red … all I see is fucking red.

Anthony Rothschild raped my little sister.

And instead of killing him, I let him go.

I. Let. Him. Go.

"And Andrey knew?" I ask slowly.

She nods. "I ended up pregnant. I wasn't sure who the father was because Owen and I hadn't exactly been careful, but it didn't matter because the moment Andrey found out, he forced me to have an abortion."

Her hands go to her belly, and my gut twists inside of me.

"He said I was damaged goods," she cries. "That I was a disgrace to the family. I told him that Anthony raped me, and he said that I got what I deserved. That I shouldn't have been with Owen."

How the hell did all of this happen under my nose?

"I had no idea," I tell her, rushing across the room and pulling her into my arms. "I had no fucking idea."

"I thought you knew." She weeps into my chest. "I mean, you were Andrey's right-hand man."

"Only because I had no other choice. If I wanted the company, I had to do what he said. But I'd never have gone along with any of that."

"I just … I didn't understand," she cries, tightening her arms around me. "I didn't understand why him raping me wasn't enough for you to end his life. I know I'm just a woman …"

"You're not *just* anything," I tell her. "You're our flesh and blood. Our sister." I step back and lift her chin and then frame her face with my hands. "You really believe if we knew that Anthony had raped you, that Andrey had forced you to have an abortion, we wouldn't kill both of them with our bare hands?"

"Oh my God, Dominick." She bawls harder. "I was in such a bad place, and I assumed you knew. Andrey had killed my boyfriend, and then he forced me to have an abortion. He was spouting out stuff about you guys needing to do damage control, and I thought you knew. I wasn't thinking clearly. I'm so sorry. I didn't know! I shouldn't have—"

"Shh. Stop." I pull her to me and kiss the crown of her head. "We should've fought harder to find out why you didn't want to come home. We thought it was because you'd lost your boyfriend and then Andrey had died. We didn't know."

I tip her chin and look into her blue eyes, the same ones as our mom. "I promise you, when Matteo and I find that asshole, we're going to make him pay. By the time we're done with him, he'll be begging for us to kill him."

"Thank you," she says, stepping back. "But, Dominick, please don't make me go back there. I like it here."

"No, you like hiding here," I correct her. "And I get it now that I know what you went through. But you have no reason to hide anymore. Andrey is dead, and Matteo and I are running shit now. The house has been renovated. You won't even recognize it."

"Since when is he Andrey to you and not *Father?*" she asks.

"Since he lost the right to that title. He did a lot of stupid shit in his life, but he's lucky he's dead, or I'd be burying him six feet under. He was a shitty husband and father, and he doesn't deserve to be called either."

She nods in agreement.

"I just … I don't know if I can go back to that city and that house. The memories … Harbor Point is tainted with everything Andrey was and what he did to me."

"The city is ours, not his," I tell her. "It's like he never even existed. Please, come home and give it a chance. We miss you and want our family back together."

She stares at me for several seconds and then finally says, "Okay, I'll come home."

My phone vibrates, and I pull it out in case it's Matteo. After I saw Peyton on the flight and she mentioned this Damien guy a couple of times, I texted Matteo to investigate her, wanting to know if she was with someone and whether it was serious.

Since finding info on someone is child's play for my brother, I'm sure it won't take him long to get me the info I need.

Matteo: We need to talk.

Fuck, this can't be good.

FIFTEEN

Peyton

A TWELVE-HOUR FLIGHT, AND DOMINICK HAS PRETTY MUCH ignored me the entire time, aside from when he's needed to order a drink and food.

He's spent most of the flight working on his laptop, sitting beside a beautiful blonde woman, who's spent the trip listening to music and binge-watching shows on her tablet.

I thought for sure that I was going to have to hide out for the flight back, but it's like he doesn't even know I exist.

Unfortunately, we're taking a detour to Harbor Point to drop them off before we fly back to home base, which means we'll be stuck spending the night in his city.

"We should go skiing this winter," the woman says, looking up at Dominick from her phone. "Remember when we went a few years ago? We had so much fun."

Dominick glances up at her and smiles, and my heart stops. I don't know who this woman is, but I've learned Dominick's smiles are few and far between, and for her to earn one must mean she's important to him.

"Sure," he says. "You plan it, and we'll go."

I shouldn't care that he's with someone. It means he'll leave me alone, which is what I want … what I *need*. But I can't help the anger spreading through my veins at the fact that he was literally flirting with me yesterday on his way to … what? Go pick this woman up and bring her back here?

She squeals and leans over to kiss his cheek, and before I can think about what I'm doing, I'm stalking toward them.

Dominick sees me coming first and raises a questioning brow. But the woman doesn't notice me until I'm standing directly in her line of vision.

"Just so you know," I tell her, "the guy you're with was hitting on me in this same plane yesterday. So, you might want to be careful."

The woman's brows furrow in confusion for several seconds before she glances from me to Dominick and then proceeds to laugh. Like a full-blown belly laugh that ricochets throughout the plane.

"Oh my God, Dominick, you were hitting on the flight attendant?" She shakes her head. "Have you no boundaries? I would expect that from Matteo, but not you."

Dominick rolls his eyes, and I stare at them, wondering why the hell the woman isn't mad. I mean, she just learned that her … *whatever he is to her* was flirting with another woman.

"Well, anyway," I say, "I just wanted you to be aware. Girl power and all that."

I'm about to turn around to walk back to the front when she speaks, stopping me in my place.

"While I agree that flirting with the employees is in bad taste," she says, side-eyeing Dominick, "my brother is free to flirt with whoever he wants."

Brother …

Oh shit.

I glance at Dominick, who smirks.

I got it all wrong.

And I look stupid.

And sound like a jealous girlfriend.

"Right," I murmur. "I'm just going to go …" I nod over my shoulder and then scurry away as the woman, who's apparently related to Dominick, laughs.

Thankfully, the rest of the flight goes smoothly. After I told Sonia that I'd made an ass out of myself, she served them their drinks so I could hide out until we landed and Dominick and his sister got off the plane.

After we finish up our duties, Sonia and I head to the airport hotel since we're stuck in Harbor Point until tomorrow morning. I put in a notice with the company I work for that I'm able to work any route heading to Coral Bay in case there's an opening, hoping to get home sooner, but nothing pops up.

So, after talking to Damien, telling him I love and miss him, I go to bed and set my alarm for six a.m.

I'm snuggling into my pillow, my eyes slowly closing, when there's a knock on my door. Because I'm in a hotel and it's late, it can only be one person …

"Peyton, open up." Dominick's masculine voice comes through the door.

I consider yelling at him to go away, but something tells me that a guy like him would only see that as a challenge. He obviously went out of his way to find out where I was, and I doubt he'll leave until he says whatever it is he needs to say. Honestly, it's better for him to talk to me here than follow me back home. The last place I want this dangerous man is in Coral Bay.

"What?" I ask when I swing the door open.

Instead of answering, he strolls past me like he owns the place, not stopping until he's in the middle of the tiny main area.

"You're not surprised I found you," he says, quirking a brow. "Does that mean you now know who I am?"

"Yes, I know exactly who you are," I tell him, crossing my arms protectively over my chest. "And in case I didn't make it clear, I want nothing to do with you."

"Really?" He chuckles darkly, stepping toward me. "Because when you were accusing me of cheating on my *sister*, what you wanted seemed a bit fuzzy."

"It was a mistake. What we had all those years ago was a one-time thing, and I would really appreciate it if you left."

Dominick eyes me for several seconds, his gaze roaming over my face and down my body, and despite being fully clothed in my pajamas, I've never felt more exposed from a single look.

"Who's Damien?" he asks.

I flinch at his out-of-left-field question and pray I school my features before he notices.

"He's—"

"Don't even think about saying he's none of my business."

Dammit.

"And don't lie."

Fuck.

I know about his reputation. And I would be stupid to lie to him and risk him finding out, but I don't have a choice because the alternative is …

"He's my boyfriend. And it's serious."

Dominick tilts his head, assessing me, and my heart pounds against my chest as I hope like hell he doesn't see through my lie.

"You sure about that?" he asks me point-blank.

I don't know why, but I have a horrible feeling he already knows the answer. Which means …

"Did you have me investigated?"

"What does it matter?" he asks. "If you're telling the truth, then you have nothing to hide."

He steps toward me, and I take a step back, hitting the wall behind me.

"Answer the fucking question," he says, his tone reminding me of *that day.* Cold, menacing … deadly. "Who is Damien?"

Oh my God. He knows.

He wouldn't keep asking if he didn't. It's like when I ask Damien about something he did that he shouldn't have, wanting him to admit it for himself, even though I already know the answer.

I should tell the truth. But I can't. Because doing so would mean putting Damien in danger, and I won't do that. It's my job to protect him.

"My boyfriend!"

"Dammit, Peyton!"

He raises his hand, and I cower before the blow can land. Only instead of hitting me, his hand lands on the wall next to me.

"Are you fucking serious? You think I would hit you?"

"I know what you're capable of!" I yell. "You've killed people! Is it so far of a stretch to think you'd hurt me?"

He backs up slightly in shock at my accusation, and I use that as my chance to escape. Ducking under him, I run toward the door, but before I can get it open enough to get out, he slams it closed. The action sends my body into the door, and with his arms caging me in, I'm trapped.

"Please," I beg, my entire body shaking, "don't hit me!"

Images of my dad pushing my mom around hit me hard, and I close my eyes, praying Dominick doesn't hurt me the way my dad hurt my mom.

"I'm not going to fucking hit you!" he barks, spinning me around so I'm forced to look at him. "Now, stop fucking lying to me. We both know who Damien is, and you're going to fucking say it!"

"No," I shout back, "I'm not! I want you to get the fuck out of my room and out of my life! I already told you—"

Knock. Knock. Knock.

"This is security. We've had a noise complaint. Please open the door."

I move to the side, but instead of Dominick opening the door, he glares at it for several seconds.

Finally, with an annoyed sigh, he takes a step back and opens the door. "Everything's fine," he tells the security guy. "I was just leaving."

"Oh, I'm sorry, Mr. Antonov. I didn't know you were here …"

Seriously? Does everybody but me know who this guy is?

"No worries," he tells the gentleman.

I assume he's going to leave without another word, but he turns around, his cold gray eyes meeting mine.

"This isn't over, Peyton," he warns, sending a chill up my spine.

Because I know his words aren't empty, and it's only a matter of time before he comes for me and forces the truth out of me, which is why I need to leave as soon as possible.

As if Dominick can hear my thoughts, he adds, "Before you think about leaving, I'll be back in the morning. And you'd better fucking be here and be ready to speak honestly."

He doesn't wait for me to answer. He simply saunters away like he didn't just threaten me.

Despite his menacing words, I know without a doubt, I will not be here in the morning.

PASSPORT
AIR
JOHN
New
London
25 DEC 18
15:45
H93815
IFK
35

SIXTEEN

Dominick

THIS FUCKING WOMAN. FOUR AND A HALF GODDAMN YEARS of keeping this secret. And even knowing that I fucking know, she still won't admit it.

"Boss," George, one of the guys who works for me and Matteo, says when I step around the corner.

"I want you on that fucking room. If she leaves, you follow her."

I stop and remember the way she freaked when she thought I was going to hit her. She had told me about her dad being violent and her mom getting away. I might be pissed, but I would never lay a hand on a woman.

"Don't touch her," I tell him.

"But what if she runs, Boss?"

"Then, you follow and call me. Don't lose her, but don't fucking touch her."

He nods in understanding and then heads down to her room while I take the elevator to the parking garage.

"He yours?" Matteo asks when I ring him on the way back to my place.

"She won't say. You find Anthony?"

When I told him what Anthony had done, he went fucking nuts. And I got it because Brielle was ours to protect and we had failed.

Once he got his shit together, he started his hunt for Anthony.

"My guys are scouring the streets," he says.

I know he's champing at the bit to get out there and look for Anthony himself rather than hang out at home with Brielle. But I didn't want to leave her alone. The second we had pulled up to the house, she'd started crying, saying she didn't want to go inside, obviously still traumatized by what Andrey put her through. But I'd assured her that there wasn't a trace of Andrey left in that house.

"We need to find him," I say as I turn onto the highway.

"We will. Before, we didn't look because we didn't care. But now, I'll stop at nothing until I have him," Matteo says in a bone-chilling tone that would even scare the hell out of me if I didn't know that my brother would rather end his own life before he would ever hurt me.

When I arrive home, Brielle is asleep. Matteo takes off, and I check in with George, who tells me there's been no movement. I grab my suitcase since I'll be making an unplanned trip to Coral Bay in the morning and then take a quick shower.

I should get some sleep. It's been a long couple of days, and tomorrow isn't going to be any better. But my mind can't stop racing, thinking about my last conversation with Peyton.

"I've moved on. I met someone else, and I need you to please leave me alone."

Did she know that she was pregnant then?

But it doesn't make sense. I'd contacted her. She could've told me on the phone. Instead, she lied. She knew how to contact me, yet she never did. She kept this huge secret from me, not giving a shit about me.

When I saw her on the plane, I thought it was fate. That it was my second chance to make Peyton mine. Now, the only thing I want is the goddamn truth.

With an old-fashioned and my laptop, I settle in on the couch to try to get some work done when Matteo calls.

"We found where he was staying."

"*Was?*"

"The entire fucking place has been cleaned out," he says, and even though I can't see him, I can hear him punch something. "We have a fucking rat. Someone must have told him we were coming. It's the only fucking way he could have known to pack up his shit and leave. I'm having our guys pull up the footage to see if we can find anything."

"Keep me informed."

"The goddamn maid? Are you fucking kidding?" Matteo grabs a vase from the end table and chucks it across the room.

"Hey, do you mind?" I bark. "I know you're pissed. I am, too, but since we're going to have to fire the cleaning crew, I'd rather not fuck up the place."

"I'm going to fucking kill her," he says, referring to the maid we caught on camera, who had placed bugs all over the goddamn house.

We'd gotten lax, not having our house swept for bugs, which made it easy for her to walk in, plant the bugs in various rooms, and then leave—allowing Anthony to hear every goddamn word we said.

"No, you're not," I tell him, my thoughts going back to Peyton and the way she feared me. "We don't hurt women."

Matteo nails me with a hard glare. "Fine. Then, I'll send her ass back to wherever the fuck she came from."

"First, we need to confirm that Anthony got to her. Then, we'll—"

My phone rings with a call from George.

"Yeah."

"She ran."

Fuck.

"Follow her." I jump up from my seat on the couch. "And send me your location. Remember, don't fucking touch her."

I hang up and grab my luggage by the door.

"Peyton ran," I tell Matteo. "Apparently, she's determined to defy me at every turn."

He shakes his head. "Women are nothing but goddamn trouble."

PASSPORT
FK
H608215
25 DEC 18
15:45
JOHN
New
Lond
35

SEVENTEEN

WAITED, WANTING TO MAKE SURE DOMINICK WAS GONE BEFORE I made my escape. And then I held off a little longer, afraid he was still around. Then, after a couple of hours, I started to worry that if I stayed too long, he would return.

So, I packed up my stuff and made my move. I had found a flight heading back to Coral Bay in a few hours and booked it. It was with a commercial airline, so I had to pay for it, but there was no way I was risking getting on a private flight. If he had known what hotel and room to find me in, he'd also know when I was scheduled to get on the plane to go home.

When I stepped out of the room, the hall was empty, and I released a relieved breath, thinking I was in the clear. But the moment I started to walk toward the elevator, I felt someone on my trail. He followed me into the elevator, down to the first floor, and continued as I made my way to the airport.

I speed-walk through the airport, past the check-in desks, and down the escalator that will take me to security. Once I'm through, I'll be in the clear because only ticketed passengers can get past security, and there's no way this guy bought a ticket.

Because it's early, the line goes quickly, and before I know it, I'm handing my driver's license over to security and being waved through.

I go through the metal detector, and just as I'm about to grab my carry-on from the conveyor belt, a gentleman lifts it and says, "Ma'am, I need you to come with me."

Are you freaking kidding me?

"Is there a problem with my luggage?" I ask.

"Please come with me," he says, walking us toward a secluded area.

It's just my luck that while I'm in a rush, my luggage raises a red flag. Luckily, I arrived a bit early for my flight.

He opens the door for me, and I step inside, ready to ask him again what's wrong with my luggage when I see the man who was following me standing in the room.

"No!" I breathe out, turning to run.

But the door is closed and locked, and I'm fucked.

"Let me out right now!" I demand even though it's fruitless. "I have a flight to catch."

He stares at me with bored disinterest, and it boils my blood. I stalk over to the door and start to bang on it, yelling for someone to help me, but nobody comes.

I refuse to give up, needing to take my anxiousness and frustration out on something, while the man who clearly works for Dominick stands in the corner, watching, his features devoid of expression.

I'm still banging on the door when it swings open, forcing me to stumble back. Dominick, dressed in the same sharp suit as earlier, saunters in, and his gray eyes, filled with disdain, lock with mine.

"I told you not to leave," he says, cornering me against the wall.

"And I told you to leave me alone!" I volley with false bravado. The truth is, I'm shaking, scared of what will happen next.

Will he demand to meet Damien?

Will he try to take him away from me?

"Let's go," he says, taking hold of my wrist with such strength that I squeal out in pain.

"That hurts!" I hiss, trying to get free of his grasp.

He loosens his hold just barely as he guides us to another door that seems to be a back way. The halls are empty, aside from his spy, who's following us to wherever we're going.

When we step into the gangway, it hits me …

"No! No, no, no!" I wriggle my wrist. "You can't kidnap me!" I can see part of a jet from here, and I know if I'm forced onto it, nothing will ever be the same.

"Stop it!" Dominick barks, now dragging me onto the jet. "I'm not kidnapping you."

"Really? What would you call forcing me onto a plane against my will?"

"Giving you a ride back to Coral Bay," he deadpans.

Fuck, this is bad.

There's only one reason he'd want to go to Coral Bay.

Damien.

We step onto the plane, similar to the one I saw him on a couple of days ago.

Holy shit, how has it only been a couple of days?

It's sleek with mahogany wood and creamy leather, screaming wealth and opulence. The flight attendant scurries around to get things ready, but she doesn't greet Dominick, telling me that she knows exactly who he is.

"Is this your plane?" I ask, too curious for my own good.

"Sit," he commands, ignoring my question.

"No."

His jaw tics, but I hold my ground, refusing to make this easy on him. He's kidnapping me, for goodness' sake, regardless if it's to take me home.

"Fine."

He shrugs, and I think he's going to relent. But then he leans over and flings me over his shoulder like I'm a damn rag doll.

"Dominick! Put me down!" I yell as he stalks toward the back of the plane.

I'm upside down, kicking and screaming, demanding repeatedly that he put me down, but he doesn't listen.

"Keep it up, and I'm going to spank your ass," he murmurs, forcing my thoughts to go back to our night together—when he fucked me from behind in the bathroom, smacking my ass.

I've been with men since him, but none of them pleasured me in the way Dominick had done that night.

I squirm, thinking about our time together, and the asshole chuckles. Fucking chuckles! I hate how well he can read my body. He barely knows me, for God's sake, yet he somehow knows my body better than anyone else I've been with.

He swings the door open and then drops me onto a bed. The room is simple yet elegant, and despite being clean, I can smell his masculine scent lingering in here.

"Now," he says, pulling a chair over to the edge of the bed and sitting on it, "we have about an hour until we get to Coral Bay, and we're going to talk."

I eye the closed door, and he shakes his head.

"The plane doors are being closed, and we're about to take off. You're not going anywhere."

I huff in annoyance and fall onto my back. Crossing my arms over my chest, I stare at the ceiling, refusing to talk to him.

"Peyton," he says in a tone that sends shivers racing down my spine, "we can do this the easy way or the hard way. It's up to you."

"And what's the hard way?" I snap, sitting back up to glare at him. "Are you going to torture me? Threaten me? *Kill* me?"

"What the fuck are you going on about?" he barks. "I just want you to admit that Damien is my son and you kept him from me. I want to hear it from your mouth that you knew you were pregnant with my flesh and blood, and instead of telling me, you chose to hide it. I want you to admit—"

"Fine!" I blurt out. "Yes, Dominick. He shares the same biology as you. But let's get one thing straight. He's not yours. He's mine, and you're never going to get anywhere near him!"

Before I finish my sentence, Dominick is across the bed, towering over me. His knees cage in my thighs, holding me there. His fingers grip my chin, and the back of my head hits the wall behind me.

"How dare you keep my fucking son from me!" he growls.

"I was protecting him!"

"From me?" The hand that's holding my face tightens. "I'm his father!"

"And you're dangerous!" I yell back. "I … I saw you."

"Saw what?"

"I saw you kill that man."

Dominick releases his hold on my face and backs up slightly. "Explain."

Four and a Half Years Ago

I'm pregnant.

Holy shit, I'm freaking pregnant.

My period is always on time. Like clockwork, it shows up. So, when it didn't, I knew something was wrong. And then it hit me—Dominick and I had not been careful. We were too caught up in our passion, in the moment. At the time, it'd felt like a fantasy.

But now, as I stare at the positive pregnancy test, reality sets in.

It was only supposed to be a onetime thing, and he proved that when he took off without so much as a note the morning after.

And now, I have to tell him I'm pregnant.

My phone dings with a text from the manager of the hotel I work at, asking if I can switch shifts with another employee. Because of my mom being sick, I quit my job as a flight attendant, wanting to be home with her, and took a job at a local hotel as a front-desk receptionist, hoping it would help build my résumé for when I finished my degree.

And now, I'm pregnant.

I can't afford a baby.

Money is already tight.

My focus should be on my mom's health.

But there's a baby growing in me.

My hand goes to my belly, and I sigh.

First things first. I need to confirm my pregnancy with a doctor. And then, if I really am pregnant, I'm going to have to let Dominick know.

As I sit on my flight to Harbor Point, I stare at the grainy black-and-white image. I'm pregnant. Due in December. In several months, everything is going to change. I haven't told my mom yet because I want to tell Dominick first.

I looked him up and learned he's a businessman in Harbor Point. He has an office downtown, so I'm going to go there and see if he's available to speak to me.

I have no idea how any of this is going to work. For all I know, he won't want to have anything to do with the baby. But I'll let him make that decision.

When I arrive at the office, security is busy talking to someone about something that sounds important, so when the elevator doors open and a woman steps out, I slide in. There's a list of offices on the inside, but none of them specify Dominick Antonov.

Hopefully, I'm in the right place.

I press the button for the top floor since it's reserved for

Antonov Enterprises Executive Business. But when I step onto the floor, the place is quiet.

I'm about to turn around and go back down when I hear voices, and then I see the nameplate on the door—*Dominick Antonov, CEO.*

I step closer as I consider knocking. I flew all this way, and it would be a waste of money to have to fly back without telling him about the pregnancy. I should've called before I came, but I was afraid he wouldn't take my call or that I'd chicken out.

I hear a voice speak on the other side of the door, so I tiptoe over and then press my ear to the wood, praying I don't get caught. How embarrassing would it be if he opened the door and I fell into the office?

"My father might've forgotten to teach me about making friends. But there's one lesson he instilled in me at a young age. If someone is bold enough to threaten you, they're willing to act on it. And if you knew my father the way you say you did, then you know what he did to anyone who threatened him."

The voice is unmistakably Dominick's, only it's much colder than the way he spoke to me during our time together. He's using his business voice. I heard it a few times, like when we met that gentleman for brunch in the Dominican Republic.

"I-I …" another gentleman says.

Dominick isn't alone.

I should walk away.

Go to the hotel I booked and try to call him.

But I've always been too nosy for my own good.

So, I continue to listen, and what I hear makes me wish I'd never gotten on that plane. Because ignorance is bliss.

But I'm no longer ignorant.

And I can never unhear what I just heard.

The father of my baby just killed a man.

Present Day

"That was you," Dominick says smoothly, not the least bit concerned that I overheard him murder a man.

"What was me?"

"My brother said a woman was seen in the lobby near my office that day. I told him to follow up and make sure she hadn't witnessed anything. I assumed he'd handled it since I never heard anything about it again."

"You killed a man."

"I've killed a lot of men," he admits. "But that man in particular was a bad man. He was trafficking women through my port and was pissed that I refused to allow it to continue."

"What are you saying? That you're some sort of vigilante?"

Dominick barks out a laugh. "Hardly."

He climbs off me and moves to the corner, making himself a drink. He takes a long sip, and I can't help but notice the way his Adam's apple bobs when he swallows.

Now is not the time to be turned on, I remind myself.

"So, you're a bad guy?" It's a question, but at the same time, it's not because I already know he's not a good guy.

After what I heard, I freaked out and took off. He managed to get ahold of me, but I lied and said I had moved on.

Instead of going home, I went to a few different bars and asked various people about the Antonov family. The women were smitten, the men envious. Some feared them, and others respected them. But almost every person confirmed what I'd already known—they were dangerous.

"Regardless of what I am," Dominick says, "it didn't give you the right to keep my son from me." He walks back to his seat and slides into it, casually placing his ankle over the knee of his other leg.

"Actually," I say, sitting up and swinging my legs around the side, "it did give me the right. Because my job as Damien's mom is to love and protect him, even if that means protecting him from you.

"I heard the violence in your voice. when you killed a man with your bare hands, and I will *never* let you get anywhere near my child.

"I watched my father abuse my mom, and I told you once that I was afraid of history repeating itself. That my biggest fear was not breaking the cycle, and you told me that I would break it. So, I did what I had to do to protect my son."

I walk past him, but he catches my wrist and glances up at me.

"You saw what I'm capable of," he says, tilting his head slightly. "Do you think it's wise to poke the beast? Who's to say I won't kill you? Then, what will be standing in my way from taking *our* son?"

"I will *always* fight for *my* son," I tell him, pulling my arm out of his hold. "Until I take my final breath, I will fight for him because I am his mother. He is just a baby, Dominick. Not your heir or a pawn. He's an innocent little boy who doesn't belong anywhere near your violence."

Dominick surprises me when he lets me walk out of the room without stopping me.

Good. Maybe I got through to him.

Maybe he understands.

Maybe he'll do the right thing and let us go.

PASSPORT

EIGHTEEN

Dominick

"A S YOU CAN SEE, NOBODY IS HERE," PEYTON SAYS WHEN WE
arrive at her apartment a few hours later.

I take in the area where she's been raising our son.
Worn-in couches and a kitchen table with chairs that have seen better days. The cabinets are the original dark-wood particle board from the '80s with Formica countertops. And the flooring is a scratched-up linoleum.

But on the walls are child's drawings, framed like they are the most precious thing in the world. Taped to the fridge are dozens of photos of Peyton and a little boy with several other people. They're laughing and smiling in every picture, and my heart swells. He has her fiery-red hair and porcelain skin, but his eyes … his gray eyes are one hundred percent mine. And the reminder that I have a son—someone with my eyes, who shares my genetics, that I've never even met—sends my blood boiling all over again.

"I want to see our son," I say to Peyton.

"He's not yours," she volleys. "He's mine. I already told you that you're not getting anywhere near him. You're violent and dangerous, and you'll have to kill me before I let you get close to my son."

"That can be arranged," I tell her, striding across the room.

Despite her false bravado, her eyes flash in fear as her back hits the wall.

Normally, I'd reassure her that I'd never hurt a woman, especially the mother of my child, but I've had enough of her shit.

"I understand you think you're protecting our son, and I can even respect that," I tell her, caging her in. "But you cost me over three years of his life, and it stops now. You made your choices, and now, you'll deal with the consequences. I'm giving you forty-eight hours to come to terms with the fact that our son has a father. One who will be in his life. When I return in two days, be prepared to move to Harbor Point."

She opens her mouth to argue, but I shake my head.

"You have nothing keeping you here. Your mom is dead, you graduated, and this apartment is leased."

"I have a job!"

"Your part-time job as a flight attendant?" I scoff. "It barely even pays your bills. You're running out of money and hoping to land a job at one of the hotels or restaurants you applied to."

Her eyes turn into thin slits. She's pissed that I know so much, but I don't care. She did it her way the past four years, and that ends now.

"Our son will have a home in Harbor Point, where he'll be given the best of everything. You can either get on board or the train will leave your ass here. You were right. I am dangerous, and I am powerful, which means I have important people in my pockets. As you know, I've killed people, yet I'm not behind bars. I do what I want, where I want, how I want, and nobody will fucking stop me."

"Cocky much?" she chokes out.

"No, just stating facts. If you don't think I'll use my connections to make sure I have our son in my life, you didn't do your research."

I step back to give her some space. She's going to need it because once I return and bring her back to my place, her days of having space are over.

"I will stop at nothing to ensure I don't lose another minute of time with our son, and I promise, I have the money and resources to make it happen."

I turn my back on her and saunter to the door. "Pack your shit, Peyton," I say as I open the front door. "I'll be back in two days, and our son is coming with me. With or without you."

I slide back into the town car and pull out my phone, needing to get shit rolling, when I notice a text from a number I don't recognize.

Unknown: An eye for an eye.

I forward it to our IT guy so he can run a trace on it, tell my driver to take me to my hotel, and then shoot a text to my assistant.

Dominick: Send packing supplies over to Peyton's apartment.

Peyton has two days, and then I'm coming for both her and our son. If I have to take her back to Harbor Point, kicking and screaming, that's what I'll do.

She played this game her way. Now, it's time to play it mine.

PASSPORT

NINETEEN

Peyton

"I WANT A TREE LIKE THAT," DAMIEN SAYS, CUDDLING INTO MY side as I close The Giving Tree—his recent favorite book that's about a tree who has a special friendship with a boy as he grows up. "Can we get a tree like that?"

He looks up at me with a serious expression, and I stifle a chuckle, not wanting my three-year-old to think that I'm mocking him.

"We'd have to grow it," I tell him. "And that would take years."

He sighs and thinks for several seconds before his eyes light up. "Or we can find a tree no one wants and then dig it up and bring it here."

"Where would we put it?"

"I don't know," he says thoughtfully. "We need a yard like Frankie."

Frankie is his friend from preschool. Ever since Damien went over to his house for a playdate, he's been begging me for a yard with a swing set and a pool.

It's tough, living in an apartment complex with a child. The place is small, and there isn't really any room to play. Because it's a one-bedroom apartment, we share a room. As he gets older, he's going to need more space, but in order to find a bigger place, I need to get a better job. I could easily go full-time at the company I work for, but that would mean flying for longer flights, sometimes even overnight, and I don't want to be away from Damien that long.

"One day," I tell him, kissing the top of his head. "Now, get some sleep. You have school in the morning."

He nods, his eyes already closing. "I'm gonna draw a picture of the tree," he mutters.

"I can't wait to see it."

I kiss him once more, then tiptoe out of the room. I'll be back in a few hours to go to sleep as well, but I tend to work in the living room to give him a chance to fall into a deep sleep.

I'm working on my laptop, applying to every job possible that will get my foot in the door with my degrees, when I hear some shuffling near the front door. The only person with a key to my apartment is my babysitter, Lisa, but she's not scheduled to come by tonight.

There's more shuffling, and I stand, wondering what's going on. Maybe Lisa forgot something when she babysat for Damien.

"Lisa, did you forget—" I start, unlocking and swinging the door open.

Only, instead of Lisa standing on the other side, two men shove me back inside. They're dressed in black with balaclavas covering their faces.

Out of instinct, I scream and then attempt to run, but one of the men catches me by my waist while the other man stalks past him, heading straight for my bedroom.

To Damien.

"Stop! No!" I yell, kicking and flailing about. "Let me go!"

The man tightens his hold on me, and I know I don't stand a chance against him, but I refuse to give up. Reaching behind me, I try to claw at his skin. I kick his shins and try to elbow his chest.

"He's not there," the guy says, stalking out of the room just as the front door swings open and more men pour into the apartment.

Before I can get a good look at who they are, the man standing in front of me hits the floor. I glance down at him and spot a tiny red hole in the center of his forehead.

Holy shit, he's dead.

I turn to see who killed him when my attacker lets go of me, falling to the floor as well. Then, I'm being swept off my feet and carried out of the apartment.

"Wait!" I beg. "My son …"

The guy said he wasn't in there. How could that be?

Did someone take him?

"Dominick has him," the man says, not stopping until we're in a black town car and driving away.

The man who saved me places a call on his phone and says, "I have her. Two need to be cleaned up." Then, he hangs up.

I want to ask him what's going on, but my heart is pounding so hard in my rib cage that it's hard to catch my breath. So, I focus on breathing.

In, out.

In, out.

When I'm somewhat calm, I glance at the gentleman, and despite his eye color being blue instead of gray, his features are similar to Dominick. Tanned skin. An angular jaw, covered with stubble. A Roman nose—but where Dominick's is perfectly straight, this guy's is a bit crooked.

"Dominick is my brother," the man says, as if he can read my mind. "My name is Matteo Antonov."

"How did you know …" I shake my head. "Your timing …" Tears prick my eyes as I imagine how scared my little boy must be. "I need to see my son. Please. Are you sure Dominick has him?"

"I'm sure," he tells me. "We'll be with them soon."

"Where? Where are they?"

Now that my heart rate is somewhat back to normal, I have so many questions. "Who were those men? Why did they break in?"

And then it hits me. "You … you killed them."

"It had to be done," Matteo says. "Dominick will explain everything."

The rest of the ride is silent. Matteo makes a few phone calls, but I have no idea what he's saying since he switches between English and another language, which I think might be Russian. When he's not making phone calls, he's texting.

The moment I see the Coral Bay airport come into view, my stomach sinks. Dominick warned me that he was coming for Damien and me, and he did. And now, he's taking us to Harbor Point.

Instead of pulling up to a terminal, the driver takes us around through another entrance and then, just like in the movies, drives us directly onto the tarmac.

There's nobody else here, and my heart drops. I pray Matteo wasn't lying and that Dominick really does have our son.

The second we step onto the plane, I scan the area, but he's not here.

There's nobody here.

I'm about to yell at Matteo, demand to know where my son is, but when I turn around, Dominick steps onto the plane with our son sleeping in his arms.

"My baby," I choke out, rushing over to them.

I pull Damien out of his arms and hug my little boy tightly.

He jostles in annoyance, but doesn't wake up, and I've never been so thankful that he's such a heavy sleeper. I could vacuum around him, and he wouldn't wake up.

"There's a bed in the back," Dominick says. "Lay him in there."

While I'm tucking Damien into bed, I think about everything that happened tonight.

The intruders—one held me back while the other went after Damien. But he was already gone.

Shortly after, Matteo showed up. He wasn't shocked to see the men. He was prepared and killed them quickly. The car was waiting for us. The plane was on standby.

At the time, I thought I was a victim of a random attack. But this wasn't random at all …

Dominick is dangerous. Violent. He's rumored to be part of a criminal organization. He runs his city with an iron fist. I witnessed him kill a man …

"Oh my God," I breathe. "This was because of him."

I quietly leave the room, closing the door behind me, and then stalk toward the front of the plane, finding Dominick, Matteo, and another man sitting in their seats, talking quietly.

Dominick sees me coming first, but before he can say a word, I'm in his face. "You did this!" I whisper-yell. "You have been in our lives for two damn minutes, and I was attacked, and my son was almost kidnapped!"

"Calm down," Dominick says. "You're going to wake up—"

"Wrong answer," one of the other guys mutters.

"Don't you tell me to calm down!" I shove at his shoulders. "And don't tell me what to do with my son. I told you to stay the hell away, and you didn't listen and now—"

"Enough!" Dominick stands and towers above me. "I fucked up," he says. "I left you at that run-down apartment with no security, and it's on me. I know this." He swallows thickly. "But it will never happen again."

"You can't know that," I hiss. "This is your world. Violence and corruption and death. I told you I wanted no part in it, but you didn't listen."

"It's too late," he says, his gray eyes locking with mine. "I was being followed, and the second they learned about you and our son, you both became a target."

"Who's *they*?"

"We're trying to figure that out right now." He sighs.

"Of course." I scoff. "You have so many enemies. You probably have to play a game of elimination to figure out which one is trying to get to you this time."

Somebody snorts, and Dominick glares.

"You knew this was going to happen," I accuse. "That's how you got to us so quickly. This is exactly why I told you I didn't want you in Damien's life. We were almost taken!"

"I handled it," he says.

"You handled it." I laugh, but it comes out manic. "You handled it? There shouldn't have been anything to handle! Normal people don't get attacked in the middle of the night! Kids don't get kidnapped while they're asleep!"

"You'd actually be surprised," Matteo says.

I nail him with a death glare.

He simply shrugs, unfazed. "I'm just saying, violence and corruption and death are everywhere. You just don't see or hear about it."

"Tell me what happened," I say to Dominick. "Who were those men who are now lying on my floor with bullet holes in their brains? They almost … almost …" I choke out, the reality of the situation hitting me hard.

My legs wobble like Jell-O, and I drop onto the sofa, afraid I'll fall if I don't sit. "They almost got our little boy," I whisper, looking up at Dominick, my vision blurry with tears.

"I would never let anything happen to him," he says, his voice cold and confident.

"Yet, had you arrived a few minutes later, he would've been taken."

"I know," he says. "I fucked up. I got a couple of cryptic texts, and we traced them back to Coral Bay, but I didn't think they knew about the two of you." He looks at me, his eyes filled with raw emotion. "We didn't know they were going to go after you and Damien, but Matteo insisted on coming to Coral Bay after he saw the texts. We were just pulling up to your place to demand you and Damien leave with us when we watched them walk up to your door."

He curses under his breath, clearly affected by what happened, but I don't have it in me to comfort him because he did this.

"I went around back while Matteo and Scotty, one of the men who works for us, took the front. I grabbed Damien while my brother got you, and Scotty handled the guys."

"Who were they?" I ask again.

"We don't know yet. Our guy is running their prints to see if anything pops up. Normally, we'd interrogate them, but …"

"But they're both dead," I finish.

"We weren't risking it with you and our son," Dominick says. "But I can assure you, once we figure out who is responsible, we will take care of them."

PASSPORT

TWENTY

Dominick

IT WAS CLOSE. TOO CLOSE. HAD WE SHOWN UP A FEW MINUTES later, Peyton and our son would've been gone—or worse, dead. Since we don't know who is responsible, we don't know what their intentions were.

We have their phones for our IT guy to go through, but I'm not taking any chances. Until we know who is after me and my family, everyone is on lockdown.

My thoughts go to Brielle. She's going to be pissed. She just got home, and now, she's about to be a prisoner in the house she despises.

The rest of the ride is quiet—though Peyton's glares are plenty loud.

Scotty takes off once we arrive at the airport, and Matteo rides with us back to the house. The entire drive home, Peyton holds a still-sleeping Damien while I watch the two of them, hating how much I've missed of my son's life. His first words, first steps. He's almost four now.

Has he asked why he doesn't have a father?

I always told myself that I would be a better dad than mine was. I wouldn't force my child into this life. I would let them follow their dreams, and I would support them.

But Peyton took it all away from me the moment she made the decision to not tell me about my flesh and blood.

I want to hate her for it, but a part of me gets it. It's the reason I didn't go after her all those years ago. She's sweet and innocent, and I didn't want to taint her with our shit. Brielle could watch a man get murdered in front of her and not blink an eye. My mother has witnessed men get tortured and then sat down for dinner like it was just another day. But Peyton merely *heard* me take a man's life and ran scared, refusing to tell me that she was pregnant with my baby.

I can admire her protectiveness. It's obvious she's a good mother to our son, giving him what she can with what she has. But she's no longer his only parent, and she's going to have to get used to me being around because they're in my life now and there's no leaving.

When we pull up to the property, Peyton's eyes widen. The home is situated on a few acres of land on the outskirts of North Harbor Point. Andrey built it over thirty years ago when he earned his first million, and it has since been renovated to be brought into the twenty-first century.

Our car stops in front of the black wrought iron gate with a large *A* in the center, and one of our men steps out of the guardhouse to ensure it's us—they know better than to assume.

After the gate opens, we drive down the driveway. The two-story home, complete with a circle drive and an obnoxious fountain in the middle—which my mother loves—comes into view. Despite Peyton trying to hold in her emotions, a small gasp leaves her parted lips.

"You live here?" she questions, letting her curiosity get the better of her.

"We all do," I tell her. "Though my mother is probably out."

After a few weeks of her rarely being at home, I asked the guard I had on her what she'd been up to, and he confirmed she was dating someone. After having her boyfriend investigated and learning he wasn't a threat, I let it go. She hasn't told us about him yet, but I'm assuming she will once she's ready. She knows we support her moving on from Andrey.

With me just having learned about Damien, I haven't had the chance to tell her about him, but I have no doubt she'll be ecstatic to learn she has a grandchild she can dote on.

"It's late," I say as we exit the vehicle and head toward the front door. "I'll show you to a guest room. Tomorrow, I can give you a tour of the place, and we can figure out which rooms you guys want."

Peyton shoots daggers my way, but doesn't argue since she's still holding our little boy in her arms.

"Do you want me to carry him up?" I offer since there are a lot of stairs and he's got to be heavy from her holding him for so long.

"I want you to pretend you never met me," she sasses, making Matteo snort out a laugh before he disappears.

She follows me up the stairs, and I stop in front of the guest room that's closest to my room and open the door, allowing her to walk through first.

She sets Damien on the queen-size bed and then places the blankets around him before she looks over at me. "You can go now," she says, dismissing me. "I'm staying in here with him."

Too exhausted to argue, I nod. "There are towels and toiletries in the bathroom, and I'm having clothes for both of you brought over. I'll bring them up once they arrive. And tomorrow, we can buy everything you need."

"What we need," she hisses, stepping over to me, "is to go home to where all of our stuff is."

"It's all being packed up as we speak," I tell her.

"And what about Damien's school?" she volleys. "He's going to wake up in the morning and expect to go to school, where all his friends are. Are you going to pack them up too?" she says, sarcasm dripping in every word.

"He's three. Once we get a handle on the threat, we'll find him a good school here."

She scoffs and shakes her head. "So, what, we're being held prisoner here?"

"Only until we figure out who the threat is."

"And once the threat is gone, can we move out?" she challenges, knowing damn well I'm not going to let our son live anywhere other than under my roof.

"Let's just take it one day at a time," I tell her. "I went almost four years without my son. If it's okay with you, I'd like to spend some time with him. You've had him to yourself all these years while I didn't even know he was alive."

"Well, if tonight is anything to go by, the only reason he's still alive is because I kept him away from you. Less than twelve hours into you knowing about him, and we're already being threatened. If you want to get to know him, you might want to work a little harder at keeping him out of harm's way." Her voice catches on the last part, her emotions seeping through.

For a moment, instead of the cold bitch she's shown me, I see the worried mother who is scared for her child's life.

As I watch her walk away and disappear into the en suite bathroom, I vow to make sure they're both protected and safe. I failed my mother and my sister, but I won't fail them.

"What do we know?" I ask, walking into my office a few minutes later.

Matteo is already sitting in the visitor seat with our IT guy. Eddy is a literal genius when it comes to all things technology. He can hack into damn near anything and find whatever or whoever we're looking for.

"Anthony Rothschild," Matteo says as Eddy turns his laptop around for me to see. "All contact leads back to him."

For a moment, I think about what he would get out of this.

He wanted to marry my sister.

He raped her when he found out that she was with someone else.

She wasn't sure who the father was …

176

My thoughts go to the text we now know he sent—*An eye for an eye.*

Suddenly, it all clicks into place.

"He knows." I glance up at Matteo, who raises a questioning brow. "We don't know what was said that day Joseph shot Andrey. Anthony was there. What would make someone so mad that he would kill his business partner?"

Matteo waits for me to continue.

"Andrey told them that Brielle had an abortion, that Joseph's flesh and blood was dead."

"Fuck," Matteo breathes. "It makes sense. Andrey was probably pissed that Anthony was with her before the wedding, and he wanted to punish him, make a point. Andrey never would've let Brielle have a baby out of wedlock."

"No, because it would've made the family look bad."

"So, Joseph killed Andrey. And then Giuseppe killed Joseph. And Anthony ran. He said it the day we were questioning him in the warehouse … 'I want what's owed to me.'"

"He didn't just mean Bri," Matteo says. "He also meant the baby."

"And the second he found out that I have a son, he went after him … *an eye for an eye.*"

"We need to take him out," Matteo deadpans. "He's not going to stop until he gets his hands on Damien."

"He's working with the mayor," I say. "I don't know why the mayor would give him the time of day, but he's the one who vouched for Anthony at the auction."

"Fucking unbelievable," Matteo spits. "It's not a coincidence that Paul Astor Jr. was nearly killed right before the election and forced to pull out of the running, allowing Eric Vanderbilt to win by default."

"No," I agree. "It's not a coincidence. So, the question is, what does Mr. Mayor want?"

"Martha." I nod at the housekeeper as I walk into the kitchen the next morning.

"Mr. Antonov," she says with a smile as she pours my coffee.

After finding out who was responsible for the bugs in our house, we were forced to fire our cleaning company, unsure if anyone else had been compromised. Thankfully, Martha has been with us for years and is loyal to a fault.

"We have a couple of new houseguests," I tell her, taking the coffee from her and having a seat at the island. "My son, Damien, and his mother, Peyton, will be staying with us indefinitely. He's three … almost four," I add, realizing I don't even know when my son's birthday is.

"Oh." She perks up, and I imagine she's already planning what she can cook for Damien. "Do you know what he likes? Or better yet, I'll ask him myself when he comes down," she says thoughtfully.

When we were younger, she practically helped raise us, and when we got old enough to no longer need a nanny, she moved into caring for the house and cooking. When I noticed her slowing down, I decided to hire an outside cleaning company to come in and do a thorough housecleaning every week.

"Morning," Brielle says, sauntering into the kitchen, dressed in workout attire. "Martha, I've missed you so much." She wraps her arms around the housekeeper, who returns the embrace.

Martha was visiting a relative when Brielle and I returned from Russia, so she hasn't gotten a chance to see her until now.

"Oh, Brielle," Martha coos when they pull apart. "You've grown into such a beautiful young woman. Welcome home, my dear."

"Thank you," Brielle says, having a seat next to me. "I wish I could say I was happy to be home, but"—she side-eyes me—"I was dragged back here against my will."

"Hardly," I mutter, taking a sip of my coffee.

While the women catch up, I go through the emails that came in while I was asleep. It's not until Brielle mentions leaving for Pilates that I enter the conversation, already knowing there's going to be a fight.

"You can't leave," I tell her.

She whips her head around until she's looking at me. "What the hell do you mean?"

"There are things you don't know," I begin.

Before I can fill her in, a little boy comes stumbling into the kitchen, dressed in dinosaur pajamas. His red hair is messy from sleep, and he's rubbing his eyes.

"Mommy?" he mutters, looking around in confusion. "Do you know where my mommy is?"

"What the hell?" Brielle breathes. "How did a little boy get in here?"

Ignoring her question, I walk over and kneel in front of him. "Hello there, Damien. My name is Dominick. Your mom is here somewhere. Why don't we go find her?"

"Who is his mother?" Brielle asks, earning a glare from me. "Don't look at me like that," she says smartly. "A child is wandering around the house."

"He's not wandering," I say, standing and holding out my hand for him to take. "He's … related to us."

I want to say he's my son, but I can't imagine that would go over well with Peyton. I have no intention of keeping my paternity from him a secret, but I bet it will go over better if I ask her how she'd like to go about it.

Speaking of which …

Loud padding down the stairs fills the air, and a few seconds later, the mother of my child comes flying around the corner.

"Oh my God, my baby!" Peyton cries, scooping Damien up into her arms. "I went to go pee, and you were gone. You scared me! You went down the stairs by yourself? Are you okay?"

He looks at her like she's grown two heads and then says, "Mommy, I'm not a baby. I'm three." He lifts his fingers to emphasize his point.

Although I don't have any kids to compare him to, I must admit, mine is damn cute.

"I know," Peyton says, her tone patient. "But stairs can be dangerous. You could've fallen and gotten hurt. You could've bumped your head."

"I didn't fall," Damien says. "I slid."

Peyton sighs, and I stifle my laugh because she's such a mom—worried about him when he's not the least bit worried himself. She would have a heart attack if she knew the shit my brother and I had gotten into when we were little.

"Wait, you slid?" she asks. "You slid where?"

"Down the stairs." He giggles and then wiggles his body, silently demanding to be let down.

When she lets him go, he takes off out of the kitchen, and we all follow and watch him fly up the stairs without a care in the world.

Peyton gasps while I laugh under my breath, and she scowls at me.

"Watch, Mommy!" Damien yells when he gets to the top.

He drops to his butt and then proceeds to slide down, hitting each step as he goes, laughing the entire way. When he's about halfway down, Peyton cracks a smile and shakes her head.

"See?" he says when he gets to the bottom. "I slid. I didn't fall."

"I see," she tells him. "But I need you to go slower while going up and down the stairs, please. You could trip and get hurt."

"Fine," he says with a sigh. "Can I go to school now?" he asks, switching the subject quick enough to give someone whiplash.

Peyton shoots daggers my way as she contemplates what to say, so I jump in, hoping making it right will earn me some points with the mother of my child.

Last night, when I spoke to my assistant about picking up clothes for them, she mentioned he'd also need some toys since they came with nothing. I'm planning to order shit, but she grabbed a bunch of stuff to hold him over until I can do that.

"Hey, Damien," I say, stepping toward him. "You don't know this, but while you were asleep, we took you on a plane."

"Really?" he asks, tilting his head thoughtfully.

"Yep. We brought you here … on a vacation. Do you know what a vacation is?" I ask, and he shakes his head. "It's where you go somewhere far away from home to have fun."

"But school is fun." He pouts. "I wanna go to school."

He crosses his arms over his chest, and Peyton smirks at me with a silent *fucking told you* written across her features.

"I know," I tell him. "But this place has fun stuff too. Like a pool."

"A pool?" he asks, his gray eyes lighting up.

"Yep. We have a pool, and I have it on good authority that right through that hall, in the living room, is a bunch of cool pool toys and a bathing suit for you."

"Yay!" he cheers as he runs in the direction I pointed.

"What did you say about him throwing a fit?" I murmur to Peyton with a smirk.

"Whatever," she mutters. "Just fix this shit so we can leave."

She goes to stomp away, but before she can, I extend my hand, halting her in place.

"I'm going to fix this shit," I say, using her words. "But my son isn't going anywhere. So, you should get used to living in this house because unless you're okay with leaving him here with me, you're not going anywhere either."

"Really?" she snaps. "Threatening the mother of your child? Such a gentleman."

"I never claimed to be a gentleman." I shrug. I lean in so only she can hear me, my breath tickling her ear. "And I'm pretty sure when I was fucking you from behind and you were begging me to do it harder, you were perfectly okay with that. If you were to be honest with yourself, I think you prefer it that way."

"You're such an asshole," she hisses, looking me in the eye. "It seems like you're a bit obsessed with our time together. This is the second time you've brought it up. Hope you have a good memory because the only way you'll ever fuck me again is in your mind."

She stalks off, and I can't help but laugh.

"We'll see about that," I call after her, earning her middle finger.

"What the hell was that?" Brielle asks, glancing from me to Peyton, who's now helping our son blow up a floatation device that's shaped like a pizza. "And why is the flight attendant in our house?"

"That's what happens when you don't wrap it up," Matteo says with a laugh as he saunters into the room and slides his arm across the back of Brielle's shoulders. "Our brother here hooked up with that woman and got her pregnant."

Brielle's body stiffens, and Matteo drops his grin.

"Hey," I say to her. "I'm not a woman, so I can't possibly know what you went through …"

"It's fine," Brielle snaps. "It's been years. I'm over it."

It's clear she's not, but in our family, showing any kind of emotion is a weakness.

"So, she … what, kept him from you?" Brielle asks, channeling her anger toward Peyton.

"Put the claws away," I warn.

I might be pissed about what Peyton did, but that's between me and her. I'm not going to have my family fighting my battles for me, and if I have any chance of coexisting with her, I can't have my sister or mom out to get her in my honor.

"She did what she thought was right," I tell her. "The important thing is that I know now, and it would make shit easier if you could get along with her, especially since she's not going anywhere."

"She's living here?" Brielle accuses, her eyes wide in shock. "What … did she find out you were worth billions and came to collect?"

"Actually, *she* doesn't want a single thing from him," Peyton says, nodding toward me. "I had no intention of telling him about Damien. But thanks to your brother stalking me when I told him to leave me alone, he found out about our son, then almost got him kidnapped. As soon as he finds the guy responsible, we'll be out of your hair."

Without waiting for Brielle to respond, she walks back over to Damien, taking his hand in hers and scooping up the giant pizza with her other hand, and they disappear out the back door.

"Well, that went well," Matteo mutters.

"Anthony is after Damien," I tell Brielle.

"What?" she gasps. "Why?"

"I think he knew you were possibly pregnant with his kid and knows Dad forced you to have an abortion."

Her face turns white.

"He potentially lost his heir and the connections to our family. I think he was trying to find a way to get back at our family and found out I had a son at the same time I did. He sent me a text—*an eye for an eye*—and then tried to have Damien kidnapped."

"That motherfucker," Brielle hisses. "Where is he? Why haven't you killed him yet?"

"He's hiding," Matteo says. "But I promise, we won't stop until we find him."

"And when you do, I want him," Brielle says. "I want to be the one to end his life."

She's never killed anyone, so she doesn't know the way it stays with you, but I'm not about to argue with her. When the time comes, I'll convince her to let us handle it. But for now, I nod in agreement.

"That doesn't explain why that woman kept your son from you," she says.

"That woman's name is Peyton," I tell her. "And she's the mother of my son—your nephew—so show her some respect."

Brielle scoffs.

"If Mom had been stronger, if she had tried to escape Andrey and left this life behind, would you have gone with her?" I ask her.

"Of course," she says without hesitation. "But what does that have to do with—"

"Peyton heard me kill someone," I say, keeping my voice down.

"It scared the hell out of her, and she ran. She kept Damien from me to protect him because she's a good mom."

Brielle swallows thickly. "But you're not him," she chokes out. "You're a good man."

"Because your standards are fucked," I say with a humorless laugh. "But to Peyton, I might as well be the Devil himself. She's not from this world. That's why I let her go all those years ago."

"And now?" Brielle asks, quirking her perfectly shaped brow.

"And now, I'm never letting either of them go again."

PASSPORT

TWENTY-ONE

Peyton

I SHOULDN'T BE ENJOYING MYSELF. I SHOULDN'T BE SITTING IN the pool—wearing a bikini that fits damn near perfectly, thanks to Dominick—while my son splashes around atop the ridiculously huge pizza floatie, but I am.

It's beautiful outside. The sun is shining down on us with just enough cloud coverage to make it so that it's not too hot. But that's the good part about living in Florida. You can hang by the pool pretty much year-round.

Martha made us the most delicious, thirst-quenching lemonade and brought out an array of finger foods that Damien and I both love. And for the first time in forever, I have nothing to do but spend time with my son.

When I think too hard, a mini me appears, wagging her judgmental finger and telling me that I should be fighting back, demanding to leave. Giving Dominick hell.

But I've accepted that I don't have a choice in being here. The man is a force to be reckoned with, so rather than waste my energy being pissed at a situation that's out of my control, I'm choosing to make the most of it. And right now, that includes sitting on the steps of the cleanest, bluest pool I've ever seen.

"Mommy, look!" Damien yells, standing on top of the float and lifting his arms. "I'm a fishy!"

He dives off, screaming like the crazy little boy he is, at the same time Dominick steps outside. I glance up at Dominick just in time to see his eyes widen in shock. Before I can ask what's wrong, he's running toward the pool and jumping in.

Damien pops through the surface of the water and shakes his shaggy, overgrown red hair—which I've refused to get cut because I'm not ready to accept my little boy is growing up—just as Dominick reaches him. He grabs Damien by the waist, lifting him out of the water, and out of shock, Damien screams, unsure who's got him.

"What are you doing?" I ask, confused as to what just happened in the last fifteen seconds.

"Saving our son from drowning!" he barks, stalking toward me with Damien in his arms.

His hair is soaking wet, and droplets of water drip down the sides of his face. As he walks up the steps, I can't help but notice the way his white dress shirt, which is now see-through, clings to his front, outlining every muscle. He moves Damien to the side of his hip, and my eyes zero in on each ridge that makes up his six-pack.

"Are you seriously eye-fucking me right now?" he hisses, forcing me to look up at his face.

"Ooh, you said *fuck*! That's a naughty word." Damien giggles because he thinks it's hilarious when an adult curses since I told him it's not allowed after he came home one day and repeated something he'd heard.

I was always a rule follower. If my mom had told me not to curse, I would've listened and probably reprimanded anyone who did.

But my son seems to take after his father more than I'd like to admit. Not only does he have his gray eyes, but he's also a rule breaker. He loves to push the limits, and he's mischievous beyond his years. He's daring and isn't scared of anything.

"I'm sorry," Dominick says to Damien, then turns his attention back to me. "Are you seriously *eyeing* me right now when I just had to save our son's life because you were too busy focusing on me rather than him?"

It takes me a few seconds to wrap my head around what he just said, but once I do, I bark out a laugh. Everything now makes sense—him jumping into the water while still dressed in his work clothes because he thought our son was drowning.

"And now, you're laughing?" he growls. "I just told my sister that you were a good mother. Maybe I should consider—"

"Hey," I bark, my laughter now gone. "I am a good mother." I pluck Damien from his arms, needing to hold my baby boy. "I'm such a good mother that when our daredevil son, at a year old, jumped into a pool without blinking an eye, I immediately enrolled him in swimming lessons, and he's been swimming like a fish ever since."

"Yeah, I swim like a fish!" Damien agrees.

I put him down, and he swims back to his pizza float, scrambling to get back onto it. I wait until I know he's safely on it before I turn back to Dominick.

"Don't you dare judge me, and you should think twice before you make threats." I glance at Damien to make sure he's busy playing with the pool rings and isn't listening before I continue. "My son is my entire life, and I would do anything to keep him safe."

"Including keeping him from me," Dominick adds.

"Including keeping him from you," I agree.

We stare at each other for several seconds in a silent standoff, and while I appreciate that he jumped without thought to save our son's life, I refuse to give in. He might not agree with me keeping Damien from him, but I will never apologize for making the decision I felt was best for my little boy.

After what feels like forever, Dominick sighs. "There's so much I don't know about him," he murmurs, glancing at Damien, "including the fact that he can swim. I want to be so pissed at you." He clenches his jaw. "You kept him from me for years, and had you not been on the flight to Russia, you never would've told me about him."

It's not a question. We both know I wouldn't have. The moment I heard him kill a man, I made my decision. Even during the late nights, like when I was exhausted and taking care of Damien on my own because my mom was too sick and needed her sleep, or times when he came home and asked why his friend had a daddy and he didn't, I never considered telling him because the thought of my son growing up the way I had—in a home with a violent man—made me sick to my stomach.

"Have you found anything out about the guy who was responsible for trying to have Damien kidnapped?" I ask, changing the subject.

"We're working on it," he says, stepping out of the water.

I try like hell not to—as he put it—eye-fuck him, but, holy shit, the man is sexy, and with his clothes sticking to him, I can make out the bulge in his pants.

My thoughts go back to our night together, and from experience, I know that bulge is real and not at all hard.

Sigh.

Why does he have to be dangerous? He's good-looking and great in bed, and he makes a decent living. I know no one is perfect, but couldn't his fault be a hairy mole or something? Did it have to be that he's a violent criminal who is eyeballs deep in the underworld?

"Hey, mister," Damien calls out, making me realize they haven't been properly introduced.

After Dominick told him about the pool stuff, we headed out to the pool house to change and have been out here ever since.

Dominick flinches at the title, and a small part of me feels bad because I know if Damien called me anything other than Mommy, it would break my heart.

"Yeah, buddy?" Dominick says.

"Wanna play with me? My mommy is kinda boring."

"Hey! I am not boring." I scoff.

"Yeah-huh," Damien argues. "You got upset when I splashed your eyes, and you're not strong enough to throw me far, like Mr. Williams does."

"Who the fuck is Mr. Williams?" Dominick barks, making Damien giggle. "And why is he touching our son?"

"You say a lot of naughty words, mister," Damien tells him, not picking up on the second part of what Dominick said.

"Damien, his name is Dominick," I tell him. "And don't even get any ideas. You're not saying them."

Damien sighs. "It's so unfair. Everyone gets to say all the words but me."

I glance over at Dominick, and despite his clenched jaw, a small trace of a smile peeks out.

"Mr. Williams is Frankie's dad," I explain to Dominick.

"Yeah, my bestest friend in preschool," Damien adds. "He's got a pool and a backyard for a Giving Tree." He looks around the property with several acres of green grass, and it's like a light bulb clicks on right above his head. "Hey, mister … uh …"

"Dominick," I repeat.

"Dom-i-nick," Damien says, sounding out the syllables. "Can we get a Giving Tree?"

Before I can tell Damien it's not happening, Dominick says, "Sure," without question, and Damien erupts in happiness.

"Good job," I mutter so only Dominick can hear me. "You just agreed to plant a big-ass tree in your yard."

Dominick's brows furrow in confusion because he's never read *The Giving Tree*, and I shake my head. I'll deal with him later. We're going to have to have a talk about questioning things before saying yes. I understand he's rich and he can give our son the world, but that doesn't mean he should.

"Can you throw me now?" Damien asks him. "And then we'll go get the tree."

Dominick stares at him for several seconds in confusion, but then he shakes his head and says, "Yeah, let me go get my swim shorts on first."

Damien cheers again, and Dominick heads inside, his wet shoes squeaking as he walks.

PASSPORT

TWENTY-TWO

Peyton

THE NEXT FEW HOURS ARE SPENT WITH DOMINICK AND Damien roughhousing in the pool while I sit on the edge and watch. For a little while, I can't help but pretend like we're a normal family—Dominick is an upstanding citizen and businessman who took the day off to spend time with his son, and I'm a stay-at-home mom, looking for a job after graduating from college.

There's no violence.

No corruption.

We're just a happy little family, and everything is perfect.

When Damien starts to rub his eyes, I tell him it's time for a nap. He starts to whine, and I'm preparing for the tantrum that's about to ensue when Dominick speaks to him.

"Hey, buddy," he says, holding Damien in his arms like he's been caring for him his entire life. "How about you go take a nap, and when you wake up, we can play with some of your new toys?"

"I got new toys?" Damien's teary eyes light up with renewed excitement.

"Yeah. They were delivered a little bit ago. We can check them out after your nap."

He stops crying, and while I know he's only giving in because Dominick is new and shiny and totally bribed him, it's nice to have someone as backup.

I bring Damien his towel and wrap it around him and then

carry him up to our room so I can rinse him off and change him into dry clothes.

He falls asleep quickly, and I consider staying in the room with him so I don't have to face Dominick or anyone else in the house. I overheard his sister's judgmental remarks about me keeping his son away from him. And although his brother is kind of funny, he's also pretty freaking scary.

Figuring it'll be better to talk to Dominick about the future without Damien around, I head down in search of him.

After checking the kitchen and living room, where I see the toys he told Damien about, I find him in what I assume is his office, at his desk, typing away on his laptop.

Once again, he's dressed in business attire—a gray button-down dress shirt, rolled to his elbows, showing off a few tattoos, some of which weren't there when we spent the night together. I can't see what's below the desk, but I imagine he's in his usual dress pants and shoes. I've never seen him dressed down. Even during our time sightseeing in the Dominican Republic, he was wearing a collared shirt and khakis.

"Are you coming in, or will you just continue to eye-fuck me from the doorway?" he asks, making me roll my eyes.

"You're going to need to watch your mouth around our son," I tell him, stepping inside. "I have enough trouble keeping him from cursing without you throwing F-bombs around. And I wasn't eye-fucking you. I was wondering if you went to bed in a suit."

He stops typing and looks up at me, mirth dancing in his gray eyes. "Who says I sleep?"

He quirks a brow, and I sit in the visitor seat across from him.

"That's true," I agree. "I thought you were asleep in the Dominican Republic, but really, you were just waiting to get away in the middle of the night." I cringe at the hurt in my tone, wishing I could take back what I said. But it's too late.

"I didn't sneak out," he says, closing the laptop and shifting it to the side. His hand goes to the corner of his chiseled jaw, and he uses it to hold his head up as he locks eyes with me. "My dad had been killed," he explains, scrubbing his hand over his stubble, "and I wasn't thinking clearly. It wasn't until I was on the plane that I realized I'd left without a note, but by then, it was too late."

I nod in understanding. "I'm sorry about your dad."

"I'm not," he says, his tone devoid of all emotion. "He was a shitty father, an even shittier husband, and his business partner shooting him saved my brother and me the trouble of taking him out ourselves."

"And that right there is why I'm scared of you," I admit. "Violence is just so easy for you. I know you're mad that I kept Damien from you, but you don't understand what I went through. Your life is filled with brutality and you're okay with that. You talk about it like you're discussing the weather.

"But you weren't there when my dad brought his violent job home and took it out on my mom. I would hear her beg him to stop as he hit her and hurt her, and then he'd spend the next several days apologizing and promising he would never do it again," I choke out, hating that after all these years, it still makes me emotional.

"You weren't there when my mom finally saved enough money and accumulated enough evidence against him so that she could escape him. Is that what you want? For me to live in fear that, one day, you're going to get violent with me—or worse, our son?"

"Dominick would never hurt you," a feminine voice says.

When I turn, I find Brielle sauntering into the office. She's dressed in a cute, short black dress that's cinched around her waist, showing off her curves, while the top is modest with short sleeves and a turtleneck. Her blonde hair is pin straight, and her makeup is flawless. She's sporting a pair of black heels with the signature red soles, and she's glaring at me like I personally offended her.

"You don't know that," I tell her.

"Yes, I do," she says, stopping in front of me. "We grew up with an abusive father who hit our mother, and Dominick and Matteo would defend her, earning themselves beatings."

I gasp in shock and glance at Dominick, who's now sitting up, clenching his jaw and glaring at his sister.

"Brielle," he warns, "I don't need you to—"

"No," she cuts him off. "I'm not going to listen to her accuse you of things you aren't capable of." She looks at him briefly before turning back to me. "My brother might be a lot of things, but he would never hurt a woman or child. I get not wanting to be a part of this world. Most days, I hate it, too, but to keep that little boy from his father, out of fear that Dominick would hurt him, is wrong."

Tears fill her eyes as she looks at me, speaking with conviction. "He spent years protecting me from our abusive father. You want to know why he still lives in our family home instead of moving out and getting his own place? Because he refused to leave our mother. He knew once he was bigger and stronger than our father, he wouldn't touch our mother. So, he stayed to protect her. The same reason Matteo stayed."

"Why didn't she leave?" I ask, needing to know … needing to understand.

"Because he would've had her killed," Dominick says.

"You've killed other people," I point out. "Why didn't you kill him?"

"Because we would've lost everything," he admits. "Andrey was a very smart businessman, and when he realized he couldn't control us with his fists, he controlled us with his money and power. My entire world was wrapped up in the business, and he made it so that if he died, we'd get nothing. So, knowing that my mother and sister were safe, I plotted his demise. But it thankfully happened sooner."

"The night we were in the Dominican Republic," I finish.

"Yes," he says with a nod. "I left the DR to come home and bury Andrey and put out fires. I told myself it was for the best because I never wanted you to be involved in this life."

"Yet you're dragging me and Damien into it."

"You can't expect him to live without his son," Brielle says, reminding me that she's still here. "That's not fair."

I swallow thickly as I take in the sadness in her eyes, in her words, and I'm at a loss as to what to do.

"I can't change the way things are," Dominick says. "My world is violent, but I will keep our son safe. I won't let anything happen to him, and I will give him everything I have to give. Money, clothes, vacations, the best school …"

"He doesn't need any of that," I choke out. "All he needs is to feel loved and safe."

"And he will be," Dominick promises, his gray eyes locking with mine. "He's already loved. But now, he'll be loved by more people. By my mother, my sister, my brother … and we will all protect him."

"With our lives," Brielle adds. "And the same goes for you. You're family now. And we take care of and protect our own." She turns to Dominick. "I'm sorry for forgetting that."

I don't know what she's referring to when she apologizes, and I don't hear what Dominick says in response because my brain is currently stuck on what she just said.

"You're family now. And we take care of and protect our own."
Family.

For so long, I've been on my own. Even when my mom was alive, she was sick. It was just me taking care of her and then Damien. I can't even recall a time when anyone cared for or protected me. The thought of someone looking after me for once feels like a fever dream.

"So, where do we go from here?" I ask Dominick. "I don't agree with your life and business choices, but I also don't want to keep our son from you."

"I'm going to let you guys talk," Brielle says, stepping back toward the door.

"Did you need something?" Dominick asks her.

"I'm going to go have drinks with Katie," she says, referring to one of her old friends from high school who still lives in North Harbor Point. "I'm assuming I need to take a guard with me."

"Take Daniil," he replies. "He'll be your guard. Anywhere you go, he goes. And have Fernando drive you."

Once she's gone, I glance at him. "Does that mean we can leave now?"

Dominick's gaze turns glacier. "You just said you don't want to take my son away from me, yet in the next breath, you're trying to leave."

"Well, obviously, I'm going to have to stay in Harbor Point. But I can't live in this house forever. I mean, it's big and all, but I need my own space, and … what if one of us wants to date? We'll have to figure out—"

Dominick growls, "Who the fuck are you dating?"

My thoughts go to Jake. We were only just getting to know each other, and if I'm honest, there wasn't much of a spark, but I still owe it to him to let him know I've moved.

"Well, no one right now. But—"

Dominick rounds the desk, eating up the space between us until he's towering over me. Out of instinct, I stand and step back, but forgetting the chair is behind me, I stumble.

Before I hit the chair—or worse, the floor—Dominick reaches around my waist and hoists me onto my feet. Our eyes lock, and for a moment, I'm brought back to the first time I met him.

"So we meet again," he says, his playful words a paradox to his broody tone. "The first time we were in this position, all I could think about was how badly I wanted to fuck you in the restroom."

I snort out a laugh. "I doubt we would've fit."

"I don't want you to date anyone else," he says, changing the subject so quick that I blink several times, trying to mentally catch up.

"What?" I breathe.

I heard him, but what does that mean?

"The thought of another man touching you"—he runs his finger along my neck and up to my mouth—"kissing you"—he traces the seam of my lips, and when I suck in a harsh breath, he slides his fingertip into my mouth—"fucking you … drives me insane." He swirls his finger along my tongue, gently pushing it in and out between my parted lips, and I clench my legs together, wishing I weren't as turned on as I am.

"I tried to keep you out of this life, but fate had other plans. And now that you're here, I'm never letting you go," he says as he removes his finger and drags my saliva across my lips.

"Give me a chance, Peaches. Let me show you that I can protect you and our son. I promise, you'll both want for nothing."

"Dominick," I breathe, my heart erratic from our closeness, "I'm … I'm scared."

I expect him to argue, but he nods in understanding.

"I get it," he says, "and I'm not going to lie to you." He cups my cheek, and without thought, I sigh into his hold. "There will be times when you see or hear shit that scares you, but just know that I will do everything in my power to keep it out of our home and away from you and our family."

"One chance," I tell him, letting my heart and gut guide me rather than my brain. "One chance to prove that you can keep us safe. But I swear to God, Dominick, if anything happens to our little boy …"

"Nothing will happen to him," he says. "I'll burn this city to the fucking ground before I let anything happen to either of you. You have my word."

"Okay," I whisper. "We'll stay."

Dominick licks his lips, his eyes locking on mine, and for a moment, I think he might kiss me. And I'd let him.

But then a tiny voice yells out, "Mommy," and we separate, both of us going in search of our son.

"Mommy!" Damien yells when he sees me. "I play with toys now." He jumps into my arms and circles his arms around my neck and then swivels around me so he can look at Dominick. "Mr. … Domick, I play with my toys now?"

I stifle a laugh at the butchered name he gave him and walk us over to the couch, having a seat with Damien in my lap. Dominick sits across from us on the coffee table.

"You can play with your toys," I tell him, "but first, I need to tell you something."

He huffs in annoyance but nods.

"You know how Frankie has a mommy and a daddy?" I say, using his friend as an example since Damien talks about them all the time.

"Yeah. He has a mommy and a daddy, and a pool, and a yard, and he can have a Giving Tree. Oh! Mr. *Domick*, can I have The Giving Tree now?"

Dominick glances from Damien to me with the most perplexed look on his face, and I get it because …

"Welcome to parenting," I say with a laugh.

"We'll talk about the tree later," I tell Damien. "But right now, I want to talk to you about mommies and daddies."

Damien nods, but I can tell I'm quickly losing his attention, so rather than draw this out, I simply say, "You know how I'm your mommy?"

He nods.

"Well, Dominick is your daddy."

Damien's brows furrow, and I can't help but smile at how much he looks like Dominick when he does that.

"You're my daddy?" Damien asks him. "Like Frankie's daddy is his daddy?"

"Yeah, buddy," Dominick says. "I'm your dad."

"Does that mean we can get a Giving Tree now?"

I snort out a laugh, and Dominick grins, shaking his head.

"Yeah, we can get a Giving Tree."

Damien jumps off my lap and throws himself into Dominick's arms, enveloping him in a hug. As Dominick hugs him back, his eyes meet mine, and I note that they're filled with so much raw emotion. Most of the time, Dominick is cold, brooding, and calculating, but I'm learning that it's a shield to protect himself from the outside world and that he saves his softness for the people closest to him. The people who have earned the right to see him vulnerable.

"Thank you, Daddy." He wiggles out of his hold and stands. "Let's go get The Giving Tree now."

Damien grabs Dominick's hand and pulls him to get up.

"Wait, where do we get a Giving Tree?" Dominick asks.

"In the forest, Daddy," Damien answers, making Dominick's eyes go wide.

"Better get to chopping," I joke. "You have a tree to bring home, *Daddy.*"

TWENTY-THREE

Dominick

DADDY.

I'm a fucking daddy.

I have a son.

With my gray eyes.

He has Peyton's red hair and skin color, but his personality is all me. The kid isn't afraid of shit—and he proved that when he flew off the float and into the water without a care in the world. And I proved I have no idea what I'm doing as a dad when I dove in after him and then proceeded to bitch at Peyton because I thought our son had almost drowned.

Of course he can swim.

Because Peyton is a damn good mother.

And she not only agreed to give us a chance, but she also told our son that I was his father.

Then, he called me Daddy … and I agreed to chop down a fucking tree.

"Okay, so tell me about this tree," I say to Damien as we sit at the island while Peyton heats up the dinner that Martha made earlier and left for us.

"It's in my …" He stops speaking and looks up at me with sad eyes.

I have no idea what I did wrong, but when tears fill his eyes, I glance at Peyton, two seconds away from freaking out.

"Mommy, my book!" Damien cries. "My book is gone. It's at home."

He jumps off the stool and runs toward the living room, and we both follow after him.

"My book is gone! I gotta go home and get it."

Tears track down his face, and my heart, which I thought was dead, squeezes in my chest, reminding me that it's very much alive and beating.

"Please, Mr. Daddy, I gotta get my book."

He looks around the large room, hoping the book will appear, but it's not here, and unfortunately, while their stuff is on the way, it'll be a few days before it arrives since the company that I hired has to pack up everything and then deliver it.

As I watch my son cry in devastation over a book that he doesn't have because I had to take him from his home in the middle of the night—because he was going to be kidnapped, thanks to a vendetta that a psychopath has against me and my family—my only thought is that I need to make this right.

Peyton starts to speak—I'm sure to try to calm him, but he shouldn't have to be calmed. He should have his fucking book. Peyton's trusting me to make sure they're taken care of, and I'm not about to fuck this up.

"C'mon," I say, lifting Damien into my arms. "Let's go get your book."

"What about dinner?" Peyton asks. "We don't have to—"

"We can eat out," I tell her. "Damien needs his book."

I snatch my keys off the table and head to the garage, thankful that I had Janet make sure booster seats were installed in all the cars I use.

Since I have no idea how to buckle a child in, I watch Peyton do it, and then we take off. She doesn't know it, but because Anthony is still missing, I have several guards following us, and they'll surround us wherever we go.

"I think we can get it at Target," she says as I pull out of the driveway and head toward town.

"Chocolate milk with whip?" Damien asks.

"We'll see," Peyton tells him. "He knows Target has a coffee shop in it," she says to me. "Whenever we go, I get a coffee, and he gets a chocolate milk with whipped cream. It's kind of our thing." She shrugs.

"Coffee and chocolate milk it is then," I tell them both.

Target didn't have the book—but it had coffee and chocolate milk—and neither did Walmart or Barnes & Noble. But after looking up other bookstores in the area, we were able to find it at the third one we went to. And the smile that spread across Damien's face when he saw it on the shelf was worth traveling all over South Florida.

"And this is *The Giving Tree*," Damien tells me.

We're currently sitting on a bench in the children's section of the bookstore—since he insisted his mom read it to us immediately so I'll know what kind of tree we're looking for—while my guys are stationed in several spots around the store and by the front door. There's going to come a time when my son learns the type of life that he's now a part of, but I refuse to follow in my father's footsteps and force it down his throat. He's going to stay innocent for as long as possible.

"This is the tree you want in our backyard?" I ask him, pointing to the large tree in the book.

"Yes." He nods. "This one has apples, but I can get apples at the store with Mommy. I just want the tree to swing on."

Peyton snorts a laugh, but quickly covers it with a cough before she says, "Damien, any tree we get will be small, and it will take years to grow. I don't—"

"I got this," I tell her with a grin, patting her knee. "You want a tree like this to swing on?" I ask him.

He nods.

"You got it, buddy. But we don't need to go chop one down … because we already have one in our backyard."

I pull out my phone and text my guys, letting them know what I need, and George responds that it will be done before we get home.

When my father cleared the land years ago to build the house, my mom insisted he keep an old tree in the back for shade. She said he was pissed, that he told her it would ruin the aesthetic, but she put her foot down, and the tree stayed.

We were never allowed to play as kids, but when we wanted to get away from our father, Matteo and I would climb the tree and hide out. And I always thought it would be the perfect tree to hold a swing.

"Let's go to dinner," I tell them. "And when we get home, I'll take you to the tree, and your mom can read us the book while you swing from it."

I wink at Damien, and he squeals in delight. And fuck if my heart isn't full. My entire life has been filled with so much damn darkness, but only a day with these two, and it's already so much brighter.

"Mommy! Daddy! It's The Giving Tree!" Damien yells as he runs toward the large tree in the back of the property, which now houses a brand-new tire swing and wooden steps leading up to the separation in the trunk, where Matteo and I used to sit and talk for hours.

"I can't believe you did this," Peyton says, smiling at me. "Thank you. This is …" She shakes her head, and her eyes fill with tears.

"What you both deserve," I tell her.

Damien goes straight for the steps first, and without issue, he clambers up the rungs and then turns around and leans against the thick branch. He's only a few feet up in the air, but George let me know he's having playground grass installed tomorrow, so if Damien were to fall, it would reduce the chance of him breaking something.

"Mommy, look at me!" Damien yells with a smile spread across his face. "I'm in The Giving Tree!"

"I see that," Peyton says, walking over to him.

Damien looks around for a few seconds, and then he comes down and goes over to the tire swing. It's low enough for him to get onto himself, so I let him do it. Once he's sitting and holding on, I walk up behind him and push him gently.

He giggles in excitement, and Peyton grins. In this moment, I swear I'll do whatever it takes to keep them both safe and happy.

I meant what I told her. I'll burn this city to the ground and go after anyone who threatens my family, starting with Anthony Rothschild. He'd better enjoy his time on this earth because it's limited.

"And who is this?"

My mom comes strolling into the living room, her face full of makeup, her hair perfectly styled, dressed in a black-and-gold pant-suit. The woman is in her early fifties, but doesn't look a day over forty, thanks to Botox and the best plastic surgeons in South Florida.

She spots Peyton first, but before I can explain—she hasn't been home, and I didn't want to tell her she's a grandmother over the phone—Damien comes running out of the kitchen with a cookie in each hand, no doubt courtesy of Martha, who has taken great joy in spoiling him.

"I got two cookies, Daddy!" He giggles, holding up the cookies for me to see. "I share with you."

He hands me a cookie, and I take it from him with a smile.

"Thank you, buddy." I take a bite of the cookie and glance at my mom, whose mouth is parted in shock.

"Did he … just call you …"

"Mother," I say, bringing Damien over to me, "I'd like for you to meet your grandson. Damien, this is your grandmother."

"I already got a grandma," Damien says. "She's in heaven. Right, Mommy?"

Peyton comes over and kneels in front of Damien. "Grandma is in heaven. But she was my mommy. This grandma is Daddy's mommy."

"Oh my goodness," my mother says. "Dominick, he looks just like you, the same gray eyes … only with red hair."

"That's because of me," Peyton says with an awkward laugh and stands. "Apparently, my Scottish genes run strong."

"Mother, this is Peyton, Damien's mom."

"It's nice to meet you," Peyton says softly.

I'm sure she's nervous because her meeting with Brielle didn't go over too well.

I explained to Peyton that my sister is protective and she'll come around. She's just fighting her own demons.

"Why are we just learning about his existence now?" my mother asks. "I don't understand."

"Peyton had planned to tell me, but she saw some things that scared her away." I give my mother a knowing look, and she nods in understanding. "So, she made the decision to raise Damien in Coral Bay, but they're here now and living with me."

My mother approaches Peyton first and takes her hands in her own. "My name is Larisa. It's a pleasure to meet you." Then, she lowers herself until she's eye level with Damien. "And since I'm your second grandmother, would you like to call me *Babushka?* It means grandma in Russian."

Damien giggles. "*Bah-bush?*" he repeats, completely butchering the word.

My mom laughs and glances up at me with watery eyes before she turns back to Damien. "Yes, my sweet boy. I'm your *babushka*. Your grandma."

"*Babush,* I got a cookie. You want some?" he asks, holding it out for her.

"Oh, no, sweetie. You eat it. Martha makes the best cookies."

Damien nods and takes a bite, and my mother stands.

"I was wondering if I could speak to you. I came home, hoping to catch you in person, but you seemed to have caught me." She grins over at Peyton and then down at Damien.

"Damien," Peyton says, "why don't we go get some milk and a plate for that cookie?" She takes his hand and smiles at my mother. "It was nice to meet you."

"It was my pleasure," Mom says. "I look forward to getting to know you both."

Once they're gone, Mom says, "They're both lovely."

"They are," I agree. "But she isn't thrilled about our lifestyle."

My mother nods in understanding. "She'll come around. You're nothing like your father, and she seems like a wonderful mother."

"She is. So, what did you need to speak to me about?"

"I've met someone," she gushes.

"I figured as much. The guard said you've been staying over at a man's house. Walter Freedman. Married for twenty-five years. Widowed for six. Two kids, who work for him at his finance firm, located in downtown North Harbor Point."

"Of course you looked him up." Mom shakes her head.

"I did … and Matteo paid him a visit last week."

Mom laughs. "I love you boys."

"And we love you."

"He asked me to move in with him," she says.

"Out of wedlock?" I half joke.

"Actually"—she extends her hand and shows off her diamond ring—"he proposed."

"Congratulations, Mother." I pull her into a hug and kiss the crown of her head. "How soon do you plan to move in with him?"

"Immediately." She glances around the house. "If you don't want to keep this place …"

I think about Damien swimming in the pool earlier today and

then playing in the backyard. "I think we'll keep it for now. Damien loves the tree in the back. George put up a tire swing for him."

Mom grins. "That's always been my favorite shade tree." She pats me on the chest. "I'm going to head back to Walter's. We'd love to do dinner with everyone soon. I want to be the one to tell Matteo and Brielle."

"Of course. But you know you have to keep the guards, right? Anthony went after Damien. We took out the two men he'd hired, but he's still out there."

"That boy." She sighs. "He's always been a bad apple. And what he did to your sister …"

"You knew back then?"

She nods and tears fill her eyes. "It wasn't my place to tell you. Not what Anthony did nor what your father forced her to do."

"I know." Even though it would've ensured we killed Anthony, I get it. Brielle confided in our mother, and she protected her the best way she knew how by helping her run.

"I hope you catch him soon." She swipes a tear and shakes her head. "Have you spoken to his mother? Maria and I spoke a while back, and she doesn't condone any of the decisions he's made. She might know something."

"Matteo questioned her a while back, but maybe I'll make a trip to see her. Wouldn't hurt."

And if he is lingering, maybe he'll catch a whiff of me near his mom and crawl out of whatever hole he's hiding in.

After we say goodbye, I head into the kitchen to join Peyton and Damien. Once he finishes his cookie, Peyton tells him it's time for bed. Having bathed him earlier, she changes him into his pajamas, and since I'm in the room, I notice he's wearing underwear.

"He doesn't wear diapers?" I ask.

"Diapers?" Damien laughs.

I swear the kid thinks everything is a joke. He might have more of my brother in him than me.

"Diapers are for babies. I don't wear no diapers." He jumps up onto his bed and holds out the book for Peyton. "Mommy, read, please."

Peyton shakes her head. "As Damien said, he's potty-trained. You lucked out. You don't have to change any diapers."

She winks, and I know she's only playing around, but her comment reminds me of how much I missed. My mom once said my dad never changed a single diaper. It was always her or the nanny.

"I would've changed diapers," I tell her, sitting on the edge of the bed, next to Damien.

Peyton glances at me, her expression sobering. "I know," she says. "And I'm sorry you didn't get the chance to."

"Who knows?" I say with a smirk, not wanting to ruin the mood with my broodiness. "Maybe, one day, I'll get the chance when we give Damien a brother or a sister."

Peyton's mouth drops, and Damien squeals.

"I want a brother!" he says. "Can I have one?"

"Dominick, that's not funny," Peyton hisses. "No, Damien, Daddy was just joking."

She glares my way, waiting for me to agree with her, but all I can think about is how sexy she probably looked while carrying my baby. Suddenly, the idea of getting her pregnant seems like a damn good idea.

"Damien, what kind of bedroom would you like?" I ask, looking around the bare room.

Peyton just finished reading *The Giving Tree*, and I now know why my son loves the book. It's the definition of unconditional love, something his mother has given him his entire life. I love my mother, and she did the best she could, but I can't remember her ever reading to us before bed, let alone a book about a tree being personified and teaching a boy about selfless love.

"We go home?" Damien asks, misunderstanding my question. "But I like my swing."

He pouts, and it makes me happy that he loves it here, but I don't like that he doesn't see this house as his home, which leads me back to my question.

"No, buddy. This is your home now. But I want to make your room yours. What theme did you have at your old house?"

Damien looks at me in confusion, and when I glance up at Peyton, she's chewing on her bottom lip.

"He didn't have one," she says. "We had to share a room because I could only afford a one-bedroom apartment. Coral Bay is ridiculous when it comes to rent, but moving would've meant having to change colleges and Damien's preschool, so I just made do."

I nod in understanding and pull out my phone. After searching for boy rooms, I turn the screen toward Damien. "If you could decorate your room with anything, what would you do?"

His eyes go comically wide as he looks at the examples of the rooms. "Can I get a pool in my room?" he asks, making me laugh.

"No, buddy. The pool has to stay outside. What else do you like?"

"I like my tree."

"That also has to stay outside," I tell him, making him pout again.

"I like cars!"

Okay, now, we're getting somewhere.

"What kind of cars?"

"Ones with tires and that go fast. Lightning McQueen is my favorite!"

I look over at Peyton for some guidance, and she smiles.

"I showed him the *Cars* movie while he was home sick a couple of months ago, and he became obsessed. We watched all three movies in one day."

I've never heard of these movies, but I note to find time to watch them with him soon.

I Google *Cars* bedrooms and turn the screen for him to look at.

"That!" He points at the cartoon car–filled room. "I want that! And a car bed!" He looks at his mom. "Mommy, you gonna sleep in my car bed with me?"

Peyton's eyes widen, and I smirk.

"No, buddy. Mommy is going to sleep in her own room," I tell him. *Or in my room, if I have it my way.*

PASSPORT

TWENTY-FOUR

Peyton

IT'S BEEN A LITTLE OVER A WEEK SINCE WE MOVED IN WITH Dominick, and we've fallen into a bit of a routine. Dominick has breakfast with Damien and me every morning before he excuses himself to work from his office. During which time, Damien and I switch between playing in the pool, the backyard—Damien mentioned once that he wished he had a swing set, and one magically appeared the next morning—and Damien's new bedroom, which looks like *Cars* threw up everywhere.

I've never seen anything get done as quickly as when Dominick snaps his fingers, but I must admit, it's rather impressive. I can see why he's as successful as he is. I've overheard him doing business from his office a few times, and he's confident and knowledgeable, and he doesn't accept no as an answer.

Sometimes, Dominick joins us for lunch. I've learned that he usually works at his office downtown, but he's working from home because he wants to be close to Damien. He also joins us for dinner every night, and we spend the evening with Damien, watching movies, playing with his toys. Then, Dominick helps with his bedtime routine. A few times, he's even read him a story before bed.

The first couple of nights here, after Damien went to sleep, I ventured out to the main area out of boredom. But with Martha always leaving before dinner, Dominick retreating to his office to work, and Matteo and Brielle being MIA, I've given up, and I now go straight to my room to watch TV or read—because after Damien's room was turned into a child's dream room, I moved to the room next door.

When Dominick said he wanted me to give him a chance, I thought he meant *us*. I even thought, when we were standing in his office, before Damien showed up, he was going to kiss me. But he hasn't made any attempt to kiss me again, and every conversation we have revolves around Damien, making me believe that it was all in my head. Which is kind of strange since he told me he didn't want me to date anyone else. That the idea of me kissing or fucking anyone else drove him nuts. But he did tell me that his parents were part of an arranged marriage, which is one reason there was no love between them, so maybe that's what he's expecting from me—a loveless arrangement. I think we're going to have to talk because that's not what I'm looking for. I haven't had much luck in the love department, but I'm too young to give up on finding it.

I hear shuffling outside my door, so I walk over and peek out, wondering who I'll see. I've run into Brielle a few times, but she tends to keep her distance, and Matteo comes and goes, but we don't see him often. If it wasn't for Dominick mentioning that both of them live here, I would never have known it.

Larisa has joined us for dinner a couple of times, and Damien seems to like her. She's sweet, and she makes a point of trying to get to know us both. Dominick says she was very withdrawn when they were growing up, so he's enjoying watching Damien soften her up. But Damien seems to have warmed up to Martha the most. It probably has something to do with their daily baking sessions and the fact that she always makes him his favorite meals, despite me telling her it's not necessary.

I always wondered what it would be like to be a stay-at-home mom, and while I enjoy getting to spend time with Damien, I can tell he's starting to get bored. He's been in structured childcare his entire life because of me being in school and having to work, and I think he's missing the socialization. It doesn't help that there are no other children here.

Which is why I've decided Dominick and I need to talk. And since Damien is in bed for the night, I figured now is the perfect time.

When I see it's only Ricky standing outside my door—the guard Dominick hired to watch over Damien and me. His job is to literally follow us around to ensure we're safe, and at night, he stands guard outside of our son's room. I'm not even sure if the man sleeps at this point—I give him a quick head nod and then head down the stairs to Dominick's office, where I know I'll find him. It's where he always is when he's not spending time with Damien.

The door is open, and I'm about to walk in when he barks out, "I don't give a shit!"

There's a loud bang, and I jump, imagining it's his fist hitting the wood desk.

"Lock him up. We need some goddamn answers. And then I'll slice his throat myself. I'll meet you there."

I hold my breath, debating whether to leave or go in, but before I can decide, Dominick storms out of the door, running straight into me. Because he didn't know I was there, I fly back, landing on the floor with a thump.

With him towering over me, flashbacks of my dad standing over my mom after he hit her flit through my mind, and I find myself closing my eyes, preparing for the worst.

Only the worst doesn't come.

"Jesus," Dominick hisses, gently lifting me off the floor and carrying me into the living room. "Are you okay? What were you doing?"

I open my eyes just in time to see him glance from me to the office door and back.

"Were you spying on me?"

He quirks a brow, and I squirm for him to put me down, but he only holds me tighter.

"You lied," I choke out.

"What?"

"You said you would keep your business out of this home. I was coming to talk to you and heard you tell someone that you would *slice his throat* yourself."

Dominick's eyes go wide.

"What if it had been Damien? He could've heard your conversation. Is that what you want? For our son to know that his father is a killer?"

"Fuck." He scrubs his hand down his face.

I notice his stubble has turned into a full-grown beard. His eyes ... they look cold, and underneath them, his tanned skin is dark, like he hasn't slept in days.

"Are you okay?"

He sighs. "Shit's hit the fan. Somebody keeps going after our shipments. We lost one, costing us hundreds of thousands of dollars, but they fucked up with this last one, and we were able to catch one of them. He's being held at the warehouse, waiting to be interrogated. I wasn't thinking when I spoke. I'm not used to having to censor what I say."

"If you'd rather we move somewhere else ..." His jaw clenches, so I add, "Not another city. But we could move somewhere else. To another home. I was actually thinking I could start looking for a job—"

"Peyton," he growls, "you're not going anywhere. I would never hurt you or our son. I would kill myself before either of you hurt in any way."

I swallow thickly, wanting to believe him. He's done nothing to show me otherwise, but it's hard to separate the two—the violent businessman and the man currently sitting on the couch, holding me like I'm the most precious thing in the world.

His phone vibrates in his hand, and he tightens his fist around it. "I have to go."

I swallow around the lump lodged in my throat, and instead of getting up, he glances at me.

"I've been distracted the past several days, but I want you and Damien here." He tucks a few wayward strands of hair behind my ear. "We'll talk when I get home."

I nod, and then he stands, sets me down on the couch, and walks out the door while I stay where I am, wondering what the hell I'm doing. I agreed to move in here, but I don't think I can do this. Even if he keeps his business out of the home, I still know what he's doing when he leaves.

"I know what you're thinking," Brielle says, stepping out of the shadows. "How can you possibly be with a man who's capable of playing cars with his son one minute and then shooting someone the next?"

She saunters over, looking put together, as always. Today, she's sporting a high-waisted, wide-legged crimson pant set with a sleeveless crop top that shows off just a hint of her flat belly. Her blonde hair looks to have freshly done highlights, and her makeup is flawless. Finishing her look is a pair of matching heels with the signature red sole. I'm not sure what she does all day, but I've yet to see her looking anything but perfect.

Meanwhile, I'm in an oversized T-shirt and cotton shorts, making me look like a homeless person.

"Get the thought of leaving out of your head," she says, stopping in front of me. "Even if you somehow convince my brother to let you go, once you're in this world, there is no getting out. Everyone's already talking. They know Dominick has a son—an heir to the almighty Antonov empire. Matteo has spread the word that Anthony tried to take him, and there's a bull's-eye on his forehead with a hefty price tag."

"You got out," I note, remembering Dominick mentioned she was in Russia for almost five years.

"And now I'm back, and not by choice. You can fight against it all you want, but it won't change anything." She walks over and joins me on the couch.

"When my grandfather was growing up, Harbor Point was overrun by violence and corruption and poverty. Little by little, my grandfather, along with his friends, Antonio Russo and Joseph Rothschild Senior started cleaning up the city. They provided protection to businesses so they could run without fear of being pushed out or robbed. They swept the streets of the shady drug dealers and pimps, and my grandfather bought the port so he could control all import and export. Then, they started buying the run-down buildings and renovating them."

"Rothschild and Russo?" I question, having heard those names before. "You mean Lorenzo and Anthony's—"

"Grandfathers," she finishes. "Though Antonio and Joseph Senior died at an early age from a heart attack and car accident, my grandfather didn't die until he was in his eighties. By the time my grandfather was set to retire, he and his friends had transformed this city. North Harbor Point was thriving, and South Harbor Point was ten times safer." She smiles thoughtfully, and it's clear she was fond of her grandfather. "But my grandfather made the mistake of allowing Andrey to take over."

I know from listening to Dominick that Andrey was their father, but they all refer to him by his name and not title.

"Most of his life, my father had been raised poor because it took years for my grandfather's efforts to make a difference. But when he was older and my grandfather was making a good living, he got a taste of what money could do. He became greedy, thrived on power and control, and despite my grandfather warning him not to, he took the business to the next level, dragging Giuseppe and Joseph along with him. He allowed illegal importation, welcomed the drug dealers onto the streets, and gave the pimps the green light because it meant more money in his pocket.

"My grandfather couldn't watch what Andrey was doing to the city that he and his friends had turned around, so he left for Russia …"

"That's where you were," I say, remembering Dominick went there and then came back with her.

"Yes, I lived there for a little over four years, until my grandparents passed away and Dominick made me come home." She smiles sadly. "I missed my brothers and my mother, but I hate it here. I hate this house, even though it's been renovated. I hate everything it represents. I hate this city. Everywhere I go, it reminds me of Andrey, and I hate him."

"If you're trying to convince me to stay, you're not exactly painting the best picture," I point out, and Brielle laughs.

It's the first time I've heard her laugh, and when she looks at me with sparkling blue eyes filled with mirth, she's even more beautiful, reminding me of Dominick during the rare moments when he lets his guard down.

"From the time Dominick was born, he was groomed to run Antonov Enterprises. Andrey hoped to create a carbon copy of himself, but when he realized that, despite his best efforts, his son actually had a heart and a conscience, he refused to give up his control. Matteo was too much of a wild card, and he hated that, even though Dominick and Matteo were vastly different, they were inseparable."

She chuckles humorously and shakes her head. "Dominick and Matteo planned to take our father out, but he must've caught wind of it because he told them that if he died, the business would be left to his best friend and business partner, Giuseppe. He used the excuse that he wasn't handing over the reins until Dominick married Daniella Russo, but everyone knew it was just his way of prolonging giving up his precious control.

"So, my brothers had to come up with another plan. For years, Dominick pretended to kiss his ass, and it paid off. About a year before Andrey died, he was diagnosed with Alzheimer's and updated his will so that Dominick would get everything should something happen to him."

"The guy sounds like a real gem," I mutter.

"However you're imagining Andrey, he was ten times worse." She swallows thickly and then locks eyes with me. "The reason I left was because he had forced me to have an abortion after finding out I was pregnant."

Before I can hold back my reaction, I gasp and then cover my mouth.

"I was in love," she admits, her gaze now faraway, like she's somewhere else. "But I was promised to another man—Anthony Rothschild," she says, "the asshole who tried to kidnap Damien. When he found out I was no longer a virgin, he raped me, and then a month later, I found out I was pregnant.

"When I told Andrey, rather than him be pissed that the son of his business partner had raped me, he told me I shouldn't have been spreading my legs and then forced me to have an abortion. I didn't know it at the time, but he must've told Anthony and his father because his father ended up killing mine.

"And when Anthony went after your son, he said it was an eye for an eye. Dominick thinks he's pissed that my dad took his supposed heir, so he wants to take Dominick's."

"Holy shit," I breathe. "And I'm just supposed to be okay with all this?"

"No," she says. "You don't have to be okay with anything, but you do have to accept that this is the world you and your son live in now.

"Dominick isn't our father. The second our father died, Dominick cut ties with Anthony's family. He refused to allow any more arranged marriages, and he started cleaning up the streets that our father had dirtied.

"He's spent the past four years building his legal businesses, expanding on real estate, purchasing and renovating run-down businesses, but it takes time to undo what our father did. And some of it can never be undone, so rather than fight against it, he's working it to his advantage so he's in control. Because if he's not, someone else will be. And what if that person is anything like Andrey?"

She quirks a perfectly manicured brow, and I nod in understanding.

"Dominick has no choice but to be ruthless," she says. "If you show a moment of weakness, you're dead. We live in a kill-or-be-killed world, and Dominick will do everything in his power to ensure we stay alive."

"And what about you?" I ask, my curiosity getting the better of me. "Where do you fit into all this?"

"I don't know." She shrugs, and for a moment, she looks how I feel—vulnerable and insecure and so damn lost. But then she sucks in a deep breath and releases it, squares her shoulders, and juts out her chin. "I'm forced to be here, the same as you. But it's pointless to fight against it. I'm pretty and rich, and I have nothing better to do than have fun, so that's what I'm going to do." She stands and smiles down at me. "The sooner you get on board, the better. Besides, it's obvious you have a thing for my brother. Just let all your preconceived notions go and let it flow."

She stands and starts to walk away, but then she stops and looks back at me. "I'm going to Kings Point with some friends to have a drink tonight if you want to join."

"What's King's Point?"

"An upscale club my brothers own."

"I don't have anyone to watch Damien."

"Martha," Brielle calls out, and a moment later, Martha peeks around the corner.

"Yes, Brielle?"

"Any chance you want to keep an eye on Damien tonight? Ricky will be here too."

"Of course," she says with a smile. "I can watch that sweet boy for you anytime. I'm only a hundred feet away."

"What?" I ask in confusion, making Martha laugh.

"My dear, I thought you knew. I live in the living quarters in the back. It's where all the full-time employees live."

"Oh, I didn't know that." I've seen the guards walk back and forth between the house and what I thought was a pool house, but I didn't know anyone lived there. "Are you sure? I could, um, pay you extra."

Martha laughs. "Oh, no. Trust me, Dominick pays me plenty. I don't mind at all."

"Perfect," Brielle says. "Be ready to go in an hour."

"Won't Dominick be home by then?" I ask.

"Doubtful." Brielle shrugs. "He mentioned getting answers, and the torturing usually takes a while."

I glance at Martha, and she doesn't look shocked at all as she goes back to wiping down the counters.

"Who our family is, along with what we do, isn't a secret," Brielle explains. "All the employees sign NDAs, but even if they didn't, the Antonov reputation speaks for itself. Nobody would dare cross us."

"Anthony did, and whoever's messing with the shipments is too."

"Let me rephrase," she says. "Nobody in their right mind or without a death wish would dare cross us."

PASSPORT

TWENTY-FIVE

Dominick

"Two shipments in less than a month," Matteo says as we walk into the warehouse. "Someone is fucking with us."

He's right. If they had actually stolen the shipments, it would be one thing. But the fact that they were only out to destroy them tells us that they were trying to send a message. They got away with it the first time, burning thousands of dollars in drugs, but our guys were prepared this time and saved the weapons.

"Do you know who he is?" I ask.

"Nope. None of the men do. He's not from these streets."

My brother makes it a point to know everyone, so for him not to know this person means we have new players in town.

"Well, hello there," I say to the man currently tied down to the metal chair.

He's dressed in a holey black T-shirt and ripped jeans—the kind from years of wear, not purchased as a fashion trend—and his shoes are old and worn. He's sporting a myriad of shitty tattoos up and down his arms and on his neck, which look like they were probably done in jail or in someone's basement. I assume he's broke, which means he was most likely paid to do this. He might not even know who hired him.

He glares up at me, and Matteo chuckles and then punches him in the face once, twice. The guy's head snaps to the side and then lolls forward, his nose dripping blood like a crimson river down his face and into his mouth. He'd probably be choking on it if he wasn't knocked out cold.

I give Matteo a look, and he shrugs.

"My bad. I haven't gotten laid in a few weeks, and you know my fight is coming up. The pent-up frustration is real." He grins at me tauntingly, and I already know whatever he's about to say is going to piss me off. "I don't know how you do it, bro. You got that sexy-as-sin woman with her curves for days, living in our house, just begging to be fucked, and I haven't heard her calling out your name once. Your level of restraint is unmatched."

"One," I say to him, "don't ever fucking refer to her as anything other than her name. She's the mother of my child—your nephew. And, two, stop knocking out the guys we're interrogating!"

Before he can come back with a smart-ass remark, the man starts to groan.

"Oh good, you're awake," Matteo says, approaching him. He grips his chin and forces the guy to look at him. "Who are you working for?"

He spits out blood, and it hits the front of Matteo's shirt.

"Wrong move," Matteo deadpans.

He walks over to the corner and grabs a bucket to fill with water, and when the man sees what he's doing, he starts talking.

"I don't know shit," he says. "I swear."

Because he had no identification on him, we don't know who he is. Our IT person, Eddy, is hacking into police records to run facial recognition on him, but that could take a while, and even when we know who he is, that might not explain who he's working for.

Matteo walks around the chair and, with one hand, yanks the man's head back. With the other, he starts to pour the water over his face, essentially drowning him.

The guy sputters at first, but when it becomes too much, he starts to choke.

"Stop," he splutters, shaking his head back and forth.

Matteo continues to drown him for a few more seconds and nods toward me.

"You must know something," I tell him. "You were caught trying to fuck up my shipment. And based on the footage, you're the same one who did it last time."

His eyes widen, like the dumbass is just now realizing we have security cameras.

"I-I don't know who hired me," he cries. "I was just given cash and told to fuck shit up. I thought it'd be easy money."

"Boss," Scotty says, walking in and dragging someone with him, "found him at the port with explosives."

Matteo curses under his breath, but I simply nod, refusing to show any emotion. Someone is out to get us, and my guess is, when the first guy didn't succeed, they knew we'd be busy, so they sent in another one to finish the job.

"Grab a chair," I tell the second guy, who's flailing about, despite being handcuffed and gagged. "Let's get this party started."

Scotty sets Guy Two in a chair and then goes about strapping him to it. But I'm not watching what he's doing. I'm watching as the men glance at each other.

Matteo locks eyes with me, and I nod.

They know each other.

"Your friend was just going to go for a little swim," Matteo says with a grin that would scare the piss out of little kids. "How about you join him?"

Without waiting, he pulls Guy Two's head back and starts drowning him with water. He didn't expect it, so he starts to choke, and when Matteo lets go, he throws up everywhere.

"Fuck!" Guy Two yells. "This isn't what I signed up for."

"Oh, really?" I say, stepping in front of him. "What did you think was going to happen when you went to a port owned by the Antonovs and tried to fuck up our shit?" I kneel in front of him and smile. "You're going to die. But how we do it will depend on your cooperation. Tell us who hired you, and we'll make it quick."

He swallows thickly, but doesn't speak, so I give Matteo a slight nod.

He goes to a cabinet and grabs gloves and pliers, and one of the guys whimpers.

With gloves on his hands, he opens Guy Two's mouth and rips one of his teeth out. A bloodcurdling scream fills the room, and a dark spot blooms on the front of his pants. He pissed himself.

"Please," Guy One whimpers. "Just kill me! I don't know the man, but he has blond hair and a tattoo." He peers up at me with a look of desperation, hoping, by some miracle, I'll take pity on him and save his life. "A tattoo of a snake on his forearm," he continues. "He gave us the money and told us if we succeeded, we could come back, and he'd pay us to do it again."

"Anthony," Matteo says, not bothering to hide what we say from the two men.

They'll be killed shortly, and dead people can't share information.

"Anthony doesn't have money," I point out. And then it hits me. "The mayor. He vouched for him at the auction. He could easily be bankrolling whatever it is Anthony's up to."

Matteo clenches his jaw. "Looks like we'll be paying Mr. Mayor a visit."

"Gentlemen," Eric Vanderbilt says an hour later.

He's sitting at the bar at North Harbor Point Country Club, having a drink with a couple of his friends. Once they've mingled with everyone, they'll move into a private room, where they'll play poker and be served by half-naked women while they ogle and grope them. He'll then pick one of them to fuck and then go home to his delusional wife, who will pretend he didn't just rail a woman half his age.

I know this because when Andrey was alive, I had the misfortune of attending a poker game with him. He wanted me to get acquainted with Eric Vanderbilt, who, at the time, was the city manager. I played my part, and I continue to do so now that he's the mayor and up for reelection soon. But I wouldn't trust the man as far as I could throw him.

"Eric, how are you?" I ask, sitting next to him.

Matteo glares at the guy to his left, and he gets up, freeing the stool for him.

"Was that necessary?" Eric asks, taking a sip of his scotch.

"About as necessary as you working with Anthony Rothschild," I say, watching for a reaction that will prove our theory.

But he doesn't react. He rolls his eyes and sets his drink down, looking over at me. "I already told you, his father and I went way back. He came to me, asking for support to start over, and I offered to back him up for the auction. You made sure he couldn't bid. End of discussion."

"When's the last time you saw Anthony?" Matteo asks, making Eric look at him.

"Not since that day." He lifts his glass to take a drink, and if I wasn't looking so closely, I would have missed the way his hand shakes.

He's nervous … acting guilty.

He downs his drink and stands. "Look, I'm not trying to get in the middle of whatever thug rivalry you guys have going on." He buttons his jacket, and the thing damn near pops open, thanks to his beer belly. "Now, if you'll excuse me, I have a poker game to get to."

He walks away, and Matteo's about to follow, but I shake my

head, wanting to see what he does once he's out of our sight. Mr. Mayor doesn't know it, but I have men watching him from every angle of the club.

I'm waiting for my guys to send me what they see when a text comes through from Daniil. It's a picture of Brielle, clearly dressed to go out, and with her is …

"Holy shit." Matteo whistles, obviously having gotten the same text as me since he's to be kept abreast of our sister's where-abouts. "Goddamn, I knew that woman had curves, but—"

"Not another fucking word," I bark, staring at the photo of Peyton, dressed in the same damn black dress she wore on our night together.

I would recognize that dress anywhere. Hell, it's front and center, along with her, every time I get myself off. But it looks slightly different in this picture. Because her body has changed from her pregnancy, it hugs every damn curve on her, and her breasts … fuck, they're spilling out.

> Daniil: Heading to Kings Point. VIP area booked. Meeting Brielle's friends there.

> Me: And my son?

"That's what you're worried about?" Matteo laughs, making me realize I replied in the group chat. "You need to be worried about who is going to be seeing Peyton in that tiny fucking dress."

> Daniil: Martha is watching him.

"Let's go," I tell Matteo, stalking out of the country club.

"Where are we going?" he asks, amusement laced in his tone.

My phone goes off, and I expect it to be another text from Daniil, but it's a zoomed-in photo of the mayor texting someone.

Sure enough, it reads, **They're getting suspicious. I'd be careful if I were you.**

"He has to be texting Anthony," Matteo says as we get into my vehicle since I drove us here.

"Anthony isn't smart enough to pull all this off by himself," I tell him, starting the car and taking off toward the club. "And he doesn't have the resources to pay people to do his dirty work. He's the puppet. But the question is, who is pulling his strings?"

PASSPORT
JOHN
New
Londo
35
25 DEC 18
15:45

TWENTY-SIX

Peyton

"WHY AREN'T YOU DRESSED?"

I turn around and sigh. "I am."

My stuff from my apartment was delivered—and I learned that Dominick had paid to have my lease terminated—but there's nothing in these boxes meant for going to a club or bar.

"It's official," I say, my hands sweeping down my body. "I'm a mom with a mom bod and mom clothes."

Brielle stares at me for several seconds and then bursts out laughing. "Oh my God. Stop it. If that"—she nods toward my body—"is a mom bod, then sign me up. Because you have curves for days and your rack looks like you bought it."

"I invest in very good bras."

She laughs again and then saunters over to my closet, where I've been hanging up my clothes as I unbox. "Oh, what about this? This is sexy and simple. Perfect for a night out at the club."

She's referring to the little black dress that I haven't worn since my night with Dominick. Soon after, I found out I was pregnant, and then after Damien was born, when I went on dates, I couldn't bring myself to wear it. It holds too many memories. When we went to bed that night, I thought it was the start of something more, only to learn the next morning that it was the end.

"Yeah, I could wear that," I tell her, snatching it off the hanger with a bit too much force.

She eyes me curiously, but doesn't comment.

After I'm dressed, I check on Damien and then thank Martha for keeping an eye on him.

"Should I leave a note for Dominick?" I ask as we walk out to the garage.

When my stuff was delivered, so was my phone, but I don't know Dominick's number, and since he's been home a lot, I haven't needed it.

Brielle grins. "No. The one thing you need to know about my brothers is that they always know where everyone is."

The garage houses several sleek vehicles, ranging from sports cars to SUVs. And I make a mental note to ask Dominick about my car. It doesn't belong in this garage, but I'll need something to drive around when the threat is gone.

"Wait," I say, stopping. "What about the guard?"

"I'm right here, Miss Wright," Daniil says, stepping out of a side door. He's dressed like he always is—in an all-black suit, complete with a matching skinny tie. "I'll be driving you tonight."

"Or … and just hear me out," Brielle says, batting her lashes, "you could follow us so I could drive Betty." She pats her hand on the red Porsche. "It's been years since I drove her, and she misses me."

"Sorry, Miss Antonova—"

"Brielle," she barks. "I hate that last name as much as I hate this city."

Daniil nods. "You know the rules, Brielle. If you want to leave, I need to drive you."

She huffs but gives in, walking over to the black sedan next to her sports car. "Fine, let's go."

She takes the back seat, and I'm not sure if I should get in the front or the back, until another guy walks out, dressed the same as Daniil.

"Hello, Miss Wright—correct?" Unlike Daniil's blond hair, hazel eyes, and boyish looks, this guy looks downright menacing. His head is shaved, and peeking out of his collar looks to be several tattoos. One of which looks like a snake running up his neck.

"Yes," I choke out.

"My name is Denis," he says. "I'll be joining you tonight."

"Okay, thanks," I tell him.

He opens the back door for me, and I slide in next to a pouting Brielle.

"Told you they know everything," she mutters.

"What do you mean?"

"Denis is one of Dominick's best men. If I were going alone, Daniil would've been fine. But the fact that Denis is here means Dominick knows you're leaving and isn't taking any chances. I've seen that man kill five guys in less than ten seconds."

When my eyes dart between her and Denis, she laughs. "Welcome to the family."

Kings Point is exactly the kind of place I imagined Brielle frequenting. The walls are a deep crimson with red lights running from corner to corner. Black-and-gold velvet couches and chairs are placed around the perimeter, and even though they're out in the open, each area looks cozy. In the middle is a sleek marble dance floor, which is filled with people gyrating and grinding all over each other to a smooth beat.

"This way," Brielle says, heading straight for the stairs.

As she saunters across the club, people make a path for her like the parting of the Red Sea. Women look at her with a mixture of jealousy and envy while several men turn their heads, their eyes lighting up with lust, but none of them dare to try and approach her.

I think it's partly because of the two bodyguards we have—one in front and the other behind us—but also, Brielle gives off a *don't fuck with me* vibe on her own. You'd never know that woman has a vulnerable bone in her body. She carries herself the same way her brothers do—like she owns the world.

Tonight, she's dressed in a simple white dress, which shows off her trim figure and ample cleavage, paired with red heels. Her blonde locks are down in loose waves, and she's holding a tiny red clutch that matches her heels.

The man standing in front of the velvet rope nods once and opens it for us. The second floor has the same color scheme as the first, but unlike the first floor, each section has floor-to-ceiling curtains you can close if you want privacy. There's a bar and dance floor similar to the one on the first floor, only half the size. This must be the VIP area.

"There she is!" a gorgeous woman squeals, running out of one of the sections.

A few more women appear as well, each hugging Brielle and welcoming her back. She gives each a two-cheek kiss, and once she's done, she takes my hand and brings me over to join them.

"This is Katie." Brielle points to the first woman, who's wearing a cream dress that leaves nothing to the imagination. She has caramel hair and green eyes, and she's downright gorgeous. "We went to high school together."

Katie smiles, but it's fake, and I have no idea what I did for her to already dislike me.

"This is Gillian and Liberty," Brielle says, moving on to two women with platinum-blonde hair and matching blue eyes, who are clearly sisters. They look like they belong on a runway or on the cover of a magazine. "We also went to high school together, and their father is a business associate of Dominick's."

Both women smile, and I force a smile back, wondering what I'm doing here.

"And this is Lola," Brielle says. "We grew up together. Her grandfather was the mayor of Harbor Point, and her father should've been as well, but—"

"He was in an accident," Lola says, "and forced to step out of the running. It's nice to meet you."

Her smile is authentic, and I release a calming breath.

"Ladies," Brielle says, "this is Peyton." I assume that's all she's going to say until she smirks and then adds, "My brother Dominick's girlfriend."

A couple of the women gasp, and they all eye me up and down with a mixture of curiosity and confusion. Lola doesn't look surprised, so I'm assuming Brielle already told her about me.

"I thought your brother wasn't looking for a relationship," Katie says, not even bothering to hide her disdain for me.

"No, sweetie," Brielle says in a sugary-sweet tone. "He wasn't looking for one with you."

Katie huffs and flips her long caramel hair over her shoulder. "Whatever. You know what they say—men don't change."

"Actually, I think the saying goes, *A woman can't change a man. But a man will change for the right woman.*" Brielle smiles as she sits on the black-and-gold velvet couch and elegantly crosses her legs. "Now, I'd like to have a good time, so rather than be petty bitches because my brothers refuse to hook up with any of you, let's drink and enjoy ourselves. There are plenty of men here tonight who will give you the attention you want."

As if on cue, a waitress walks in and sets down a round of shots.

Brielle takes two, handing one to me, while the other women grab their own.

They raise their glasses, so I follow along.

"To having a good time." Brielle raises her glass, and all the women follow, clinking their glasses against hers.

I throw my shot back, and it burns, going down, but I can't deny how smooth it is. Brielle hands me another, and I swallow that one down as well.

"Let's dance!" she says, grabbing my hand and guiding me out of the VIP area and over to the dance floor.

The other ladies follow, and thankfully, with the alcohol flowing and the music pumping, they seem to forget about my connection to Dominick and have a good time.

We dance to several songs, then stop to take a couple of more shots before we're back at it again. With all the bodies so close, it's hot, and I'm glad my dress is sleeveless. I can feel beads of sweat dotting my forehead and the curve of my back, but I'm actually having a good time. It probably helps that alcohol is running through my veins, and with the music so loud, I don't have to converse with any of Brielle's friends.

I can't remember the last time I went out since my son was born, and I make a note to do this more often. It's easy to get lost in being a mom, but now that I'm out of school, I need to make more time for myself. All these women have their hair and nails done, and while I've never had the extra money to do anything like that before, once Dominick gives me the okay to get a job, I'd like to start doing more things for me.

I'm dancing with Brielle, my arms above my head and my body swaying to the music, when a pair of arms slide around me from behind. For a moment, in my tipsy haze, I think it's Dominick, but when Brielle's eyes bug out, I step forward and turn around, coming face-to-face with a man who is definitely not Dominick.

"Hello there," he says, flashing me a boyish grin that might work on most women, but does absolutely nothing for me.

With his messy blond hair and green eyes, he's cute, but he doesn't hold a candle to Dominick's gray eyes and sexy smirk.

"Hi," I say back, giving him a polite smile before I turn back around and move closer to Brielle, hoping he'll get the message.

But apparently, he doesn't because a second later, his hands are back on me—only, instead of going to my hips like they did last time, he has the audacity to run them down my ass.

I spin around and get in his face, ready to tell him not to ever touch me again, but before a single word makes its way out, he's ripped away from me by …

"Oh shit," I breathe, my eyes meeting Dominick's.

"You see this man?" Dominick says, his tone so cold that even in this overly hot club, shivers race up my spine. "You let him touch you, and now, what happens next is on your conscience."

He turns his back on me and nods toward the two men who have surrounded the guy that had his hands on me.

It takes a second for my alcohol-induced brain to compute what he just said, but once I do, I race toward him, grabbing the curve of his elbow.

"Dominick, wait."

He stills but doesn't look at me.

"Please," I yell over the music. "I didn't let him touch me. I was about to tell him not to do it again, but then—"

Slowly, he turns to look at me, and the moment I take in his glacial gray eyes, I realize my mistake. If I didn't let him touch me, then that means he did it without my permission.

Dominick nods toward the men, and they grab the guy by his biceps, dragging him off the dance floor.

Oh God, they're going to kill him, and it will be my fault. Sure, he shouldn't have touched me, but we're at a club, and things like this happen. I would've told him not to do it again, and he would've moved on to another woman.

But now …

"Stop, please!" I shout, about to run past Dominick to beg his men not to kill the guy.

But before I can get to them, Dominick hooks his arm around my waist and hauls me into an area similar to the one I was in with Brielle and her friends. Only this one is bigger and situated in the corner and the curtains are closed.

When we get inside, Dominick barks something to one of his men, who nods and closes the front curtain, leaving us in total privacy.

Dominick picks me up and sets me on the mini bar that is used to hold and serve liquor, and instinctively, my legs wrap around his torso.

"Dominick, please," I beg. "Don't kill—"

"Enough," he barks. "I don't want to hear you begging for that man's life to be spared. It was bad enough I had to watch him groping what is mine. You will not defend him."

His words both turn me on and piss me off because …

"Fuck you! I was handling him just fine. And the last time I checked, I'm not an object you possess. If I want to let him or anyone touch me, I—"

My rant is cut off when his fingers wrap around the base of my throat, and he pushes my head back until it hits the wall behind me.

And then his mouth is on mine. The kiss starts off one-sided, Dominick licking the seam of my lips, but when I get a taste of him, I can't help but groan into his mouth.

With my lips momentarily parted, he thrusts his tongue into my mouth, deepening the kiss. His tongue massages mine, and I slide my hands over his abs, needing to touch him in some way. Between his jacket and dress shirt and pants, there are too many articles of clothing separating my hands from his flesh, and I sigh in annoyance, making him break the kiss.

"You're mine," he growls, his eyes locking with mine. "Mine to touch." He tightens his grip on my throat with one hand and runs the other one up my naked thigh. "Mine to kiss." He brushes his lips against mine gently and then nips my bottom lip, making me hiss. "Mine to fuck." He shoves his hand between my legs, and like the horny bitch I am, I spread them more to help him gain better access.

His fingers delve under my panties, and when they slide between my wet folds, he groans. "Fuck, baby. You're soaking wet. Does that turn you on? Me staking my claim on you?" He removes his hand and brings his glistening fingers up to his mouth, sucking on his pointer and middle fingers. "So damn perfect."

The front curtain moves slightly, and I'm reminded of what we were arguing about before he distracted me with his mouth and fingers.

"Dominick, please," I say, framing his face with my hands. "I want to be yours, but I can't be with someone who can kill a man for touching me. I get it—violence is part of your world. But it can't be part of mine. He was wrong to put his hands on me without permission, but it shouldn't equal a death sentence, and I can't have that on my conscience."

He stares at me for several seconds, then nods and takes a small step back. I feel my stomach drop, thinking we've reached the end before we even got started.

I told him how I felt, and he can't give me what I want … what I need. It's better that we know this now, but it still hurts.

Dominick pulls out his phone, presses a button, and puts it to his ear. A moment later, he says, "Make sure he stays alive," with his eyes trained on mine. "And no permanent damage," he adds before hanging up.

Hope blossoms in my chest.

"Thank you," I tell him, leaning in and kissing his lips.

He kisses me back, and within seconds, we're right back where we left off—kissing and groping and grinding on one another.

He reaches around and fists my hair, tugging my head back so I'm forced to look at him, our mouths only millimeters apart.

"Tell me you want me," he demands. "Tell me you want me to fuck this cunt until you're screaming my name."

He cups my pussy, and I squirm in my spot at the mere thought of him inside me. I had only spent one night with him years ago, but he was one of the best lovers I've ever been with.

I don't know what our future holds, and there's so much we need to discuss and figure out. But the one thing I do know is how much I want this man. It's been months, and I know he'll leave me satisfied.

"I want you," I tell him. "Please, fuck me and make me scream your name."

His mouth collides with mine, and his tongue delves between my parted lips.

My hands go to his jacket, tugging the material off him, and then I unbutton his shirt, wanting to feel his skin beneath my fingertips.

He spreads my legs wider and goes back to fingering me. I'm soaked, and even with the music blaring around us, I can hear the noise my pussy is making as he thrusts his fingers in and out of me.

"Fuck," he groans, breaking the kiss so he can lick his way along my jaw and up my neck.

He sucks on the flesh just below my ear, and I clench my thighs in want. There's just something about the way Dominick touches me. Like the only way he can find his pleasure is through me.

His fingers hit the spot deep within me, and when his thumb grazes my clit, that's all it takes to send me over the edge.

"Jesus, woman." He chuckles, stroking me through my orgasm. "How long has it been? That only took thirty seconds."

"How about you shut up and fuck me?" I murmur, bringing my lips back to his.

The orgasm was good, but I know what his cock is capable of.

I reach for his pants, unbutton and unzip them, and then pull his hard length out of its confines. It's long and thick and smooth, the way I remember it being. And my mouth waters at the thought of tasting him. But now isn't the time. There are people just outside of this enclosure, and I want him inside me.

Before I can guide him into me, Dominick lifts me off the bar and pushes me against the back wall. He rips my panties off my body so they're no longer in his way and then thrusts into me, filling me so full that I don't know where he ends and I begin.

"You feel this?" he asks, pulling out slightly and then pushing back in. "You feel me inside of you?"

"Yes," I moan. "Now, fuck me!" I beg.

He's teasing me with this bullshit, and he knows it.

He tilts my head up and peers into my eyes, his own filled with lust and possession. "Tell me you're mine, Peaches, and I'll fuck you how you need."

"I'm yours," I tell him without thought.

"And nobody will ever touch your body but me?"

"Nobody will ever touch my body but you," I breathe, desperate for him to fuck me.

He captures my mouth with his and then thrusts back into me. Only this time, instead of stopping, he keeps going. He fucks me hard and deep, and with the alcohol lingering in my system, every touch, every kiss, every caress feels like so much more.

"Fuck, Peaches," he moans against my lips. "I've thought about your mouth, your body, your fucking pussy so many times over the years, but my memory didn't do it justice."

At his words, my insides tighten around him, and he groans.

"That's it, baby. Come all over my cock. I want to feel your juices dripping down my balls."

His dirty talk is my undoing. I let go and come so hard that black spots dot my vision. I hear Dominick say that he's coming, and I feel him swell inside me, but I'm too overwhelmed by my own orgasm to give anything else much thought.

"Let's go home," he says as we work to catch our breath. "There are so many things I want to do to you tonight in our bed."

He lifts me off him, setting me onto my feet, and I glance down at his cum running along the insides of my thighs.

"Dominick!" I gasp, glancing up at him. "You came inside me."

He quirks a brow. "And?"

"And I'm not on birth control," I hiss. "Until I am, we need to use condoms."

He scoffs. "I'm not fucking you with anything between us," he says, lifting me back onto the mini bar and spreading my legs.

He grabs a couple of napkins and wipes the sticky substance off my flesh. Then, he leans down and gives the inside of my thigh a kiss before he looks at me with a soft smile that is too close to disarming me.

"No protection?" I snort out a laugh. "I hope you like having a house full of kids."

His smile disappears, and I mentally smirk, thinking I scared him—as intended.

That will serve him right, refusing to use—

"I missed it all last time," he murmurs, placing his hand on my belly. "The next time you're carrying my baby, I'll be there for every moment of it. And if you even think about running, I will follow you, and I won't stop until I catch you and bring you back."

"I'm not … Dominick! I'm not getting pregnant again," I tell him, ignoring the part about me running and him catching me because we both know I'm not going anywhere. I'm in too deep to leave him. And the truth is … I don't think I want to.

"Why not?" he asks. "You heard our son. He wants a brother. Though I'm sure he won't mind if we give him a little sister."

He smirks, and I groan.

"You owe me a pair of panties," I tell him, hopping down and readjusting myself. There's still cum dripping out of me, but there's nothing I can do until I get to a toilet. "And I'm getting on birth control."

Ignoring my comment about my ripped panties, he says, "So, what you're saying is, I have until you go to the doctor to get you pregnant?"

He tugs on my hair, tilting my head to the side, and peppers kisses along my neck.

"I want to watch you grow my baby," he murmurs against my neck, causing goose bumps to prickle my skin. "Tell me you want that too."

I shake my head, confused and turned on and orgasm-drunk.

"Don't think I forgot about what you told me in the Dominican Republic. You want to get married and have two, maybe three kids, all close in age so they're not lonely, like you were as an only child. You want date nights and romantic getaways. All the shit your mom never got. I can give you that, Peyton," he says, kissing the corner of my mouth. "You just have to let me."

"It's not …" I start to argue, but my thoughts become foggy when Dominick's finger slides under the material of my dress and starts to massage my clit.

"Dominick," I whine, both turned on and annoyed that I can't resist this man.

"That's it, baby," he says, lifting me back onto the mini bar. "Feel how good this feels."

He continues to work my sensitive bud, and before I know what's happening, my legs are spread, and he's pushing his cock back into me.

Unlike last time, he fucks me with smooth, languorous strokes that match the way he's massaging my clit. I don't know if it's the liquor or the previous two orgasms he gave me, but my body feels like Jell-O, every part of me hypersensitive. When I come around his cock, screaming out his name, I'm almost positive I pass out for several moments.

"Good girl. Take all my cum," Dominick says as he lifts me into his arms. "I promise, Peaches," he says as he carries me out of the VIP area and toward what looks like a back door, "I'm going to give you everything you could ever want and more."

TWENTY-SEVEN

Dominick

A S THE TOWN CAR DRIVES THROUGH THE STREETS OF NORTH Harbor Point, Peyton sleeps peacefully in my arms. I could've put her down, but there's something about holding her that brings me comfort. Four years ago, I felt it in her presence. She illuminates my dark world. She doesn't belong. My mom and Brielle are hardened from the life we live. But Peyton is still sweet and innocent. It's selfish to force her to stay in my world, to expect her to accept the violence, but letting her walk away isn't an option.

But I meant what I said—I'm going to give her and our son everything they could ever want. For the first time, I want something more than success—I want a family. And I want it with Peyton.

The car pulls through the gate and rounds the drive, stopping in front of the door. Fernando opens the door, and I slide out with Peyton still in my arms.

I spot Martha sitting in the kitchen, playing solitaire, and she smiles warmly at me.

"Damien hasn't woken up. He's such an angel." She eyes Peyton in my arms. "They both are."

"Thank you. You can go now," I tell her, carrying Peyton upstairs.

When I get to my room, I set her on my bed and start getting her undressed. I put one heel on the floor and start to take off the other when she opens her eyes and glances around in confusion.

"We're home," she says, sitting up.

I chuckle. "Yes, you fell asleep in the car."

"I'm in the wrong room."

She starts to move her feet, preparing to get off my bed, but I grip her ankle, halting her in place.

"I meant what I said," I tell her, dropping the other heel onto the floor and running my hand up her bare calf and thigh. "You're mine, and you belong right here with me. This isn't only my room anymore … it's ours."

I spread her legs, and the bottom of her dress rises, exposing her bare cunt, thanks to me ripping her underwear earlier. I run my finger down her slit over the material, and she breathes out a soft moan.

I glance up and find her looking at me, her eyes half lidded, filled with a mixture of sleepiness and lust. I should let her get some sleep, but I can't get enough of her.

"Tell me you're mine," I say to her, needing to hear her say it again.

I'm like a drug addict, craving my fix.

I crave her touch, her smell, her words.

I have to know she's mine.

"Dominick," she whispers, "I … I don't know if I can be who you need me to be. I want to be. I feel this"—her hand comes up and presses against my chest, right above my heart—"the chemistry between us. I've felt it since the moment we met. But we're so different, and I don't know if I can accept this life."

Fuck, her honesty kills me. Most women would tell me what I want to hear. But not Peyton. She gives it to me straight every single time.

"You're mine," I tell her, crawling up her body so our faces are only inches apart. "You and Damien are mine."

I caress her lips with mine, and after a few seconds, she kisses me back. She tastes like the perfect mix of liquor and something that is just Peyton.

"You're mine," I repeat, licking across the seam of her sweet lips.

"I want to try," she murmurs against my mouth. "But I can't make any promises."

I capture her mouth with mine and deepen the kiss. It's not the answer I want to hear, but it's a start. I didn't get to where I am without determination and devotion. And I have both when it comes to her.

Peyton tugs at my jacket, wanting it off, so I reluctantly climb off the bed so I can get undressed. As I unbutton my dress shirt and drop it to the floor, she removes her dress and bra, her heavy tits falling like beautiful raindrops, leaving her completely naked. I notice the tiger stripes along her lower belly, knowing they're from carrying our son, and my heart clenches. She was beautiful over four years ago, but now, she's downright gorgeous.

As I kick off my shoes and reach down to remove my socks, I catch her watching me, and she isn't wrong—the chemistry between us is hot as fuck.

But she wants more than sex in a club. She wants a relationship, a partner to have a family with. She wants what her mom wanted, but her father wasn't capable of giving it to her. And I want to be the one to give her everything she wants. The thought of another man giving her anything has me seeing red, and I know that I'll never be able to let her go. I'll kill any man who touches her, and the only way to prevent that from happening is to ensure she never leaves me.

When I'm down to only my briefs, I reach for them, but before I can take them off, Peyton pops up and grasps them first. With her body flush against mine, she kisses me slowly and deeply as she slides my briefs down my thighs, then fists my cock in her delicate hand.

She strokes it up and down while we kiss, and it takes everything in me not to toss her onto her back and fuck her into tomorrow. Instead, I enjoy her touch, letting her control the situation.

She breaks the kiss, trailing her lips across my stubbled jaw and then along my neck and down my throat. When she gets to my chest, she circles my nipple with her tongue, then does the same to the other one.

"Peaches," I groan, fisting my hands at my sides.

"Hmm," she hums, knowing exactly what she's doing to me.

She runs her tongue down my torso, kissing each of my abs before sliding onto her belly until she's face-to-face with my cock.

"I never got to explore in the Dominican Republic," she says, placing a kiss on the tip of my crown.

She swirls her tongue along the slit, and I fist the back of her hair, wanting to push her mouth onto my shaft. Thankfully, she opens her pretty little mouth and takes me all the way down her throat, gliding her tongue along my shaft.

Then, she glances up at me and, with mischief in her eyes, says, "Fuck my mouth. I know you want to."

And because she's right, I do as she said. With my fingers wrapped tightly around her hair, I slide her mouth on and off my length, slowly picking up speed. She suctions her cheeks, firmly wrapping her lips around my cock, and takes it as I fuck her mouth. With every stroke, my cock gets wetter, the feel of her mouth on me almost as good as when her tight cunt takes me, until she's dripping saliva down the sides of her mouth and all over my shaft while she grinds her cunt along the bed, trying to get herself off as well.

I can feel the pull in my balls, and I know I'm close, but I'll be damned if she comes from the friction of the goddamn mattress.

I pull my cock out of her mouth, and she pouts. Before she can ask questions, I pull her into my arms and lie on the bed with her on top of me. I give her a hard kiss. Then, I flip her around, so her bare cunt is in my face and my dick is in hers.

She doesn't have to be told what to do. She immediately goes to town on my cock, licking and sucking, while I give the hood of her pussy an open-mouthed kiss.

With her legs hugging my face, I get to work, feasting on her pussy. She's soaking wet, and I can taste my dried-up cum from earlier, but it only turns me on more, knowing she's been sitting here with my cum coating her walls.

I spread her lips open, and my mouth latches on to her clit. I lick and suck, determined to get her off before she makes me come.

It's close. My balls tighten, but before I blow my load, Peyton loses the battle, coming all over my face. Her cunt gushes, and I lap it all up, licking her through her orgasm as I come down her throat.

"Holy shit," she breathes, rolling off me and wiping her swollen lips. "That was …"

"It's only the fucking beginning," I tell her, repeating my words from four years ago.

Only this time, I'm not referring to our night together. I'm talking about our future.

"You're mine," I tell her, scooping her up and carrying her into the shower.

"So you keep saying." She smirks, reaching up and palming the side of my face. "But those are just words. If you want me to be yours, then you're going to have to show me that you deserve to be mine. And, Dominick … stop destroying my damn panties!"

PASSPORT

TWENTY-EIGHT

Peyton

T HE WALLS ARE A LIGHT SHADE OF GRAY, UNLIKE THE WHITE in the room I've been staying in. The furniture is black. The bed is bigger, more comfortable. And for a moment, I question where I am until the memories from last night surface—going to the club with Brielle, Dominick showing up and almost having that guy killed for touching me, having sex with Dominick in the club, in his bed, in the shower … in his bed again.

I'm in his bed.

I peel my lids open, but he's not in bed with me. He left … *again*.

I sigh, wondering if I'm ever going to learn my lesson with this man. Then, I spot a note propped up where he should be, addressed to *Peaches*.

Peaches,

Five years ago, I made the mistake of not leaving you a note, and I'm nothing if not a man who learns from my mistakes. Our son woke up, and I figured you'd want to sleep in. Join us downstairs when you're ready.

—Dominick

I can't help the butterflies that flutter in my belly. The man is such a contradiction. One minute, he's threatening to slice a man's throat, and the next, he's letting me sleep in and leaving me sweet notes. I'm starting to realize that if I want to be with him, I'm going to have to accept that Dominick is a complex man. I was worried about him being violent toward me, but he's yet to do anything but bring me pleasure.

That doesn't mean I'm letting my guard completely down. My father didn't show his violent side at first. But eventually, his true colors came out.

After showering, brushing my teeth, and getting dressed, I head out to find Dominick and Damien, but before I get to the stairs, I run into Brielle, who's dressed to impress with a knowing smirk on her face.

"Looks like you made your decision," she says, tilting her head toward the door I just came out of. "And from the way you guys were going at it all night, it sounded like it too."

"Oh my God," I groan, noting to be quieter in the future.

I'm not used to living with other people and having sex. Anytime I had sex after Damien was born, I went to the guy's house, not wanting to bring him around my son.

Matteo walks over and slides his arm around my neck. He's dressed in his usual jeans, T-shirt, and tennis shoes, and with his tattoos running up and down his arms and neck, he reminds me of the stereotypical gangsters you see in the movies. It's comical how different he and Dominick are, yet they're extremely close.

"Don't be embarrassed," he says, glancing down at me. "It's nothing neither of us hasn't done ourselves. Besides, I believe I have you to thank for my big bro's good mood. He told me to take the day off because he wants a family day."

Brielle laughs. "A what?"

"A family day," Dominick says, appearing at the top of the stairs. "And get your hands off my girlfriend." He flinches as he says the word, and I wonder why, until he adds, "We're going to need to get married soon so I can call you my wife. Girlfriend sounds fucking juvenile."

I snort out a laugh, thinking he's joking, but he doesn't crack a smile.

"Dominick," I warn, "I said I'd give us a chance. That doesn't mean marriage. And if you don't like the term *girlfriend*, don't use it. Honestly, it's probably too soon anyway."

He glares, Matteo laughs, and Brielle tries to hide her grin. I duck from under Matteo's arm and walk past Dominick, but he lowers his hand to my belly to stop me.

"We're having a family day today," he says. "Sundays used to be family dinners, but Damien wants to do something fun, so we're all going to the aquarium."

"Hell yeah," Matteo says. "I'm down."

"I love the dolphins," Brielle says.

"Our mother's going too," Dominick says as Brielle and Matteo head downstairs.

I should follow after them to go say good morning to Damien, but I stay where I am, needing a moment to get composed.

"What's wrong?" Dominick asks, spinning me around.

"Nothing," I choke out, but he gives me a look that says he's not buying what I'm selling. "It's just that … my mom was always so sick, so we could never go anywhere or do anything. I spent most of his younger years taking care of her before she passed. I'm glad he has this."

"Has what?" Dominick asks, seeking clarification.

"A family." I look up at him. "It might not be perfect, but I'm happy he finally has a family. Now, I just have to hope you don't do anything to take it away from him, like go to jail or die."

It was meant as a joke, but as the words pour out, I realize I'm serious. It's a real fear. While the violence scares me, what scares me even more is loving and losing another person. I lost my father to violence, my mother to disease. I don't have anyone left but Damien and now Dominick. The thought of losing him, of my son losing him, is crippling.

"Peaches," Dominick murmurs, pinching my chin between his thumb and forefinger, "none of us are going anywhere. Not if I can help it."

"Did you have fun at the aquarium today?" I ask Damien as I give him a bath.

We got there for opening and stayed until closing. The kid is officially obsessed with marine animals, and the only way we could convince him to leave was to promise we'd be back soon. Of course, it helped that Dominick bought him stuffed animals of all of his favorite sea creatures.

He slept during the drive home, but I had to wake him up to give him a bath because there was no way I was putting him into his bed after all the animals he touched.

"Yeah," he says. "I wanna bring my stuffies to school to show Frankie. Can I go back tomorrow?"

He looks at me with bright eyes, and my heart cracks because even when he does go to school, he won't see Frankie.

"Remember that we moved in with Daddy?"

He nods.

"We live too far away from Frankie, so you can't go to school with him anymore. But maybe we can talk to his parents and visit."

Damien pouts. "I wanna go back to school."

"I know, and you will—"

"Tomorrow?" he cuts me off.

"No, not tomorrow. Hopefully—"

"It's not fair!" he cries, his tiny fists hitting the water and splashing. "I wanna go to school!"

He starts to cry, and I take a calming breath, reminding myself that he's overtired and emotional. Moving to a new place and everything changing have been a lot for me, so I know it's a lot for him as well.

"And you will," I tell him, pulling the drain plug and grabbing the towel.

I intended to get him out before he had a full-blown meltdown, but the second I pick him up, he arches his back and loses it—kicking and flailing about, tears pouring down his face.

"What the hell is going on in here?" Dominick barks, appearing out of nowhere.

I jump, assuming that he's pissed that Damien is being loud and unruly, and hold Damien closer, preparing to protect him from Dominick's wrath.

"He's—" I begin, but Damien cuts me off.

"It's not fair!" he wails. "I wanna go to school. I wanna see Frankie and Gracie and Ms. Judy. It's not fair!"

Dominick stalks toward us, and I retreat, the back of my legs hitting the side of the tub. I'm cornered with nowhere to go, and I need to protect my baby.

I tighten my hold on Damien and try to turn around to get him out of harm's way, but before I can, Dominick plucks him out of my arms.

I open my mouth to yell at him, to stop him from hurting our son. He's just a little boy, and sometimes, he's going to throw temper tantrums.

But before I can get a word out, Dominick says, "Hey, buddy, it's okay," his voice soothing as he holds Damien close to his chest, not caring that his wet body is soaking his clothes. "What's the matter?"

Damien sniffles, several tears sliding down his cheeks, and Dominick wipes them away.

"Talk to me, buddy. Tell me what's wrong. I'll make it better. I promise."

His soft tone—the opposite of what I was expecting—causes me to choke up.

He wasn't going to hurt him.

He wants to fix it.

"I want to go to school," Damien says, fresh tears filling his eyes. "But Mommy said no."

Dominick glances at me and then back to Damien. "If you want to go to school, then you can go to school."

I should tell him that giving in to Damien's demands during a meltdown sets a bad precedent, but something in Dominick's eyes tells me to let it go. We can talk about it later. He's clearly distraught from Damien crying, but not in the way I thought.

"Tomorrow?" Damien asks, optimistic.

"Yeah, buddy, tomorrow." Dominick wraps the towel around Damien and kisses his forehead. "We'll find you a school tomorrow."

Dominick carries Damien into his room and helps him get dressed into his pajamas while Damien tells him everything he wants to do at school. Dominick listens patiently, telling him he'll make sure the school has everything he wants and needs.

Guilt fills my insides like lead. I thought he was mad, but he wasn't. He was distraught because he cares so much and doesn't want to see our son upset.

"Daddy," Damien whispers after a few minutes, "can you read me *The Giving Tree?*"

"Of course, buddy," Dominick says, walking over and grabbing the book off the shelf.

He slides onto one side of the bed while I go to the other since it's big enough for all three of us.

Dominick opens the book and starts to read, and when he gets to the page about the boy going to school, Damien asks, "I go to school?"

Dominick looks down at him with love and warmth in his eyes. "Yeah, we're going to find you a school."

"Can I bring my stuffies?" Damien asks.

"You can bring whatever you want," Dominick says, making me stifle my laugh.

"As long as it's okay with your new teacher," I add.

"Okay," Damien says with a yawn, snuggling into Dominick's side. "I go to sleep now and go to school tomorrow."

Dominick continues to read the story, but before he even makes it through a few more pages, Damien is snoring softly.

"You okay?" I ask Dominick when he makes no move to leave Damien's bed.

"You thought I was going to hurt him," he says.

I was hoping he hadn't noticed, but Dominick doesn't miss a beat.

"I'm sorry. I just—"

"Andrey used to beat us," he says, changing directions and giving me whiplash. "If Matteo or I cried, he would beat the hell out of us and say that we now had something worth crying about. He told us men didn't cry and to stop acting like pussies."

He glances down at Damien and sighs. "When I heard him crying from downstairs, it brought back memories of Andrey beating us. Of my mom begging him to stop and then him hitting her. Eventually, she stopped fighting him, knowing she wouldn't win, and Matteo and I learned not to cry. I never want my children to feel like they can't express themselves, and I will never lay a single hand on them or you."

His eyes meet mine, and I know he's telling the truth. I could feel the conviction in his tone, in every word he said. He might be a violent man, but he'll never be violent toward us.

"C'mon. Let's get some rest," he says, standing and walking over to my side to help me up. "We have a busy day ahead of us tomorrow, and if I were to guess, he'll be up at the crack of dawn, ready to go to school."

I let him pull me up and fall into his arms. "You're right about that," I tell him, leaning into him and kissing his jaw. "I give him until five a.m.—at the latest."

Dominick groans. "Then, we'd better get to bed as well." He glances at his watch and then looks at me with a sparkle of mischief in his eyes. "We have less than eight hours for me to make you come as many times as possible and give our son a sibling."

He waggles his brows, and I roll my eyes as I walk past him. He's not going to give up until he's filled me with another baby.

While I should be insisting that he not do that, the thought of having another baby with Dominick doesn't seem like such a bad idea anymore.

Jesus, I internally groan. I can't believe I'm even considering it.

Then, I turn around and see him leaning over and giving our son a kiss on his forehead, and my ovaries damn near explode.

If he keeps doing shit like this, I'm going to lose the fight against him …

But the truth is, I think I'm okay with that.

PASSPORT

TWENTY-NINE

Dominick

"THE QUARTERLY REPORT STATES …" MY WORDS TRAIL OFF as my eyes catch Peyton standing in the doorway, dressed in yoga pants and a tank top that show off every curve.

Her hair is up in a messy bun, and her feet are bare. The sunlight from the foyer illuminates her, making her look like a damn angel.

My angel.

I've been working from home while she and Damien get adjusted, but now that he's enrolled full-time at the local private school, I should go back to the office.

But every time I consider it, she walks by, dressed in her tiny cotton shorts or gym clothes—since she's been working out in our gym—or the barely there bikini she wears when she goes swimming, and I have no desire to be anywhere but here.

I continue to speak to my team, but I cut off the camera and pat my leg for her to join me. She does so without argument, padding into the office and climbing into my lap.

I never knew how good it would feel to have a woman in my life and in my home. I was raised in a house that lacked any kind of normalcy, but Peyton and Damien are showing me what that looks like. Before them, my life revolved around my business, but now, it includes breakfast and bath time and bedtime stories, sex in the middle of the night with the woman I'm falling in love with, and I can't imagine going back to the way my life was before them.

Greg, my senior analyst, continues to throw out numbers regarding the new development project we're preparing to present to the city council. Normally, I wouldn't give a shit, but with the mayor going rogue, I need every *t* crossed and *i* dotted. I don't know who he's working with, and this project is too damn important to risk getting denied.

Peyton wraps her smooth thighs around my waist and starts peppering kisses along my stubbled jaw and neck while I answer the questions that are thrown at me.

When she starts to unbutton my shirt, her cold hands brush against my flesh, and I suck in a harsh breath. I glance down at her, but she's not looking at me, too busy placing open-mouthed kisses on my chest.

Another member of my team starts to present her ideas, and while I should be paying attention to whatever she's saying, my only focus is on the woman who's moved on to unbuttoning and unzipping my pants.

"Mmm," she hums, pulling my cock out of its confines. "I love when you go commando." She slides down my legs and drops onto her knees, spreading my legs and taking my shaft into her mouth.

"Mr. Antonov?" someone says, reminding me that I'm still in a damn meeting. "What do you think?"

"I think …"

Peyton swallows my entire cock, choking on it when it hits the back of her throat, and I damn near lose my shit.

"I think …"

She reaches up and cups my balls, fondling them gently, and I choke out, "I have a call coming in. Discuss this, and I'll call you right back."

Before any of them can argue, I end the call and lean back, moaning as Peyton fucks me with her mouth. Her saliva coats my dick, dribbling down to my ball sack, and I fist her hair, needing to touch her in some way.

"Fuck, baby," I groan. "You're such a pretty little distraction."

She hums around my cock, continuing to bob her head up and down, and I tighten my hold on her hair, close to coming down her throat. But then I remember my mission to get her pregnant before she gets on birth control, and I yank her head up.

"Hey!" She pouts like I just took away her favorite snack as I lift her onto my desk, not giving a shit that her ass is crumpling all the files I have laid out in front of me.

I yank her yoga pants and underwear down her legs and then shove two fingers inside her cunt.

"Fuck, woman, you're drenched. Does sucking my cock turn you on?"

"You already know it does," she says, glaring at me because I didn't let her finish.

I pump my fingers in and out of her, then curl them up, hitting the spot that I know will set her off. I usually prefer to take my time, but I need to get back to my meeting, and I want her to get off before I shove my cock inside her and hopefully fuck a baby into her.

Within a few strokes, she drops her head against my chest and comes all over my fingers, using me to stifle her moans.

"Such a good girl," I say, pulling my fingers out and sucking on them. "You taste so damn good. Later, I'm going to feast on this pussy."

I pull her legs toward me, forcing her head and back to hit the desk, and then I line up my cock at her opening. It's glistening from her orgasm, and I know despite my size, I'll slide in easily.

I waste no time thrusting into her warm, wet cunt, and then I drop on top of her, caging her in my arms. She wraps her legs around my waist and her fingers around my biceps to hold on, and then she throws her head back with a loud moan.

"Fuck," I groan. "You feel the way you fit so perfectly around me, your cunt gripping my cock?"

"God, yes," she moans. "Please, Dom, fuck me harder."

Recently, she started calling me Dom. I've never been given a nickname, never allowed anyone in enough for them to give me one—aside from Matteo, who has called me bro our entire lives, despite me telling him not to because it sounds unprofessional. I didn't think I'd like her calling me anything other than my name, but I do. I like that she feels comfortable enough to give me a nickname.

I sit back on my knees and, gripping her hips, increase my pace, fucking her hard and fast. Her cunt clenches around me, choking my cock like a vise. Then, she climaxes again, her eyes rolling upward while she screams my name, unable to hold back. I allow myself to let go, coming deep inside her, coating her walls with my seed.

When our breathing has somewhat slowed, she sits up on her elbows and looks at me. "I need to find a clinic. You're on a damn mission to get me pregnant."

I chuckle and pull out, watching as my cum dribbles out of her pretty pink pussy. "Yeah, I am," I admit, using two fingers to push my cum back inside her. "But you don't need to go to a clinic." I glance back up at her, tuck myself back into my pants, and then step in between her thighs, helping her sit all the way up. "I added you and Damien to my insurance. You have full coverage, so you can go to a proper doctor."

She releases a soft gasp, and I give her a quizzical look, unsure of what caused her reaction.

"We've never had insurance before," she says softly. "The companies I worked for never offered it, or it was too expensive, but I made too much to qualify for any assistance."

"I told you that I would make sure you both have everything you want and need, and I meant it."

"Including birth control?" She quirks a brow.

"Including birth control."

"What's the catch?" she asks.

"No catch. I would never tell you what to do with your body, but my hope is that I'll knock you up before you get on birth control. The thought of you swollen with my baby growing inside of you has me wanting to live inside your sweet pussy until I knock you up."

I cup her mound, and she laughs, shaking her head.

"You're such a caveman."

"Nah"—I palm the side of her face—"just a man who has finally found the woman he wants to spend his life with and doesn't want to waste any more time."

Her eyes sparkle, and I know whatever is about to come out of her mouth will be something sarcastic.

"Well, I already had one baby out of wedlock, and I'm not planning to do it again," she sasses.

"That's an easy fix," I tell her. "We can get married today."

She chokes out a laugh. "If you think I'm marrying a man I haven't even gone on a date with, you're out of your mind."

"A date?"

"Yeah, you know, when a man takes a woman out, usually to dinner or a movie. I know you're not very experienced in this whole relationship thing, but generally, before a man knocks up a woman, he courts her. They date, get engaged, and then married, and then the babies come."

"Well, we already have Damien." I shrug. "So, I don't see why we can't just skip to the marriage part."

I smirk, and I expect her to laugh, but instead, her smile disappears, and something about it rubs me the wrong way.

"Hey," I say, tilting her chin up so she's forced to look at me. "What's going on?"

"Nothing." She shakes her head and pushes me back so she can slide off the desk. "You're right. Who needs to date when we already have a baby? At the rate you're going, I'm sure we'll have another baby soon enough."

She gathers her yoga pants and underwear and puts them on. "Sorry for interrupting your meeting. I actually didn't come in here for sex."

"You can interrupt me anytime you want." I give her a soft kiss on her lips, and she sighs into me. "What did you need?"

"I was going to see if you wanted to have lunch," she says with a smile that feels almost forced.

"I'd love to, but I really need to get back to my meeting."

"No worries," she says, walking out and leaving me with this weird feeling.

I don't know what it is, but it doesn't sit right with me.

I try to pinpoint where our conversation took a turn, but before I can, Matteo strolls in.

"What's going on?" he says, dropping into the visitor seat. "Jesus, bro." He sniffs and then gags. "It smells like a fucking brothel in here."

I glare at him. "Sex with the mother of my child cannot be compared to a whorehouse." I sit across from him. "What do you want? I have a meeting I need to get back to."

"I just wanted to touch base regarding the shipments. Everything appears to be back on track. I added more security at the warehouse, and so far, we haven't had any more issues. I wish we knew who was behind it because I imagine they're not done, and we don't know where they'll strike next or why." He sighs and shakes his head. "It just feels different. I can't figure out their motive. I had the mayor followed, and nothing. I don't think he's behind it."

"They'll fuck up sooner or later, and we'll handle them like we always do. Until then Daniil needs to stay with Brielle any time she leaves the house, Ricky is posted at Damien's school, and Denis will go anywhere Peyton goes when she's not with me."

"How do you do it?" he asks, confusing me with his question. "You fell into this domestic life so easily. The wife, the kid …"

"We're not married—yet."

And then it hits me.

Peyton's smile fell when I jokingly told her we could skip straight to getting married.

Does the idea of marrying me upset her?

"You will be soon enough," Matteo says with an eye roll. "I just don't know how you do it. After watching our parents' dysfunctional marriage, why would you even want *that*?"

I think about his question for a few moments. We were raised in a fucked-up household. Andrey was violent and abusive, manipulative and unpredictable. Our mom was checked out and in survival mode. Brielle was nothing more than a bargaining chip. Matteo had it worse than me because our father thought he was stupid and worthless. At least with me, he saw potential.

But then I think about Peyton and the way she smiles at me. The way she loves our son. She's such a damn good mom during the day, and at night, when it's just the two of us, she lays her head on my chest, and we talk about everything and nothing, and I feel so damn complete. I never knew it could be like this until her. And now, I can't imagine my life without her.

"Because what our parents had isn't the only option," I tell him simply. "And if you stopped fucking women who only wanted you for your wallet and dick, you'd see that."

He scoffs and stands. "I'm good, bro. I'll leave the domestic life to you."

"Hey, Dom," Peyton says, appearing in the doorway. "Oh, sorry."

"You're good," Matteo says, walking toward the door. "I was just leaving."

"I'm making dinner tonight if you want to join," she says.

"Thank you, but I need to get back to the docks to handle some shit. Lorenzo and I are hitting up a new club in South Beach." He waggles his brows. "It's ladies' night."

"Oh, is it like Kings Point?" Peyton asks, perking up.

"It's similar," Matteo says. "Why? You want to join us?"

"Can we?" Peyton asks, glancing at me. "That club was nice, and I had fun dancing … until you tried to kill that guy."

She glares, and I chuckle.

"Dominick doesn't go clubbing," Matteo says.

Peyton's face drops, similar to the way it did when I told her I was too busy to have lunch with her.

"Oh," she says. "That's okay."

She plasters on a fake smile, and our conversation from earlier comes back to me. She wasn't upset about the talk of marriage. She was upset because I ignored her idea of going out on a date.

Fuck, she wants me to take her out on a date.

She walks over to my desk and sets down a plate that I didn't notice she was carrying. "Here's your lunch. I didn't want you to go without eating."

She kisses my cheek and then leaves, and I immediately start brainstorming where I'm going to take her out. It's our first date and long overdue, so it needs to be perfect ...

"All right, I'm out of here," Matteo says, interrupting my thoughts. "If you need me, you know how to reach me. If I don't answer, it's because I'm balls deep in a woman."

"You're so fucking crass," I tell him as he walks away.

I glance at my seat, ready to get back to work, then to my sandwich. I'm behind from working from home, but instead of having a seat, I take my plate and go in search of Peyton so we can eat together, like she wanted, and then I can bring up us going out on a date. I'm sure Martha or Brielle would be willing to watch Damien.

I find her in the kitchen with Martha, who's shooing her away.

"I can help, you know," Peyton says. "Besides, it's not like I have anything better to do. Damien is in school, and Dominick is working."

"Well, I'm sure you can find something to do that doesn't involve trying to steal my job," Martha says with a laugh. "What do you usually do for fun?"

"I don't know." Peyton sighs. "I've always worked. Since before Damien was born, I worked and went to school. I thought after I graduated, I would finally be able to start my career, but ..." Her words trail off, and even though I can't see her face, I can imagine the longing in her features.

She's bored. She's always worked, and now, she's sitting around, twiddling her thumbs while I run my empire. Most women would die for her life, but Peyton isn't most women.

My thoughts go back to our time in the Dominican Republic. She wanted so badly to go to school so she could have a career in hospitality. When I mentioned her having another baby, she brought up her working. But I didn't think about it because the women in our world don't work.

But Peyton isn't from our world.

"Dominick," Martha says, pulling me from my thoughts, "are you finished with your lunch?" She glances at my untouched plate.

"No." I slide onto the stool next to Peyton. "I wanted to have lunch with my future wife." I shoot her a wink, and the most beautiful blush warms her cheeks. "And"—I turn toward her—"I was thinking, tonight, we'd go out … on a date."

Peyton's brows kiss her hairline. "Really? Are you sure? I mean, I know you don't like to go out …"

"I don't like to go out clubbing with my brother, trolling for ass," I clarify. "Taking you out is another story."

"What about Damien?" she asks.

"Oh, I can watch him," Martha offers.

"Where are we going?" Peyton asks with a genuine smile that shows off her twin dimples.

"It's a surprise," I tell her since I haven't thought that far.

Peyton eyes me speculatively. "A surprise? This'd better be a good date." She playfully glares.

"Oh, it's going to be good," I tell her. "It's going to be so good that you'll be begging me to marry you and give you all the babies."

Peyton snorts out a laugh. "I can't wait to see what you have planned."

Me too, I think to myself. *Me fucking too.*

PASSPORT

THIRTY

Peyton

I'M GOING ON A DATE WITH THE FATHER OF MY SON. A MAN I never thought I'd see again, let alone date. All those years ago, when I'd overheard him in his office and ran, I had accepted that I was going to be a single mom. That I would have to be both parents for Damien. And for the next several years, I focused on being just that.

Now that Dominick is in our lives, I can't imagine going back to raising Damien without him. Not that I'm not capable of it. I single-mom'd like a boss. But somewhere deep down, I longed to give my son the home my father had cheated my mom and me out of. Dominick is everything I wanted the father of my son to be—caring, loving, protective, patient. He might be scary and violent outside of our walls, but within them, he's an entirely different man.

A man that I want to date.

I never thought I'd think those words. He's the head of a criminal organization, for God's sake. He threatens and hurts people to get his way. He deals in weapons and drugs and many other illegal imports. But he's more than that. He's tender and smart, and he looks at me and Damien like we're his entire world.

At the end of the day, isn't that all we want in life? To be loved. To spend our life with someone who makes us feel good? I lost my mom too soon, and all I wanted was more time to love her. So rather than pushing Dominick away for the life he grew up in, I'm choosing to embrace who he is and love him the way he is.

Holy shit … I love him.

I shake my head and laugh at myself because I shouldn't be surprised. I never stood a chance against Dominick Antonov. He's motivated when he wants something—or in my case, someone—and he's determined to make me his.

"The dress fits you perfectly," Brielle says, strolling into Dominick's—er, and my—room.

Since the night we had sex in the VIP room at the club and then spent the rest of the night together, I've been sleeping in his room. Little by little, all my stuff has moved from the guest room to his room. The guy is a sneaky bastard, but I kind of love it. He's always up to something, and generally, it's for Damien's or my benefit.

I run my hands down the off-the shoulder white maxi dress, giving myself a once-over in the full-length mirror hanging in the wardrobe. And I say *wardrobe* because it's too big to be considered a closet. It's bigger than the bedroom I shared with Damien in our apartment.

"Thank you for lending it to me."

I fluff my red hair that's hanging down in loose curls and lean in to check my makeup.

"I don't mind," Brielle says, "but we're going to need to go shopping soon. Dominick attends way too many events for you to keep borrowing dresses from me."

I scrunch my nose up at the thought of shopping, and Brielle laughs.

"Have you ever shopped with unlimited funds? Trust me, it's lots of fun."

I laugh and grab my clutch—also lent to me by her. As much as I loathe shopping, she's right. I do need to buy some new clothes. If I plan to send my résumé out, I'm going to need business-appropriate attire for interviews.

I pull my heels on and head downstairs with her.

Martha said she could watch Damien tonight, but Brielle offered, saying she would be home anyway, so Martha could enjoy her evening.

Damien is sitting in the living room with Dominick, doing the homework his teacher assigned them. It's just a coloring page, but he takes it so seriously. It's cute.

When they notice Brielle and me, Damien smiles, and Dominick's eyes light up with lust. I immediately think back to the past few times we've had sex and how he's ripped several articles of clothing of mine in desperation and impatience to get me undressed.

"Don't even think about it," I say to him. "This is your sister's dress, and I need to return it in one piece."

He frowns. "Why the hell are you borrowing my sister's dress?"

"Because she refuses to buy her own clothes," Brielle tattles. "But I already told her we're going shopping. We'll need your black card. She has a lot to buy."

Dominick grins, and I roll my eyes.

"Mommy, you going buh-bye?" Damien asks.

"I'm going out with Daddy," I tell him, walking over and sitting next to him on the couch. "You're going to hang out with Auntie Brielle until bedtime."

"Okay," he says. "And I go to school tomorrow?"

"Yep. You're going to school tomorrow," I answer. "Did you get your homework done?"

"Yeah, Daddy said I'm so smart 'cause I know all my colors and numbers." Damien grins up at me, and my heart melts.

The bond between Dominick and Damien is strengthening every day. It doesn't matter how busy Dominick is. He makes time for our son. And since we discussed him yelling in the house, he hasn't done it again. I've tried to come up with reasons why I should get on birth control, but he's making it damn hard. I've always wanted to have my children close in age, and Damien is about to turn four in a couple of months. I've tried to tell myself it's because I want a career, but I don't see why I can't have both. I raised Damien while going to school and working, and now, I'm done with school and have Dominick as a partner.

"Daddy's right," I tell him. "You are so smart. Can I have a hug and kiss since I won't be home when you go to bed?"

He leans in and gives me a hug and a kiss and then jumps off the couch to give Dominick one too.

Dominick lifts him into his arms and hugs him tightly. "I love you, buddy. Keep a good eye on your aunt and make sure she doesn't get into any trouble."

Dominick smirks at his sister, who rolls her eyes.

"C'mon, Damien." She reaches out to take him from Dominick. "Let's go make a snack for our movie."

"Cookies?" Damien asks, his eyes twinkling in excitement.

"Chocolate chip." Brielle grins.

"Yay! Bye, Mommy. Bye, Daddy!"

Brielle carries him into the kitchen, and Dominick bridges the gap between us.

"Despite you wearing my sister's dress, you look beautiful." He leans in and kisses the corner of my mouth so as not to mess up my lipstick. "You ready for our date?"

"I am."

PASSPORT

THIRTY-ONE

Peyton

"WHERE ARE THE GUARDS?" I ask as Dominick drives down I-95.

Usually, we're driven in the town car by one of Dominick's drivers and accompanied by at least one guard, but tonight, Dominick is driving us in his sports car, which reminds me of him—sleek, expensive, and clean, but not flashy. Because he doesn't need to prove himself to anyone. He loves the finer things life has to offer, but not to show off.

"They're around," he says, laying his hand on my thigh and squeezing. "But I want tonight to be about us."

"Have you found Anthony yet?" I ask, knowing it's driving him insane that he can't find him.

The guy had better enjoy his freedom because after what he did to Brielle—I was sickened when she told me—Dominick and Matteo are going to kill him when they finally get their hands on him.

"Not yet." He grips the steering wheel tighter. "As much as I despise him, I think he's a small player in this game."

He rarely talks about business with me, saying he doesn't want to burden me with shit that I don't need to be concerned with, but I like when he does because I don't think he talks to many people. Aside from Matteo and Lorenzo and his business associate Jaimie, who he mentions once in a while, I don't think he trusts many people.

"I assumed it was him going after our shipments, but I'm starting to question it," he admits. "The mayor is up to some shit, and I think there's someone else involved. We haven't been able to pinpoint who or why, but Anthony was left nothing when his dad died. The company was sold off, and Joseph's wife took the life insurance, using it to move out of town and start over."

He takes the exit toward Miami, and I briefly wonder where we're going tonight. Hopefully, it's somewhere to eat because I'm starved.

"So, if he was left nothing, then he has nothing to lose, and it would make sense that he's coming after you, right?"

Dominick eyes me with a smirk. "Correct, except he had to have paid the guys who fucked with our shipments. And Anthony doesn't have money."

"Then, he has to be getting money from somewhere," I muse, feeling like I'm part of a romantic suspense book. "Or he knows someone with money."

"Ding, ding, ding." Dominick grins. "We thought it was the mayor since he'd backed Anthony at the auction, but he swears he's not working with Anthony, and we haven't found any evidence that contradicts his statement."

"So, you think someone else is coming after you?"

"It wouldn't surprise me. Since Andrey died, I've made a lot of enemies, refusing to do business like him. Usually, when someone comes after you, it's to make a point. But so far, nobody has come forward with any demands."

He pulls into a parking garage, and I realize I was so focused on our conversation that I wasn't paying attention to where we were going.

"So, what are you going to do?" I ask, unlocking my seat belt.

Dominick turns toward me and cups the side of my face with his warm, large palm. "I'm going to enjoy my night with my beautiful girlfriend because all that shit will still be there tomorrow, but tonight is about us."

I roll my eyes, trying to play off his sweet words, but the blush that creeps up my neck and face gives me away.

"There she is," Dominick says, rubbing my cheek. "My Peaches. I love when you blush for me." He leans in and softly kisses my lips. "Stay right there."

He turns the car off and gets out, rounding the front and then opening my door. I eye him for a few seconds, soaking in this gorgeous man. Tonight, he's dressed in a sharp charcoal suit that fits him like it was tailor-made. And it probably was.

Extending his hand, he helps me out of his car and threads his fingers through mine.

He guides us to an elevator and presses the number one. I want to ask where we are and what we're doing here, but the suspense of it all is kind of fun.

When we step out of the elevator, we're met by an older gray-haired gentleman, sporting a sleek tux. "Good evening, Mr. and Mrs. Antonov."

I glance at Dominick, and he smirks, all too pleased with me being referred to as his wife.

"Welcome to the Miami Museum of Art."

I whip my head around to look at Dominick again, who simply nods at the gentleman.

"We're at an art museum?" I ask even though I already know we are.

"You still love art museums, right?" Dominick asks, following the gentleman as he walks us down a narrow hallway and out a back door.

"I do. I love all museums, especially ones filled with art."

But how does he know that?

"But first, dinner," Dominick says, pointing to a table and chairs that are situated outside, overlooking the water.

"Dom," I breathe, my heart beating rapidly in my chest as I take in the romantic scene in front of me.

We're at an art museum.

On the beach.

Having a candlelit dinner.

Then, the gentleman lifts the silver tops covering the plates. And I'm done.

Because sitting on my plate is none other than pancakes, bacon, and eggs.

"Breakfast for dinner," I choke out, tears filling my lids. "You …" I shake my head, and Dominick smiles warmly at me. "You remembered."

Over four and a half years ago, I told him all the things I loved, and he not only remembered, but he's combined them to create the perfect date.

"I once let you go," he says, reaching over the table and taking my hand, "because I thought it was for the best. The truth is, it probably was. I never wanted you to be caught up in my shit. Immersing you in my world is dangerous, and with the enemies I have, loving you is a weakness I can't afford. Despite all that, I still love you and want you because the idea of not having you and our son in my life is unfathomable."

Oh my God … he just said … he just said he loves me.

"You love me?"

Dominick chuckles and shakes his head. "All that, and that's what you focused on? Did you not hear the part about my world being dangerous and me having enemies?"

"Yeah, but I already knew that." I shrug. "What I didn't know was that you loved me."

He scoots back, and I take that as my cue to get up and round the table, climbing into his lap so I'm sitting sideways across his thighs.

"Yes, Peyton, I love you. I'm pretty sure I've loved you since the moment you fell into my lap on the plane. But I didn't want to admit it."

He loves me. This hard, cold businessman, who shows no mercy to anyone, loves me. I should be focused on the facts that his world is dangerous, that he has countless enemies, and that our son needs a guard with him at school to keep him safe. That every moment I'm with him, our lives are at risk.

But the only thing that matters is that he loves me. He listens to me, values me. He is a hands-on, loving father, and he wants to give us a wonderful life.

This is what I've always wanted. What my mom wanted, but died without ever having. To be loved so fiercely by a man that he would do anything for me, including creating a thoughtful, perfect date. It seems so trivial, but isn't that what life is all about? Falling in love and finding happiness.

And Dominick Antonov makes me happy.

"I love you," I tell him, "And I'm so glad we found our way back to each other."

My mouth crashes down on his, and as we kiss, all thoughts of breakfast and the museum are lost. All I want is to love Dominick and be loved by him.

I have no idea who's around or watching—and I honestly don't care—as I reach down and unbutton and unzip his pants. Without breaking our kiss, I pull him out and stroke his long, thick shaft, getting it nice and hard, while Dominick reaches into my panties and massages my clit. We're supposed to be on a romantic first date, yet all I can think about is him fucking me senseless.

I swirl the pre-cum dripping from his slit around his head and use it as lubricant to stroke him hard and slow while he matches my pace, rubbing my clit while sinking a couple of fingers into my center.

"I'm so close," I murmur against his lips, my body coiled so tightly that I have no doubt when my release hits me, it's going to be earth-shattering.

"That's it, baby," Dominick says. "Come all over my goddamn fingers so I can shove my cock inside that warm pussy."

His dirty words are my undoing. I come so hard that fireworks, in vibrant colors, burst behind my lids. He fingers me through my orgasm, not stopping until I sigh in pleasure against his chest.

"Fuck, Peaches, do you have any idea what your orgasms do to me?" he asks as he reaches down with his other hand and tears my panties from my body.

"Dominick!" I chide. "At this rate, I'm going to have no underwear left."

"Good," he says. "Now, lift."

He taps my ass, and I rise, swinging my leg around so I'm straddling him. He guides the head of his cock into me, and inch by inch, I slowly lower myself onto his hard length. It's the first time I've been on top, and I've never felt so full. When my butt meets his thighs, we groan in unison at the way he fits so snugly inside of me.

"It feels like you're hitting my cervix," I joke, then blush when I realize how unsexy that sounds.

Of course, Dominick simply grins, taking it as a compliment. "You riding me, baby? Or do you want me to fuck you from the bottom?"

I attempt to ride him, but in the position I'm in on his lap, I can't use my feet to lift myself up and down. When I pout, he chuckles, captures my mouth with his, and grabs my ass cheeks.

We work together—him moving me up and down and me swiveling my hips to hit the spot that feels good—and within minutes, we both find our release.

I never knew it could be like this. The connection we share goes deeper than anything I've ever felt. I didn't know what I was missing until Dominick, and now, I can't imagine going a day without him.

"Best dessert before dinner," he says with a smirk that has my eyes rolling upward.

How a man can be so deadly and serious yet cheesy astounds me.

"Come, baby," he says, pulling out and grabbing a napkin to stop his cum from ruining our outfits. "Let's get cleaned up and eat. Our night is only beginning."

Breakfast for dinner.

An entire art gallery to ourselves.

And a walk along the beach, where he had a picnic with dessert—actual dessert—waiting for us.

"You realize you've set the bar high," I tell him on the way home.

"I'm okay with that," Dominick says, focusing on the road.

It's late, nearly two in the morning, but I don't feel tired. It's probably the adrenaline buzzing through me from our evening together. Tonight was amazing. More than amazing. And I never wanted it to end.

"Just remember that when—" My words are cut off by the sound of Dominick's phone ringing.

Matteo's name flashes across the screen and my stomach sinks—for him to be calling this late, it can't be good.

"Yeah," he says over Bluetooth after accepting the call.

"I just left the precinct. Four of our guys were arrested for distribution tonight."

"Let me guess," Dominick says, his jaw clenched in anger. "The mayor."

"According to my guy, he signed off on it. Had the cops searching everywhere for them, determined to bring them in. The guy is starting to piss me the fuck off."

"Could you be arrested?" I ask Dominick, thoughts of him ending up in jail and leaving Damien and me flashing through my head.

"We could," Matteo answers before Dominick can, "but it wouldn't hold."

"I'll contact Michael in the morning," Dominick says. "It should give you time to handle things on your end."

"On it," Matteo says.

"Who's Michael?" I ask.

I should probably stop asking questions, but Dominick has never told me to mind my business, and he's never refused to answer me. If I'm going to be in this life with him, then I want to be in the know. Knowledge is power after all.

"Our attorney on retainer," Dominick says to me. Then, to Matteo, he says, "Meet me in my office downtown tomorrow morning so we can go over things."

"You're going to the office?" Matteo asks in confusion, most likely because Dominick has been working from home since Damien and I moved in, only going into the office on occasion.

"Yeah. I promised my future wife I'd keep the violence out of our home. And I am a man of my word."

He ends the call, and a chill spreads through my body at his words. Dominick is pissed. But he's containing it for me. I love that he's willing to do that, but also …

"I don't want you to hide your emotions from me. I like knowing what's going on. I want us to be open with each other and talk. I can handle it."

Dominick pulls up to the wrought iron gate, and the guard lets us through. The garage door opens, and he pulls into the bay and turns off the car.

"What you said means a lot to me," he says, stroking the side of my face. "And I will talk to you, but whoever is doing this is starting a war, and I won't bring that into our home. I couldn't protect my mom and sister, but I will do everything in my power to protect you and Damien. You two have filled these walls with love and laughter and fucking light, and I won't darken it with this shit."

I nod in understanding. "Okay, but just promise me you'll be safe." I frame his stubbled jaw with my hands. "I've grown quite fond of you. And it would suck to lose the man I love and the father of my children."

"Children?" He quirks a brow.

"Well, with how many times you've come in me, I'm bound to be pregnant by now."

I roll my eyes, and he barks out a laugh.

"Just admit you want to have more of my babies," he says, a twinkle in his eye.

"I mean, it wouldn't be the worst thing in the world," I admit. "At least it would give me something to do all day. Between you working and Damien going to school, I'm bored out of my mind here."

I slide out of the passenger seat and close the door, and Dominick meets me by the door to the house.

"Be ready to leave tomorrow at seven … and dress professionally."

"To drop Damien off at school?"

I get out and walk him into his class every morning, but yoga pants and a tank top are as dressed up as I get, even if the other rich, stuck-up moms glare at me judgingly.

"No." He chuckles. "To go to work with me. As much as I love seeing your peach of an ass in those tight pants you wear around the house, I don't think it's appropriate in a place of business."

My eyes widen. When I said I wanted him to talk to me, I didn't mean I wanted to be a part of whatever they were plotting.

"I am not capable of killing anyone," I blurt out, making him double over in laughter.

"Fuck, baby. I needed that." He slides his arm across my shoulders and walks us inside. "Contrary to popular belief, I don't go around killing people on a regular basis," he says.

I raise a brow, silently reminding him of his conversation with Matteo, and he shakes his head.

"Touché," he says with a laugh, pulling me into his side and giving my temple a kiss. "Tou-fucking-ché."

PASSPORT

THIRTY-TWO

Peyton

He was being serious. He brought me to work with him, but not to his office downtown. No, we're standing in the beautiful lobby of Hotel Blu, a resort that—according to Dominick—has three pools, a state-of-the-art gym, a luxury spa, a private golf course, and many other amenities.

"I can't believe you own this," I say in awe.

He told me before he owned a few hotels, but I never pictured them to look like this.

Actually … now that I'm thinking about it, this place screams Dominick. It's luxurious yet understated. It screams wealth, but isn't ostentatious—similar to his home.

"And when we get married, you'll own it as well," he says nonchalantly, like he didn't just mention us getting married and sharing his assets with me in one breath. "Which is why I thought you'd like to work here."

"You want me to work here?" I breathe out, scanning the place with new eyes.

It's my dream job. What I worked through school for. But …

"I don't want to be given a job just because I'm sleeping with you. I mean, I know the sex is good, but …" I smirk, half joking, but Dominick doesn't laugh.

"There are two things I don't mess around with: my family and my businesses. If I didn't think you were capable, I wouldn't have brought you here."

He takes my hand and saunters through the hall and into a room marked *PRIVATE*. It's an office, just as luxurious as the hotel, with a sleek mahogany desk and a comfy brown leather couch.

He slides one of the visitor seats back for me and then rounds the desk, sitting on the other side. He reaches into his briefcase and pulls out a file, which he pushes across the desk, opening it for me to see.

I eye what he's showing me for several seconds, and then I glance up at him in shock.

"That's my résumé." I flip through the pages. "And my grades and internships. You have my letters of recommendations."

And then it hits me. When I submitted applications to local hotels on a job finder site, I applied to this one.

"Based on your degree and experience, I'd like to offer you a paid internship position. Vaughn, the hotel manager, has been asking to be considered for a position at the new hotel when it's complete. Since it's going to be a little bit before that happens, I told him he could start training his replacement."

"And there's no one else in-house who wants to move up?"

"Nobody that has the glowing résumé you have." He leans back and steeples his fingers over his torso. "You said your dream was to work in hospitality at a hotel. Now, you can have it."

"Why are you doing this?" I ask curiously. "I thought you wanted me pregnant. Won't it be pointless to go through the trouble of train-ing me, only to have me take maternity leave?"

"You're not pregnant yet," Dominick says. "And maternity leave is allowed. If you decided to stay home with our baby, then we'd hire a replacement, and when you were ready to go back to work, you'd already know what you were doing. But who says you can't do both? Men have kids and jobs all the time. Why can't women?"

"Are you saying you'll be a stay-at-home dad while I focus on my career?" I smirk, expecting him to laugh me off.

Instead, he simply shrugs. "We'll cross that road when we come to it. If it means we hire a nanny, then that's what we do. But wanting to expand our family doesn't mean you can't follow your dreams."

He gets up and comes over to me, sitting in the seat next to me and turning it to face me. "I want a life with you, Peyton, and I don't want to follow in Andrey's footsteps. My mother felt trapped and oppressed, and I never want you to feel like that."

He reaches out and cups the side of my face, and instinctively, I sigh into his touch.

"If you genuinely don't want another baby with me right now, get on birth control. I'll hope it doesn't work …"

He grins devilishly, and I swear my panties dampen. The man wanting to breed me shouldn't be so hot, but it totally is.

"But I'll support whatever you decide. I thought about you for years, our short time together staying in my head on replay, and now that I have you, I'll take you however I can get you."

"You're making it hard to think clearly," I choke out, overcome by his sweet words.

"Then, take some time to think about it," he says, leaning in closer and placing a chaste kiss on my lips. "The job is yours. I'll introduce you to Vaughn, and he'll show you around today. If you want to train with him, then you can do so. If you want to work at another one of my hotels, you can do that. If you want to stay home, go for it."

"You're being very accommodating," I joke. "And the job sounds like something I'd want, but I don't want to be given it because you love me."

He rests his hand on my hip, and I smile to myself, loving that Dominick craves my touch. The man always has to be touching me in some way. Even at night, if I roll away from him in my sleep, he finds me and drags me back into his arms.

"I know moving here wasn't in your plans," he says. "But I'm going to make sure you never regret it. And if hiring you to work at one of my hotels makes you happy, then it's a win-win because any of them would be lucky to have you as an employee."

"You flatter me." I wrap my arms around his neck and lean on my tiptoes to give him a kiss. "Keep it up, Mr. Antonov, and you'll be rewarded tonight when we get home from work."

I waggle my brows, and he chuckles.

"Oh, really? That's all it takes?" He glides his hands around to my ass and gives my cheeks a squeeze. "Putting your ass to work was the key to your pretty pussy all along?"

"You know what they say," I tell him with a laugh. "Happy wife, happy life."

Today was, without a doubt, one of the best and most exhausting days I'd had in a long time. I'd forgotten how much work went into running a hotel, and I'd never worked in one with this much extravagance. But Vaughn was amazing and didn't treat me with kid gloves, despite Dominick's threat for him to be good to me before he left to go to his office downtown.

I shadowed Vaughn all day, taking notes on my phone and learning more from him in one day than half my classes had ever taught me.

Before I knew it, it was lunchtime, and Dominick texted that he would pick up Damien from school and that when I was ready to go home, a car would be waiting for me.

I teared up at his text—because I hadn't experienced having a partner before—and then got back to work.

Now, it's almost six o'clock, and I'm on my way home, excited to come back tomorrow. I've never minded working—it's all I've ever known—but doing what you love makes it that much better. And I already love working at Hotel Blu. It's clear Dominick only hires efficient, knowledgeable employees, and a sense of pride runs through me when I remember him showing me my file. He might love me and want me to be happy, but he wouldn't have hired me if he didn't feel I was capable.

When I get home, the living room is empty, so I follow the voices into the kitchen, stopping in the doorway to take in the sight in front of me.

Dominick is at the stove with Damien standing on a chair next to him. He's explaining to Damien how to know when the pancakes are ready to be flipped, and Damien is watching intently.

"Bubbles!" Damien yells loud enough to make me flinch, but Dominick just laughs and nods, not the least bit annoyed by our son's overenthusiasm.

"That's right," he says. "You ready to flip?"

When our son nods, Dominick takes Damien's hand around the spatula, and the two of them flip the pancake together.

"Yay!" Damien cheers. "I did it!"

"You did," Dominick agrees, pride in his eyes for something so inconsequential as flipping a pancake. "You ready to do the next one?"

I watch for a few minutes as Dominick and Damien make breakfast for dinner. My heart is so full of love and happiness, and I know there's no going back. This is our life now. In Harbor Point, with the man I never thought I'd have a future with, but who has quickly become a vital part of my world. But not just my world. Damien's too. He's already fallen in love with his dad and become attached, and I could never take that away from him.

"Mmm, it smells delicious," I say, walking into the kitchen and making my presence known.

"We're making pancakes!" Damien says, lifting one up to show me.

"Hey, baby." Dominick leans over without leaving Damien and gives me a quick kiss, causing butterflies to attack my chest. Dominick might be ruthless in other aspects of his life, but in our home, he's soft and romantic. "How was your day?"

I tell him about everything I learned today while they finish cooking. Then, as we sit down to eat, the garage door opens and closes, and Matteo and Lorenzo come sauntering in. I only have eyes for Dominick, but I would be blind if I didn't notice how good-looking all of them are. I can't even imagine the heads they must turn when they go out together.

"What's up, little man?" Matteo fluffs Damien's hair and then has a seat at the six-person table next to him.

Matteo is dressed in his usual jeans and T-shirt, making him look more gangster than billionaire with his dozens of tattoos running up and down his arms and across his hands and knuckles. If Dominick hadn't told me they were business partners and Matteo was worth as much as Dominick, I never would've believed the man had money. Dominick says he dresses like that because he handles the streets, and if he walked around in a suit, he'd lose the respect of the men they employ.

While he looks mean, from the little bit of interaction I've had with him, he's a jokester who doesn't take much seriously. But Dominick says not to be fooled, that his brother is ten times more ruthless than him—and that alone is scary as hell. Because I can't imagine anyone more ruthless than Dominick.

"Dominick," Lorenzo says, having a seat at the end of the table. "Mrs. Antonov."

He nods toward me, and I burst out laughing at his formality.

I don't know much about Lorenzo besides that he's best friends with Matteo, he runs a company that partners with Antonov Enterprises a lot, and he has a younger sister that Dominick was supposed to marry before their dad died and they threw the arrangement out the window.

Unlike Matteo, Lorenzo is dressed in a pair of charcoal slacks and a button-down shirt, the sleeves rolled to his forearms. He's sporting several tattoos as well—a contradiction to the formal attire.

As I glance between the three of them, I find it funny how different they all are, yet they clearly work well together, if their newest expansion project is anything to go by.

Dominick drove me by it the other day to check on it, and it's going to top the one in Coral Bay. When he told me he was a major investor in that project, I was in awe. In the hospitality industry, Antonov Enterprises and Russo Property Group—Lorenzo's company—are spoken about with reverence and respect. To say they are two of the top players in the industry would be an understatement.

"You can call me Peyton," I say to Lorenzo. "Dominick and I aren't married. We're not even engaged."

I take a bite of my pancake and feel Dominick glare at me, but his possessiveness doesn't scare me.

Matteo barks out a laugh. "Careful there, bro. You look like you're about to suffer from a brain aneurysm."

"Feel free to fuck off," Dominick mutters, making Matteo laugh harder and Lorenzo join in.

"Daddy, you said a bad, bad word," Damien says with a laugh.

"Yeah, *Daddy*." Matteo smirks. "No swearing."

Dominick glares at his brother, which only makes Matteo's grin widen.

"Can I have another pancake?" Damien asks.

Before Dominick or I can answer, Matteo reaches over and grabs one for him, plopping it onto his plate. "Here you go, little man."

"Thanks." Damien smiles up at him. "You want a bite?"

He stabs a piece and holds it out for Matteo, who takes a bite without thinking twice, and my heart warms. These men can easily be cruel and cold, yet they're always loving and caring toward my son, proving that violence is a choice—one my sperm donor chose to make when I was growing up.

"Damn, these are good," Matteo says. "Did you make them?"

Damien nods proudly. "Daddy and I made breakfast for dinner." He giggles because he thinks he's getting away with something when we eat food like pancakes for dinner.

"I got the surveys back," Lorenzo says, delving into business.

"Not now," Dominick says. "I'm having dinner with my family. We can discuss business later."

Lorenzo's brows shoot up, but Matteo isn't shocked since that's

Dominick's go-to answer anytime anyone tries to talk business while he's with us.

"I need to head into the gym to get some training in before the fight," Matteo says to Dominick. "Wanna join?"

Before he can answer, I blurt out, "You're a fighter?"

Thoughts of my sperm donor come to mind, and I wonder if they fight in the same organization.

"Yeah," Matteo says. "I have a fight coming up in a couple of weeks."

"What organization are you a part of?" I ask.

"Underground," he says. "I prefer to fight without rules." He smirks. "You ever been to a fight?"

I nod. "My dad was a fighter for the World Boxing Association."

Matteo's eyes go wide. "Who is he?"

"Bobby Johnson … but everyone called him—"

"The Executioner," Matteo finishes for me.

It doesn't surprise me that he knows who he is. He's one of the world's biggest boxers, next to Mike Tyson and Floyd Mayweather.

"Yep, that's him," I say with a shrug.

"Holy shit, that's insane. He's amazing."

"Yeah, he was also an abusive POS who used to beat on my mom until she finally left him," I mutter.

Matteo's grin disappears. "Shit, I'm sorry. Want me to take him out for you?"

"Bad word, Uncle Matty," Damien says as I gape at Matteo, shocked that he just offered to take out my sperm donor.

But then a playful smile spreads across his face, and I cackle.

"I'm good, but thank you."

"All right." He shrugs. "But if you change your mind, just let me know. I could totally take him out. Speaking of which"—he glances at Dominick—"want to come spar with me down at the gym? I could use some actual competition." He side-eyes Lorenzo, who shrugs.

"It's not my fault. I don't want to ugly up my mug," Lorenzo says, reverently stroking the sides of his face with his thumb and forefinger. "I've got a date with Hillary, and she happens to like my pretty face."

"That's because she's shallow," Matteo points out. "Of course she only cares about your looks."

"It's not like that," Lorenzo volleys. "And you're just being a little bitch about her because you saw her first, but she wanted me."

"Watch your mouth," Dominick growls at the same time Matteo barks out a laugh.

"Only because she knew you were husband material," Matteo says, "and she's looking to be a trophy wife."

"You're not husband material?" I ask.

He might be a little rough around the edges and a major jokester, but he's always so nice to Damien and me.

"My brother is a perpetual bachelor," Dominick says dryly. "He'd rather jump off a tall building than settle down."

"That's just because you haven't found the right woman," I tell Matteo, who clearly disagrees based on the look he's giving me. "Look at Dominick. He had no desire to settle down, and now, he's working overtime to knock me up and make me his wife."

It's meant as a joke—sort of—but Matteo's eyes bug out.

"What?" he hisses. "You're trying to have another baby? Are you fucking mad?"

"Language," Dominick comments.

"A baby?" Damien asks. "I want a baby brother!"

"You guys are ridiculous," Matteo says, standing and violently pushing his chair in, making Damien jump.

"Were you not raised in the same house as me?" he says to Dominick, sounding more serious than I've ever heard him before. "Were you not there when our sister was … hurt? All the times our mom suffered at the hands of our piece-of-shit father? I get that you don't want to deny your son, and Peyton comes with him, but why would you willingly bring more innocent people into this fucked-up world?"

Matteo glances from Dominick to Lorenzo. "Your mom and

dad are dead," he says to Lorenzo. "Everybody we've ever tried to keep safe has been hurt in some way or another. It's irresponsible and reckless to—"

"Enough," Dominick snaps. "The world isn't perfect, and ours is even less, but you can't expect us all to live our lives alone."

He stands and walks over to Matteo, getting in his face, and for a second, I worry they're about to fight right here, in the dining room, in front of Damien.

"I know Andrey was a piece of crap, but that's on him, not you. Neither of us is *him*, nor will we ever be. You want to live your life alone? Fine. But don't judge those of us who are trying to find a sliver of light here."

Dominick shocks me—and I'm sure everyone else—when he pulls his brother into a tight hug. "I love you, Matteo, but you have got to stop blaming yourself for what happened to Brielle and Mom. We did everything we could, but Andrey was a sick bastard who got what was coming to him."

He pulls back but keeps his hands on his brother's shoulders. "If you only believe one thing I tell you, believe that you deserve to be loved. My son loves you, I love you ..."

"And so do I," Brielle says, stepping into the dining room.

She's dressed in yoga pants and a tank with her face makeup-free and her hair up in a loose ponytail—more than likely having just gotten home from the Pilates studio where she attends classes several times a week.

"And I don't blame either of you for what happened to me," she adds. "So, stop blaming yourselves. You've protected me your entire lives."

Dominick backs up, and Brielle gives Matteo a hug.

"I was in love once," she chokes out. "And it was the best feeling in the world. Don't knock it until you try it."

"Even after everything you went through, you're telling me you would be okay with falling in love again?" Matteo asks incredulously.

"In a heartbeat," Brielle says, making my heart hurt for her because all she wants is to find love. She might have a rough exterior, but deep down, she's a hopeless romantic. "I want a man who will love me with every ounce of his being, and I won't settle for anything less."

Matteo sighs and shakes his head. "I'm happy for you guys," he says, looking at Dominick and then Lorenzo. "But I just can't do it. It's not for me, but I promise, I will do whatever I can to keep your families safe. Whatever happened to Bri and Mom will never happen again if I can help it."

"Thank you," I say to Matteo. "That means a lot to me."

Matteo clears his throat and nods. "I need to head to the gym. Can we go over shit later?"

Dominick nods, but I can tell he's not ready to let his brother go, so I say, "Hey, Dom, why don't you go to the gym? Damien and I are good here."

"You sure?" he asks.

"Yeah. Just try not to ugly up your face too much." I shoot him a playful wink, and he chuckles.

"You got it." He gives me a quick kiss, then kisses Damien on the top of his head. "I'll be home later. Be good for your mom," he says to Damien before he and Lorenzo follow Matteo out, leaving Brielle and me alone with Damien.

"So, you're looking for love, huh?"

She rolls her eyes. "In this town, it's pretty much impossible. Everyone knows who I am, so they either want to date me to get an in with my brother or because they think it's a challenge."

"You could try online dating. They have sites for everyone. I'm sure they have a site for Mafia princesses."

Nobody ever says that word, preferring to use the term *organization*, but I think it's safe to assume that whatever their family is part of, it's related to the Mafia.

Brielle snorts out a laugh. "Right, and what would they call it? Mafia Dating 'R' Us?"

I laugh. "Plenty of Crime." When she looks at me in confusion, I add, "You know, like Plenty of Fish … Plenty of Crime."

"There's a site called Plenty of Fish?" She laughs.

"Yeah, I joined it when I was looking to date a couple of years after Damien was born."

"And how did it go?"

I scrunch my nose up in disgust, remembering all the losers I went on dates with. "It was filled with a bunch of smelly fish."

PASSPORT

THIRTY-THREE

Dominick

"**S**O, BASED ON THE NUMBERS, WE'RE LOOKING AT ABOUT TWO years to finish," Lorenzo says, sliding the papers over to me. We're sitting at North Harbor Point Country Club, in the private bar that's only available to VIPs, having a drink.

I went a couple of rounds with Matteo at the gym, and to say he's ready for his fight is an understatement. When he clocked me in the jaw and I stumbled back, I tapped out. I have several business meetings with investors this week, and the last thing I need is to look like I was brawling.

So, we came to the country club to get a drink and go over the business plans for the South Harbor Point expansion. Everything is coming together, and with the bids Lorenzo has gotten, the investment will be well worth it.

"I was thinking, once this project is done, if you wanted to get off the streets …" I begin, but Matteo is already shaking his head.

"I know what you're doing, and I appreciate it, but if I'm not running shit out there, someone else will be. I get you want to be a better man for your woman and son, but going soft isn't the way to do it." Matteo swallows the last of his scotch and sets the empty glass down. "You handle the business, and I'll handle the streets. It's how we work. It's how we stay on top."

I nod in understanding because he's right. As much as I'd love to go clean, we're in too deep, thanks to Andrey.

"Look who it is," Matteo says, nodding over to where Mayor Vanderbilt is walking in and sitting down with his wife, who looks more plastic than flesh.

"We've been tracking his phone and movements for weeks now, and we have nothing," Matteo says. "My guess is, he has a burner."

Eric must feel us looking at him because he glances over and flinches, quickly turning back to his wife.

"Guy reeks of guilt," I murmur, finishing off my drink.

"I was at the county clerk's office, picking up the permits," Lorenzo notes, "and Lorna, the receptionist who's always flirting with me, let it spill that he was in a few days prior, trying to find anything he could to prevent our permits from going through. Of course, he couldn't because our plans are airtight."

"He's up to something," I say, "and as soon as we find out what he's hiding, I'm done playing his bullshit games."

"Oh shit, I gotta go." Lorenzo stands. "Hillary's meeting me at my place."

"You looked into her background, right?" I ask.

Lorenzo's worth damn near as much as we are, and it wouldn't be off base to assume a woman wants to use him for his money. I'd never come out and say it, like Matteo did, but I still want to make sure Lorenzo is careful. With his parents gone and his sister away and in college, we're the only family he has.

"Of course I did," he says. "She's twenty-five. She has a degree in communications …"

Matteo snorts. "You mean a degree in gold-digging? Everyone knows women who get a bullshit degree like that are only in school to look for a husband."

Lorenzo glares at his best friend. "You're starting to piss me off. She's a good person, and you'd know that if you just gave her a chance. You hung out with her once."

"And I saw all I needed to see." Matteo shrugs. "She's a gold digger, and you'd better make her sign an ironclad prenup before you put a ring on her finger."

Lorenzo huffs in frustration, then turns his attention to me. "I'll send the rest of the bids your way tomorrow morning so you can look at everything. But the project is heading in the right direction and on schedule."

Once he leaves, I turn to Matteo, wanting to talk to him about something serious. "I'm going to ask Peyton to marry me."

It's something I've been thinking about since the moment she stepped into my life, and with her making no effort to get on birth control, I'd like to do it before I knock her up again. I'll never regret our time together, but I'd like to make an honest woman out of her now. Give her and Damien my last name.

"I kind of figured," Matteo says with a shake of his head. "When?"

"I was thinking about taking them away this weekend. She starts working at Hotel Blu on Tuesday, after the holiday weekend, and I imagine once she's all in, I'll have to pry her away to take a vacation."

He nods in understanding.

"I plan to put her in my will, God forbid something happen to me, but I …" I look at him, and even though he's hell-bent on not wanting a family of his own, I know he meant it when he said he would do everything in his power to protect mine. "I need to make sure if something happens, they're taken care of. That you'll take care of them. You're the only person I'd want to fill my shoes."

"Are you asking me to fuck your wife and take over as Damien's daddy if you die?" Matteo deadpans, and the image of Matteo and Peyton having sex has my blood boiling.

"What? No!" I bark, and then he grins.

The motherfucker grins.

"I'm just fucking with you." He laughs. "Though, if something happens to you, she'll want to eventually fuck someone else. Why not me?"

His mouth curves into a shit-eating grin, and I reach over and slap him on the back of the head, making him laugh harder.

"I just want you to make sure they're taken care of," I say with a sigh, this conversation exhausting me. "And Brielle too. I don't know where her head is at since she came home, but I was thinking maybe, eventually, she might want to work at Antonov Enterprises. She mentioned she hates everything about the name, but I'm hoping she'll change her mind one day."

"Yeah, I was shocked when she said she wanted to fall in love. After everything she's been through …"

"Peyton's the same way." I chuckle. "She reads these romance books and thinks it's all real. But I'm determined to give her the fairy tale, starting with a weekend away and a proposal that would have those guys in the books jealous."

Matteo snorts out a laugh. "Never thought I'd see the day when my ruthless boss of a brother would be comparing himself to romance books."

I pat him on his shoulder and stand, ready to go home to my family. "That's what the right woman will do to you."

PASSPORT

THIRTY-FOUR

Peyton

"**D**isney World?" I smile at Dominick when we drive up to the main entrance.

When he got home from sparring with Matteo, he told me to pack a bag, that we were going away in the morning and not to ask where because it was a surprise.

"Mickey Mouse!" Damien shouts from the back seat, pointing to the big mouse overhead. "I go on all the rides?"

"All of them," Dominick tells him, glancing in the rearview mirror and smiling at our son. "I considered taking you to the DR," he says, "since that's where we spent that first night together." He waggles his brows, and I feel myself heating at the memory. "But I wanted it to be a family trip, and I remembered Damien mentioning he's never been here."

I recall that conversation. Damien and Dominick were watching cartoons, and *Mickey Mouse Clubhouse* came on. Dominick asked if he'd ever been to Disney World, and Damien looked at him like he was crazy. Because he didn't know it existed. We couldn't afford it before, and he's not old enough to talk to his friends about their vacations.

Of course, Dominick pulled the videos up on his phone, and by the fifth video, Damien was begging to go. I was surprised Dominick had been since his parents didn't seem like the type to go to theme parks, but when he said he had gone there on a school trip, that made sense.

When his mom came by last night to visit, Damien told her about the trip, and she asked if she could go, saying her fiancé was out of town on business. Even though she had no idea where we were going, she said she would love to spend time with her grandson, which led to Brielle wanting to join. Matteo said he'd hold the fort down and he'd see us when we got back. Now that I know the destination, I'd bet Matteo had already known, and that was why he didn't want to go.

"Auntie Bri, you go on all the rides with me?" Damien asks.

"Of course," Brielle says.

"*Babu*," Damien says, butchering *Babushka*, like he always does. "You go on all the rides with me?"

Larisa grins down at Damien. "As long as you hold my hand. I'm a little scared of that big mouse."

Damien giggles. "I'll hold your hand, *Babu*."

Once we get inside, we rent a stroller because I already know Damien will never last walking all day, and then we take off to the first ride.

The day is filled with fun and laughter. We go from ride to ride, and even though it's about Damien, everyone has a good time. I get to know Larisa more, having a chance to talk to her while we wait in the long lines, and see a softer side of Brielle as she plays with Damien. My heart hurts for her—because she was forced to give up her unborn baby—and I hope that, one day, she meets a man who deserves her, and she has the chance to become a mom.

Of course, Dominick insists on buying Damien a souvenir from every ride, and by the time night falls and we're heading back to the car to go to our hotel, Damien is passed out in Dominick's arms while Brielle, Larisa, and I carry the millions of toys and stuffed animals.

"Did you have a good day?" Dominick asks as we look out over our terrace at the lit-up theme park and hotels in the distance.

We're staying in a suite at a beautiful resort on Disney property. Larisa and Brielle offered to get their own room, but I wasn't having it. This is a family trip, and they're family.

"It was like a fairy tale. Thank you." I lean over and give him a kiss. "Today was truly magical."

A loud pop sounds in the distance, and I jump, glancing out and seeing it's the beginning of the fireworks.

"Oh my God," I breathe. "We can see them from here?"

When Dominick doesn't answer, I turn around and find him down on one knee, a ring box in his hand.

"Dominick!" I gasp. "What …"

The fireworks continue to go off in the background, but my only focus is on the man in front of me.

"My world isn't a fairy tale," he says, looking up at me. "And nothing about it is magical. Most days, it's dark and dangerous and filled with corruption.

"I thought I had my future mapped out. I accepted my life for what it was. But then you fell into my lap"—he chuckles, and I do, too, remembering how we met—"and everything I'd thought I knew felt like a lie. I was drawn to your goodness, to the light you emanate, but out of every fucked-up thing I'd done in my life, keeping you for myself felt like the biggest sin, so I let you go." He shakes his head and sighs. "But fate intervened, and you came back into my life, bringing along the greatest gift I could have ever asked for, and I knew there was no way I could let you go again."

He stands and opens the black box, and I choke on a sob. Not because the ring is beautiful, but because his words are.

"If getting to love you and keep you for the rest of my life is a sin, I'll gladly go to hell." He takes the ring out of the box. "Peyton Wright, will you make me the happiest man on earth and become my wife?"

"Yes!" I breathe out as he slides the ring onto my finger. "I would love nothing more than to be your wife."

I jump into his arms, wrapping my legs around his torso, and kiss him passionately as the fireworks continue to go off.

"And, Dominick," I say once we break apart to catch our breath, "I will gladly follow you to the pits of hell if it means I get to spend my life with you. I've always preferred the heat to the cold anyway."

Dominick carries me back inside, and I jump when Brielle says, "Congrats!"

"Oh my God. You were watching?" I ask, trying to get Dominick to put me down.

"Dominick asked me to take pictures. I'm so happy for you both." She rushes over and gives us each a kiss on our cheeks. "Go celebrate, and I'll send you what I took later."

"You had her take pictures?" I ask him as he lays me on the bed once we're in our room. "That's so sweet."

"I see all the pictures you take of Damien. I figured you'd want some from tonight. She was told to stay hidden, but she obviously couldn't help herself."

He crawls up my body and kisses my lips and then trails hot kisses along my jaw and over to my neck. I want to feel him inside me, be connected as close as possible, but I also love when he takes his time worshipping me. When he gets to my collarbone, he stops so he can remove my clothes.

Thankfully, I'm wearing cute pajamas, so the pictures will be good. But I wonder if I can convince him to do an engagement shoot with me. I've always wanted to do one …

"What are you thinking about?" he asks, breaking me from my thoughts.

Since I wasn't wearing a bra, with my shirt off, my breasts are exposed and on display for Dominick. He licks one nipple and then the other.

"I was thinking about what it would take to convince you to do an engagement photo shoot with me," I admit truthfully.

Dominick smirks. "I'm sure I could be persuaded."

The glimmer in his eye is playful, and I love this side of Dominick, so I go along with it.

Sitting up, I push him off me so he's on his back, and then I straddle his thighs.

"Take your shirt off," I tell him as I slide down, my center rubbing against his cock, covered by his sweatpants.

When I'm off him, I settle between his legs and pull his pants down, his hard length springing out and making my mouth water.

I waste no time wrapping my fingers around his shaft and taking him into my mouth. I start slow, teasing his head, sliding the tip of my tongue into his slit, while I gently roll his balls in my palm, knowing he loves when I play with them.

"Jesus, fuck," Dominick groans, delving his fingers into my hair and tightening his hold on my scalp.

Once his cock is wet with my saliva, I start to suck him off with a purpose. Bobbing my head up and down, I suction my cheeks and work my mouth and tongue over his hard length.

"Fuck, baby," he moans.

I assume he's going to come down my throat since he knows I'm good with it, so I'm shocked when he uses his grip on my hair to pull me off him.

Before I can question it though, he's grabbing me by my hips and lifting me over his cock. As I take him into me, we both moan at how good it feels.

"Your mouth is fucking perfect," he breathes when I'm completely filled by him. "But this pussy, coming inside you and risking the chance of getting you pregnant ... that is what will persuade me."

I shake my head and chuckle under my breath because I shouldn't be surprised. The man is determined to get me pregnant before I can get on birth control. Little does he know, I have no intention of getting on birth control. Was I wary at first? Yes. But now, I know my future is with Dominick, and I want the same thing he wants—to fill our home with love and add to our family.

I place my hands on his hard chest and start to ride him, my hips moving in a way that I know will have us both coming shortly. He feels so good like this, with my pussy sucking him in and the head of his cock hitting the deepest part of me.

As my orgasm approaches, Dominick sits up and wraps his arms around me so our chests are touching. His mouth captures mine, his tongue tangling with my own, and in this position, with our bodies connected in the most intimate way, we both find our release.

With our bodies still sensitive and our breathing heavy, he takes the hand with my beautiful engagement ring and brings it to his lips.

"This ring means that you're mine," he says, glancing up at me with love and adoration in his gaze. "You don't ever have to persuade me to do anything. Whatever it is you want, I will give it to you—always. You and our son are my world, and I will do everything in my power to ensure you're happy … including taking cheesy-ass engagement photos."

PASSPORT

THIRTY-FIVE

"Wow! This place is insane."

"Welcome to The Underground," Dominick says as he guides me through the crowd of people who are all drinking and smoking and …

"Are they placing bets?"

Dominick chuckles. "Hundreds of thousands of dollars get exchanged during the fights down here. When my brother fights, it can get into the millions."

"But he's undefeated," I say as we step into the VIP area, where we'll be watching the fight. "Why would anyone bet against him?"

According to Dominick, the warehouse where the fight is taking place is owned by the Antonovs. When the last place got shut down, Matteo asked if he could set up a cage here, and Dominick agreed. They host several fights a month, and I was shocked when Dominick told me how much they bring in from the admission alone.

The Antonov brothers are clearly smart businessmen, and I told Dominick that I would love to one day learn all about his business ventures. There's a reason why their company made several Forbes lists this year.

When I moved in with him, I thought I would be in the middle of a Mafia romance novel, but I quickly learned that the days of Al Capone are no longer, and while they deal with territories and have plenty of illegal businesses, their legitimate businesses overpower the others.

"All businesses are corrupt," Dominick pointed out one night when we were talking. "Some are just more willing to get dirty to get what they want."

"They bet against him, anticipating that this will be the time he gets knocked down," Dominick says when we have a seat on the black leather couch. "People thrive on jealousy. For every person who loves my brother and hopes he wins, there are two hoping he doesn't."

"That's mean," I say, and Dominick chuckles.

"That's life." He presses his palm to my cheek. "The higher up you get, the more people want to see you fall."

He places a soft kiss on my lips, and I wish we were somewhere private instead of here. From the moment Dominick and I reconnected, I haven't been able to get enough of him.

Since we returned from our family trip, we've settled into a routine of sorts. We have breakfast together, one of us drops Damien off at school, we go to work—where I love learning about everything that is involved in the hotel industry—we have dinner as a family and spend time with Damien until bed, and then we spend the rest of the night lost in each other. Sometimes, life feels so perfect that I can't help but wait for the other shoe to drop.

"Not here," he murmurs against my lips when he notices me squirming in my seat. "I don't share, and not a single person in this place deserves to see an ounce of your pleasure."

Where we're sitting is roped off, but we're close enough to everyone else to see and hear everyone talking and placing bets. We're surrounded by several of Dominick's guards, so although people can see us, nobody can get near us.

There are metal detectors at the door, and bouncers check everyone as they come in to ensure nothing goes down.

"Wow, this place is insane!" Brielle says, forcing Dominick and me apart. "About time I get to watch Matteo in action."

"You've never been?" I ask her.

"Nope, I was too young and innocent." She glares at Dominick. "They'd never let me go anywhere or do anything."

"It was for your own protection," Dominick notes.

"Yeah, yeah." She rolls her eyes. "I can't wait to see Matteo kick some ass."

"Both Irvin and Matteo are undefeated," Dominick says. "It's going to be a damn good fight."

"And who are you betting on?" I jokingly ask.

"I have a hundred K on Matteo," Lorenzo says, walking over with his arm hooked around a beautiful woman's neck.

He reaches over to Dominick, and they do that weird handshake-with-a-bro-hug thing guys do. Then, he introduces us to …

"This is my fiancée, Hillary," Lorenzo says, smiling adoringly at the woman, who smiles and shows off her ring. "I proposed last night, and she said yes."

"It's nice to meet you," I tell her, standing and giving her a hug. "I'm Peyton, and this is my fiancé, Dominick."

Dominick gives her a slight nod with no smile, and I glare at him to be polite. Both he and Matteo have mentioned they're not fans of Lorenzo's girlfriend—who is apparently now his fiancée—but she seems nice enough.

We've only just sat back down when Hillary says, "So, Dominick, Lorenzo tells me that you're partnering on the waterfront expansion in South Harbor Point. That's exciting."

"I'm here to watch my brother fight," Dominick says tersely, "not be interviewed."

When I glance at him in confusion, he says, "Hillary used to be a reporter."

My eyes widen at that tidbit of information because why in the world would Lorenzo be dating a reporter of all people when they have so much to hide?

"I'm retired," she says with a forced smile.

"Oh, what do you do now?" I ask politely, refraining from asking how a woman who looks to be in her twenties can already be retired.

"I'm in between jobs. I moved here from Georgia—"

"Really?" Dominick asks, cutting her off. "I could've sworn you were from Coral Bay, and I don't believe getting fired for not showing up to work is the equivalent of retiring. But I could be wrong."

"Oh! I'm from Coral Bay," I tell her, trying to ignore Dominick's rudeness. "New Town. How about you?"

She swallows thickly, her eyes darting between Dominick and me, and there's clearly something off with her, but Lorenzo obviously cares about her, so I'm not about to ostracize her, like Dominick is doing.

"Yes," she says slowly. "I moved from Georgia to Coral Bay for a job, but the producers and I didn't see eye to eye, so they let me go before I could quit. And now, I'm trying to figure out what I should do next."

"I totally get that," I tell her. "Any ideas on what your next move will be?"

"Based on the size of that ring, I'm thinking trophy wife," Brielle deadpans.

"Bri!" I hiss, wondering what the hell is wrong with her and her brothers.

Dominick snorts out a laugh, and Brielle shrugs.

"Stop your shit," Lorenzo says, glaring at Brielle. "Nobody has said a word about you being home for weeks now and doing nothing with your life, so don't judge others." He protectively wraps his arm around his fiancée, who I notice flinches but quickly schools her features. "Hillary is working as my assistant while she figures things out, and she's doing a damn good job."

Brielle shoots daggers at Lorenzo, but thankfully, the music gets louder, and the lights lower slightly, indicating the start of the fight. Usually, on televised fights, there are several smaller fights leading up to the main event, but apparently, here, there's only one fight.

Since we're above the people on the ground level, we can see without standing, but that doesn't stop me from getting up and walking toward the front so I can get a better view of Matteo fighting.

It's been years since I've watched a fight—since my parents were still together—and as he gets announced and walks out with the music pumping and his entourage flanking him, I can't help the way my heart pounds in my chest. I know Matteo isn't my dad. He would never hurt anyone he claims to love. But that doesn't stop my brain from connecting the two. I wanted to be here to support Matteo, but now, I'm wondering if that was a mistake.

Thankfully, Dominick comes up behind me and encircles his arms around my waist, resting his chin on my shoulder.

"So, how much did you bet?" I ask, watching as the other guy comes out and gets booed.

"I don't bet," he says. "I hate him fighting, but it's what he feels he needs to do to exorcise whatever demons he has, so I support him."

"You're a good brother," I tell him, reaching up and kissing the corner of his jaw.

The fight begins, and the guys circle each other for a few seconds before Irvin takes his first swing, missing Matteo's face by an inch. Matteo retaliates by rushing Irvin and lands a few strategic hits. The fight goes on for several minutes, and when I ask Dominick how long each round is, he tells me that there are no rounds. They fight until one can't fight anymore.

They're both evenly matched, their punches and kicks landing, and when Matteo stumbles back, I worry Irvin is going to get the upper hand. But then it's as if Matteo gets a second wind because he comes back harder, faster, more determined. Every punch is delivered in rapid-fire, and before we know it, Irvin is knocked out cold, and the ring announcer is congratulating Matteo on his win.

The crowd goes crazy, and I'm about to ask Dominick if we can go down and see Matteo when an alarm sounds, making me jump.

"Fire alarm," Dominick says as everyone starts to push their way out of the warehouse. "Stay with me."

He threads his fingers through mine, and I follow him out of the VIP area.

At first, I assume someone's pulling a prank, but when the smoke starts to filter in, obscuring our vision, I know it's not a mistake. Someone set the warehouse on fire.

Dominick, Lorenzo, and the guards get us out through a back exit. When the door opens and I suck in a breath of fresh air, I realize how bad the smoke was in there.

"Where's Matteo?" I ask as Dominick flits between making calls and barking orders and texting.

"He can handle himself," Lorenzo says.

"Fuck! The warehouse at the port is on fire as well," Dominick hisses, glancing at Lorenzo. "Lorenzo, you drove here?"

"Yeah," he says.

"Daniil, I need you to take the women home." He looks at Hillary. "Her too. I want the house on lockdown. I've already told Ricky to stay with Damien."

Daniil nods, and then we're rushed into the town car without Dominick. I want to tell him I love him, to stay safe, but it all happens too quickly, and before I can get a word out, we're being whisked away.

The ride home is filled with tension. I wish I could be with Dominick, but I know I would only be a distraction. He'd be too worried about keeping me safe, and he wouldn't be able to focus on dealing with whatever was going down.

The second we arrive at the house and step inside, I know something is off. I can feel it. For one, the house alarm didn't go off, and it's pitch-black, like the electricity is out.

Brielle must feel it, too, because she pauses at the doorway and glances at Hillary and me, putting her finger to her lips for us to remain quiet.

And then I hear it.

Damien's cries.

Without thinking, I gasp loudly and take off toward the stairs.

Only Brielle stops me and shakes her head. "Whoever is up there is armed."

My heart pounds in my chest.

This can't be happening again.

Someone has my baby.

Daniil is outside.

Ricky should be protecting him. Where is he?

Brielle walks quietly over to Dominick's office, and I follow while Hillary stays frozen in her spot near the door.

"Here," Brielle says, handing me a gun. "It's loaded. Don't shoot unless you need to. We don't want to risk hitting Damien."

I nod in understanding and then follow her upstairs, gasping in fear and heartbreak when we find a body lying on the floor, bleeding out.

Ricky.

Whoever is in here shot and killed him.

"Enough," a man says, forcing me to look away from Ricky to see where the voice is coming from.

I hear Damien's muffled cries, telling me whoever has him has covered his mouth.

His room is empty, so Brielle and I follow the sounds that lead to the other wing of the house. There are two sets of stairs—one that stems from the living room and the other that leads toward the back of the house. If you're planning to go to the backyard or pool, you can take the back stairs instead.

We both must realize this is what whoever took him is doing because we pick up our speed, racing down the steps. I can hear whoever has my son descending, his footsteps loud against the marble.

And then we see him. A man I don't recognize is holding my son in his arms.

He reaches for the back door when Brielle yells, "Stop!"

I'm not sure why she made our presence known, but when the guy stops, I'm assuming it was just for that. To catch him off guard.

He turns around, not even bothering to hide who he is, but I don't know him.

"Anthony," Brielle hisses, and my heart drops to my stomach.

It's the asshole who raped her, who broke into my apartment and tried to steal my son.

And he's come back, determined to succeed.

"Take one more move, and I'll blow his brains out," Anthony says, pointing the barrel of a gun at my son's temple.

I whimper at the thought of him ending my baby boy's life.

Anthony glances at me. "Let Dominick know that it's not personal," he says with a smirk. "It's just business."

"You don't want him," Brielle says, her voice calm and confident. "You want me. I'm the one you wanted to marry. Give him back to his mother and take me."

I'm petrified of what's happening in front of me, but the fact that she's willing to take my son's place warms my heart.

I hold my breath, praying Anthony will agree, but instead, he laughs.

Fucking laughs.

"You?" He scoffs. "I don't want you. You're damaged goods, bitch. You were *supposed* to be mine. That baby was supposed to be mine. But your family took everything away from me. And now, I'm going to do the same to you."

He points his gun at Brielle, and I scream in panic. Everything happens quickly. Damien wiggles out of Anthony's hold and darts toward me at the same time a gun goes off.

Anthony flies backward, his body hitting the back door and then sliding down and slumping against the floor.

I pull Damien into my arms and hold him close, trying to protect him in case anyone shoots at us.

"Fuck you!" Brielle yells, making me look up.

She's standing over Anthony, and I realize when Damien got away, she shot Anthony before he could shoot her.

"I hope you rot in hell," she says, kneeling in front of him with her gun still pointed at him even though it's clear he's no longer a threat.

Anthony chuckles. "You think you've won," he chokes out, his breathing labored as he slowly dies. "You have no idea what you're in for." He laughs again, only it's garbled this time.

And then he goes silent, his threat hanging in the air.

PASSPORT
AIR
HGKB15
FK
25 FEB 18
15:45
JOHN
New
London
gate 35

THIRTY-SIX

Dominick

"**A**RE YOU FUCKING KIDDING ME?" I BARK AS I WATCH OUR warehouse, filled with millions of dollars' worth of product, burn down.

"Four of our guys are dead," Matteo says, rounding the corner. "Whoever did this ..."

His voice is drowned out by the sound of my phone, notifying me that our home security just went down. I stare at it, trying to make sense of it all, when all the pieces click into place.

"The warehouse fires were a distraction," I tell Matteo, running back to the car. "The house is under attack!"

While Lorenzo drives, I call Daniil, who answers on the first ring.

"Boss, we have a problem," Daniil says, confirming my suspicions. "Anthony took out a portion of the security system. He had to have known what he was doing because the guard gate wasn't touched, so nobody suspected a thing.

"I was checking the perimeter when I heard a gunshot. By the time I made it inside, Brielle had shot Anthony. Everyone is okay. But ... Ricky is dead, and Martha is hanging on by a thread. He must've shot them when he got in."

Fuck. I hate that the people I care about, who care about my family, are dead or injured. But the relief I feel, knowing that my sister protected my fiancée and son, is strong.

"He was acting alone?"

"We're doing a sweep of the house now, but according to the cameras, he was."

"We'll be there in ten minutes. We're across town."

I hang up and shake my head. Since I had my phone on speaker, I don't have to repeat anything to Matteo or Lorenzo.

"This was a fucking setup," Matteo growls. "We underestimated that fucker."

He bangs his hand against the seat next to him, and I feel his frustration tenfold.

My family was depending on me to keep them safe, and I failed. This should be the moment when I admit that they're better off without me, but I can't live without them, so that means I'm just going to have to work that much harder to keep them safe.

"I don't believe it," I say. "Anthony isn't that smart or resourceful. He's working with someone."

And when I find out who, I'm going to end their fucking existence.

When we arrive at the house, I go straight for Peyton and Damien, who are sitting in the living room, hugging each other.

"Daddy!" Damien yells, flying into my arms when he sees me. "The bad man got me while I was sleeping, but Auntie Bri shot him dead."

Fuck, I hate that my kid has been through this. That his innocence has been ripped from him because of my fucked-up world. He should be in bed, dreaming about happy shit, not getting kidnapped and witnessing murders.

"I'm so sorry, buddy," I tell him, sitting next to Peyton and pulling them both into my arms. "Nobody is ever going to hurt you again."

"Dominick," Peyton chides, "you can't make promises like that …"

"Yes, I can," I hiss. "Because neither of you is ever leaving this fucking house again. We're upping security, and you're homeschooling Damien."

I give Damien a kiss on his forehead, then give Peyton one. "I need to handle the police, and then we're going to go to a hotel for the night."

"Thought you just said we're never leaving the house again."

She raises a brow, and I glare at her.

Smart-ass.

"Dominick, there's something you need to know," Brielle says when I walk over to where she's talking to my team of men.

We need to call the police. Too many deaths occurred. But before we do that, we need to make sure we have our ducks in a row.

"When Anthony was dying, he said we might think we've won, but that we have no idea what we're in for."

Her words are confirmation that he wasn't working alone. I was hoping I was wrong, that Anthony's death meant my family would be safe. But someone else is out to get us, and because they were using Anthony as a front and he's dead, we have no idea who it is.

"You did good," I tell Brielle, pulling her into a hug. "I can never thank you enough for saving my son."

"It felt good to be the one to end that bastard's life," she murmurs against my chest. "I just wish I could've gotten more info out of him before he died. But I did get this …"

She slips something into my pocket, and without looking, I know it's his phone.

I thank her and hope that it will unlock some answers to our questions.

After calling the police and having Peyton, Brielle, and Hillary give their statements, I take my family over to Hotel Blu to stay in the penthouse suite while the police turn the house into a crime scene investigation.

Damien insists on checking on Martha, so I call the guard I have there, and he informs me that she pulled through surgery and is recovering in the ICU. After what she's been through, I'm going to insist she finally retire. She deserves some peace and quiet.

With the knowledge that Martha will be okay, Damien thankfully falls asleep quickly, and Brielle excuses herself to her room. Matteo stayed behind to oversee things at the house, and Lorenzo took his fiancée home.

"What are you doing?" Peyton asks, looking up from the book she's been reading for the past half hour.

"Searching for new houses."

There's no way I'm moving my family back into that house. It has too much history, too much corruption hidden in the walls. My son witnessed a murder there, and I'll be damned if I bring him back.

Besides, we need somewhere safer. The way Anthony and whoever he was working with was able to get in proved that it wasn't as safe as I need it to be.

Peyton nods in understanding, and her lack of argument tells me that she agrees. I pull her into my side, and we scroll through listings. She comments on certain ones, and the ones she seems to like, I note to look into them further.

When she falls asleep, I put the laptop away and carry her into bed, holding her in my arms and praying that nothing ever touches her or our son. I finally got them back, and I'll be damned if I lose them.

PASSPORT

EPILOGUE

Dominick

"**D**OMINICK, IT'S ENOUGH!"

I glance up at my gorgeous fiancée in confusion, but I don't have to wait long for her to elaborate.

"Damien and I are sick of being cooped up in this house. Don't get me wrong. It's beautiful and perfect. Damien loves his room and the fact that you managed to find a house with the perfect *Giving Tree* to replace the old one. But you need to let us out. It's like we're in jail!"

I take a deep breath, not wanting to upset her further, knowing we're never going to see eye to eye on this. It's been three months since we lost Ricky and came way too close to losing Martha.

Despite us having access to Anthony's phone, he wasn't as stupid as we thought because he left no trace of any evidence of him working with or for someone else, so we are no closer to knowing if we have a bigger threat looming over our heads or if Anthony said what he did to fuck with us.

Shortly after everything went down, we started searching for a new house. Since my mom was already pretty much living with her fiancée—who is now her husband—she moved in with him. Brielle chose to move in with us, unsure where she wants to live, and Matteo—despite me asking him to live with us—moved into a condo in one of the developments we own, saying it was time for him to have his own place.

At first, Peyton was busy setting up the new place, so she didn't fight me on my refusing to let them go anywhere. We set a wedding date, and then she was busy with Thanksgiving. But then Damien began to complain that he wanted to invite his friends from school to his upcoming birthday party, and she started asking when he was going back.

"I'd hardly call a twenty-thousand-square-foot home jail, but to each their own," I say dryly.

"Dominick," she says, rounding the desk and climbing into my lap, "I understand you want to keep us safe"—she runs her fingers through my hair, and I lean back, gripping the curves of her luscious hips, wishing we could just stay in this bubble forever—"but Damien misses his friends, and I miss working, and … you're going to have to let us out because I need to go to the doctor."

"What?" I sit up and lift her onto my desk, and then I search her for what could possibly be wrong.

"Stop." She laughs, swatting my hands away. "I'm fine, but my period is late, and I need to have my pregnancy confirmed."

Her period is late.

Pregnancy confirmed.

"You're pregnant?" I breathe out, my hands going to her soft belly.

"I think so." She smiles. "But this time, I want to do it the right way. With you by my side."

Fuck, she's pregnant. If she thinks I'm going to let her out of the house now, she's wrong. She just gave me even more reason to keep her safe in our house. With the brick wall—topped with electric fence and barbed wire—that runs around the perimeter of our property, the state-of-the-art guard gate and wrought iron gates, and the additional guards manning the area, this house is a fortress that will protect my family.

"Say something," she says, her brows furrowed in concern.

"I love you." I press a kiss to her supple lips. "I can't wait to marry you and have this baby with you. I'll take care of it."

"Thank you," she says with a soft smile.

I'm sure she thinks she's being let out of the safety of our home, and she'll be mad when she learns she's not, but I will stop at nothing to ensure that my family is protected.

"What the hell is this?"

Peyton glares at me, but I ignore her as we walk over to meet the doctor.

"This is Dr. Drescher," I tell her. "She's one of the best OB-GYN's in South Florida, and she'll be confirming your pregnancy and making sure everything looks good."

"No." Peyton steps back and shakes her head. "No. This is not happening. I love you, but if you don't let me out of this goddamn house, I'm going to scream it down."

The doctor shuffles uncomfortably. "I can come back …"

"No," Peyton says again. "You will not come back. We will go to you, like a normal couple. I'm assuming you have an office?"

The doctor nods.

"Great!" Peyton says. "We'll meet you there."

The doctor is torn between staying and going, so I nod at her, letting her know we'll meet her at the office.

Once she's gone, I step toward Peyton, who's looking at me like she wants to murder me with her bare hands.

"Peaches—"

"No, Dominick!" she yells. "Don't you *Peaches* me. This is insane. We are going to the doctor, and Damien is going back to school, and I am going back to work!"

She captures my face in her hands and looks up at me with her beautiful emerald eyes. "We are not going to live our lives like this anymore. I love that you want to keep us safe, but we're not living. Please," she begs.

My heart cracks in my chest because I hate the thought of her being upset, but I also want her to be alive.

"If something happened to you or our son …"

"I get it," she chokes out. "I get it. I want nothing more than for all of us to be safe, but we're not enjoying our life together. I want to go on dates with my fiancée, to take our son to the park and the movies and the museums. I want family trips and dinners out. I love our home and our life, but you're making me resent it and you."

Fuck, I know she's right.

"Okay," I tell her. "We'll go to the doctor and then let the school know Damien will be returning next week. But, Peyton, you don't go anywhere without guards and never in anyone else's car."

"Okay, thank you." She kisses me and then pulls back. "Now, let's go confirm this pregnancy."

Since we didn't want to get Damien's hopes up yet, Brielle stayed with him while we headed over to the doctor's office.

Martha listened to me, and the day she was let out of the hospital, I moved her into a small cottage—of her choosing—on the water, where she can retire and spend the rest of her days relaxing. I also promised she was welcome to visit anytime she wanted.

Dr. Drescher had the morning blocked off for us, so her nurse takes us back. She gets Peyton's blood pressure, has her give a urine sample, and collects some blood.

When she's done, she leads us into a private room and gives Peyton a paper gown to put on, and then says she and the doctor will be back in a few minutes.

"How are you feeling?" I ask while she changes out of her clothes and puts on the gown that shows off her pert ass and sexy back.

"Okay," she says, sitting back on the medical bed. "I haven't really had any morning sickness, like I did with Damien, so that has me a little nervous."

I walk over and take her hand in mine, bringing it up to my lips. "If you're not pregnant and it's a false alarm, if you want to get on birth control …"

She smiles warmly at me and palms my cheek. "I don't want to get on birth control. Life is short and precious, and I want to have another baby with you. If it's a false alarm, then we'll keep having fun trying."

The doctor knocks, and after Peyton says she's dressed, she and the nurse come back in. While the nurse sets up a machine, the doctor asks Peyton questions, like when her last period was and how her last pregnancy went.

"The urine test came back positive," the doctor says with a smile. "Based on your last period, you're most likely not far enough along for an abdominal ultrasound, so we're going to do a transvaginal one to confirm your pregnancy and try to get an estimated due date."

Peyton lifts her legs onto the stirrups, and I try to ignore the fact that the woman is about to shove a decent-sized fake dick into my fiancée by focusing on her and the monitor.

A few moments later, the screen gets fuzzy, and then a small flutter appears, followed by a loud whooshing sound.

"Oh!" Peyton breathes. "That's the heartbeat."

She glances at me with tears in her eyes, and I swear my heart has never been so damn full. This woman is truly the light in my dark world.

"It's strong and healthy," the doctor says. "And based on the size, you're about nine weeks pregnant with a due date of May 23."

"Really?" Peyton asks. "But I had some bleeding last month."

"It happens," the doctor says. "But everything appears to be normal …" She continues clicking and then grins. "Well, lookee here." She points at the screen. "It seems someone was hiding."

I'm holding Peyton's hand, so when she squeezes it, I glance down at her in confusion.

"Who's hiding?" I ask.

"Holy shit," Peyton gasps. "There's two?"

"There is," the doctor says. "You're pregnant with twins."

"Oh my God." Peyton laughs. "Apparently, you don't do anything half-assed."

She smiles at me, but I'm too shocked to smile back because, holy fucking shit, she's pregnant with twins. That's not only one baby to protect, but two. And she's going to have to carry them both.

"Is that healthy?" I ask, realizing how stupid I sound once the words are out.

"It's perfectly healthy," the doctor says with a small smile. "The goal will be to get as close to term as possible, but with twins, sometimes, it's normal for them to come sooner. Since you had a C-section with your son, we'll be able to schedule one for this pregnancy. For now, I'm going to prescribe you a prenatal vitamin. Keep the stress to a minimum, eat healthy, and drink plenty of fluids, and we'll see you back in four weeks."

She hands the probe to the nurse, and then she prints out black-and-white photos of the two tiny little dots that represent our babies. Then, they excuse themselves so Peyton can get cleaned up and dressed.

"I can't believe we're having twins," Peyton says with another laugh. "You sure you still want to be a stay-at-home dad?"

There's a twinkle in her eye, and I can't help but pull her into my arms and kiss her hard. This woman has given me everything I could ever want, and now, she's about to give me two more babies.

"I'll be whatever the hell you want me to be," I murmur against her lips, "as long as I can be with you."

"You have me, Dominick," she says, wrapping her arms around

my neck. "Until death do us part. And even then, I'm sure you'll find me in the afterlife."

"Damn right I will," I tell her, kissing her soft lips. "And then I'll drag you from heaven to join me in the pits of hell. Because you, Peyton soon-to-be Antonov, will always be my sweetest sin."

Peyton

Eight Months Later

As I lie on the couch with my family surrounding our two precious little bundles of joy, I can't help but feel so blessed. This pregnancy was a mixture of sweet and rough. Dominick gave in and let Damien go back to school—with the agreement that not one, but two guards would be on the premises at all times. Thankfully, they blend in, and the kids don't think anything of it.

We got married on Christmas Eve, and the wedding was beautiful. Only our close friends and family were there, in a small church, where we exchanged our vows and then signed the papers for Dominick to be added to Damien's birth certificate and for both of our last names to be changed.

He surprisingly let me work, but when I hit six months pregnant and my blood pressure was a bit high, I was forced to quit to go on volunteer bed rest before it turned into mandatory bed rest. With that news came Dominick's need to delegate.

We've yet to replace Martha, though I don't believe she could ever be replaced. But he insisted on having someone come in and cook healthy meals for us, and then he hired a nurse to come daily to check on me. It was a bit over the top, but I quickly realized it was the only way he would calm down, and the last thing I wanted was for my husband to have a heart attack.

Brielle offered to throw me a baby shower, but the truth is, our circle is so small that it would've just been us, so instead, we went shopping and to lunch and then spent the afternoon setting up the nursery. We decided to wait to find out the genders of the babies, so we had the room painted in soft yellows and greens and blues and bought enough clothes to last until we could go shopping.

I made it to thirty-six weeks and then my water broke. So, we went in, and they performed a C-section. Then, we got to meet our beautiful, healthy little boys.

Yes, I gave birth to twin boys, and Damien is absolutely beside himself. They aren't identical, but at only a few weeks old, it's hard to tell them apart.

Justin—named after my mother, Justine—seems to be calm. Adam—his name was picked by Damien—is cranky and demanding, reminding me of his father.

Since we arrived home, everyone has been so helpful. Brielle has been making sure that Damien is taken care of while Larisa helps with the babies. Even Martha has come by several times to visit.

We've hired a nighttime nanny to help because breastfeeding two babies is not easy, especially while recovering from surgery. But Dominick and I still take turns getting up.

"Do you want to hold Justin?" I ask Matteo, who has been watching from afar since we got home, but has made no move to come near either of the babies.

"Nah." He chuckles. "Pretty sure I would break him or drop him."

I'm about to tell him that's not true when the front door opens, and Daniil walks in, a serious expression on his face.

"Boss," he says to Dominick, "we have an issue."

My heart drops.

It's been quiet.

We started to think what Anthony had said was a lie to scare us.

But deep down, we always knew the other shoe would drop.

"What's going on?" Dominick asks as Matteo stands and walks over to join them.

"The police are here," Daniil says, "and they're looking for Matteo. They have a warrant for his arrest."

I gasp at the same time Matteo curses under his breath.

"And to what do I owe the pleasure?" he asks the officer who is standing in the doorway.

The officer steps inside and starts to read him his rights. I don't understand it all, but from the little I do, he's being arrested for money laundering.

Matteo scoffs when the officer finishes. "Really? That's what you guys have on me?" He glances at Dominick, and they exchange a look. "You know this shit isn't going to stick," Matteo says as they cuff him and take him away.

"Just doing my job," the officer says.

"Why are they doing this?" I ask Dominick once they're gone.

"Because they want Matteo put away," he says, turning to Daniil. "Lock the house and the property down," he says in a tone that sends a chill up my spine. "There's only one reason someone wants Matteo behind bars. They don't want him to interfere in whatever they have planned."

Gah! I hope you loved Dominick and Peyton's story, but this series is far from over. You can preorder Matteo's story, *Deadliest Desire*, on Amazon.

Not ready to say goodbye to Peyton and Dominick just yet? You can read Dominick's first time at the movie theater on my website under bonus content.

ABOUT THE AUTHOR

Nikki Ash is a *USA Today* Bestselling author of contemporary romance, focusing on single parent, secret baby, and surprise pregnancy romances. She spends her days and nights getting lost in words. When she's not writing, she's reading. From the Boxcar Children, to Wuthering Heights, to the latest single parent romance, she has lived and breathed every type of book.

Nikki resides in South Florida with her husband, two children, and dog that she considers to be one of her kids. When she's not reading or writing, she's traveling the world with her family—in search of inspiration.